THE
PRISONER'S
DEFENCE

and other First World War stories

THE PRISONER'S DEFENCE

and other First World War stories

selected by
ANN-MARIE EINHAUS

First published 2017 by
The British Library
96 Euston Road
London NW1 2DB

Introduction and notes copyright © 2017 Ann-Marie Einhaus

Cataloguing in Publication Data
A catalogue record for this book is available from the British Library

ISBN 978 0 7123 5671 8

Typeset by Tetragon, London
Printed in England by TJ International

CONTENTS

INTRODUCTION

Ann-Marie Einhaus

In Britain and beyond, thousands of short stories were published about the First World War. Besides poetry, which is the best-known genre of war writing in Britain, no other literary form shows us the total reach and global scale of the First World War as well as short stories do. The inventor of the mystery story, Edgar Allan Poe, famously defined the short story as a "brief tale" that can be read "at one sitting".* Usually too short to be published on their own, such tales appeared in all manner of magazines, in some of the big daily papers, and in collections of stories. Newspapers and magazines addressed very varied audiences at home and abroad, consisting of both civilians and combatants, so the reach of these "brief tales" was immense. In the period 1914–18 and the two decades beyond, short stories were everywhere.

This was not due to the war itself: by 1914, the British market for fiction was already set up for the publication of vast numbers of short stories, since magazines were a mainstay of the British and American publishing industries. They ranged from specialized professional or interest-based publications to mainstream magazines with large circulation figures, such as *Blackwood's Magazine*, the *Saturday Evening Post*, or the *Strand Magazine*. Most magazines took a predictable hit under wartime conditions, not least because of shortages of paper and shifts in reader interests, but nevertheless the market survived the war intact. Although short stories had

---

* Edgar Allan Poe, 'Review of *Twice-Told Tales*', in 1976. *Short Story Theories*, ed. by Charles E. May (Athens, Ohio: Ohio University Press, 1976), pp. 46–7.

always been popular magazine fare, they were arguably particularly suited to wartime publication: their brevity offered brief moments of distraction for readers, and useful copy for editors in times of increasing paper shortages.

Although commercial magazines and periodicals were usually aimed at audiences at home in the first instance, they were also read by British men and women serving abroad, and many magazines encouraged their readers to donate used issues to soldiers at the front. Mainstream publications such as the *Strand Magazine* targeted particularly broad readerships and consequently offered space for a wide range of stories designed to appeal to men, women and even children on the assumption that a magazine issue would be shared among the whole family.* There was consequently a thriving market for short fiction in which writers of the calibre of Joseph Conrad, Rudyard Kipling and D. H. Lawrence published successfully alongside a host of authors whose names would be unknown to most readers and critics today. In addition to magazines, popular newspapers such as the *Daily Mail* and the *Evening News* also published short stories: most of the war stories written by soldier-writer "Sapper" H. C. McNeile, for instance, first appeared in the *Mail*. Short stories were bought along with the day's, week's or month's news and features, consumed in their particular context, and discarded (except for those that were subsequently included in a short story collection).

Short stories, moreover, played a part in wartime fundraising efforts. The war witnessed the publication of gift books that collected short stories alongside poetry and letters. Authors'

---

* For a more detailed account of short stories in magazines, see Ann-Marie Einhaus, *The Short Story and the First World War* (New York; Cambridge: Cambridge University Press, 2013), pp. 43–9.

willingness to "donate" a story to a charitable cause testifies to the popularity and monetary value of short fiction. Two examples of such fundraising books (and their well-meaning but rather laborious titles) are *King Albert's Gift Book: A Tribute to the Belgian King and People from Representative Men and Women throughout the World* (1914) and *The Queen's Gift Book in Aid of Queen Mary's Convalescent Auxiliary Hospitals for Soldiers and Sailors Who Have Lost Their Limbs in the War* (1915). The latter volume was introduced by the popular author John Galsworthy (of *Forsyte Saga* fame) as a book "in the nature of a hat being passed round, into which, God send, many hundred thousand coins may be poured".* It contained contributions from the literary notables of its day, including Galsworthy himself, J. M. Barrie, John Buchan, Hall Caine, Arthur Conan Doyle, Joseph Conrad, Jerome K. Jerome, "Sapper", Maud Diver and Mrs Humphry Ward.

British readers thus encountered short fiction as a matter of course, whether they picked up their favourite magazine to read after work or at weekends, read the newspaper on the way to work, or were given a copy of a fundraising gift book as a patriotic present. It is hardly surprising, then, that writers of short stories quickly adapted their plots, settings and protagonists to match wartime reality. While by no means all short stories published during the war addressed the conflict directly, many writers began to incorporate the war into their work even where it was not their explicit subject. Popular genre fiction in particular was easily adapted for wartime audiences. Soldiers, nurses and anxious sweethearts made excellent romance protagonists, while German spies and saboteurs slotted

---

* John Galsworthy in *The Queen's Gift Book in Aid of Queen Mary's Convalescent Auxiliary Hospitals for Soldiers and Sailors Who Have Lost Their Limbs in the War* (London: Hodder & Stoughton, 1915), p. 7.

neatly into the emerging patterns of popular crime and detective fiction. In Jane Potter's words:

> Writers and publishers adapted quickly to the new atmosphere of a society at war. Almost immediately bookshops and newsstands were filled with [...] novels that featured blushing heroines and their soldier-sweethearts, periodicals, especially those aimed at women and girls, containing practical articles on how to help the war effort, and a host of other media that promoted civilian support and patriotic thinking.[*]

Writers of romance or comic fiction—such as Ethel M. Dell or May Edginton—likewise turned to wartime settings and protagonists. Thriller or mystery writers of the calibre of Edgar Wallace or E. Phillips Oppenheim, and indeed Arthur Conan Doyle, populated the pages of magazines with German spies masquerading as Swiss waiters, Belgian governesses or Polish noblemen, as in H. B. Marriott Watson's 'The Safe' (1916), included in this volume. The war also crept into more "literary", modernist short fiction of the period. Modernist writers' responses to the war included the intrusion of war news into private reflections in Virginia Woolf's stream-of-consciousness story 'The Mark on the Wall' (1917) and the adventure of an illicit wartime liaison between the narrator of Katherine Mansfield's 'An Indiscreet Journey' (1915/1924) and a French officer. They also included the ferocious and unsettling female ticket collectors who take revenge on a tram-conductor Lothario in D. H. Lawrence's 'Tickets, Please' (1919). As these modernist stories have

[*] Jane Potter, *Boys in Khaki, Girls in Print: Women's Literary Responses to the Great War 1914–1918* (Oxford: Oxford University Press, 2005), p. 55.

been included in a number of other recent anthologies, however, they do not feature in this volume.

During the war, a number of editors preserved a small part of the flood of "war stories" published in magazines by collecting them in book form. During the 1920s and 1930s, more story collections followed, including a big international anthology, *Great Short Stories of the War* (1930), with a foreword by the British war poet and memoirist Edmund Blunden. It contained sixty-six stories by authors from nations that had been involved in the war—England, America, France, Italy and even Austria and Germany. This collection was testament to the emerging view that the war had been a tragedy for all the nations and peoples involved. Naturally, new stories about the First World War were still being written, as a thriving market for such literature continued to exist during the inter-war period. Even after Britain entered the Second World War, many writers of short stories, such as Mollie Panter-Downes and Elizabeth Bowen, referred back to the earlier conflict as they wrote about the new one. Only following the Second World War did the pace of writing and collecting First World War stories slow down considerably—though some short stories about the war are still being written today, such as Andrea Levy's excellent 'Uriah's War' (2014), about West Indian volunteers serving in the British army. This volume, however, concentrates on the war years and the war's immediate aftermath and deliberately excludes stories published later than 1933.

Wartime short stories reflected the extent to which the war affected the everyday life of their readers. In December 1916, for instance, roughly half-way through the conflict, workers at the Newcastle-based W. G. Armstrong, Whitworth & Co. munition works edited and published a Christmas magazine for Armstrong employees. It was titled *"Carry On": The Armstrong Munition Workers' Christmas Magazine*, and sold in aid of the Northern War Funds. This publication has been preserved in the British Library. As a mixture between a magazine and a fundraising gift book, *"Carry On"* was also meant to be "an interesting and lasting souvenir which will serve as a reminder in days to come of a time when Britain was a nation in arms".* We can read *"Carry On"* as a kind of literary time capsule that reveals a glimpse of wartime life and interests. The content and the cover design of *"Carry On"*—which pictured an attractive young Armstrong "munitionette" in her work uniform, adjusting her cap—suggest that the magazine was aimed particularly at a female readership, though by no means all Armstrong employees were women. As well as poetry, cartoons and jokes, the magazine contained sixteen short stories. *"Carry On"* was intended as a Christmas gift, so we can imagine that they were meant as reading for the festive period. Not all of them addressed the war directly, as readers must have craved some escape from the ongoing conflict. However, 'As It Is Written: A Strange Story', the very first war story in the magazine—also included in this anthology—is an interesting example of a wartime morale-boosting production. It features an unsuccessful Zeppelin attack on an English munitions factory and makes strong claims about the Germans' inability to match British morale. *"Carry On"* offers us a local snapshot of wartime reading and wartime concerns in one English city, which illustrates the reach of the war with regard to readers' everyday experiences. As stories, poems, articles and advertisements in this souvenir magazine demonstrate, by December 1916 the war had a firm hold on most aspects of life, from the local (and national)

---

* *"Carry On": The Armstrong Munition Workers' Christmas Magazine*, 1 December 1916, p. 2.

economy and standards of living to fashion, family and relation-
ships, entertainment and food.

Whereas most of the war fiction in the *Armstrong Munition
Workers' Christmas Magazine* firmly homes in on local concerns
and the specific interests of munitions workers, other short stories
can reveal the global nature of war. The majority of war literature
still read today centres on the Western Front, but this was by no
means the case with short stories at the time. The close proximity
of the Somme and Flanders meant that soldiers on leave from the
Western Front were regulars in topical short fiction, but other front
lines and services equally appeared in the pages of magazines and
collections of the period. The Home Front and the experiences
of women and children were not excluded. A number of stories
included here reflect this attention to the Home Front, particularly
Annie Edith Jameson's 'One of the Old Guard' and May Edginton's
'War Workers'. The navy also received its fair share of attention in
the naval stories of authors such as "Bartimeus", whose sketch 'The
Navy-Under-The-Sea' features in this volume. More exotic locations
and protagonists also abounded, such as the war in Africa in Francis
Brett Young's story 'Armistice', or the Indian hero in Frederick
Britten Austin's adventure tale 'The Magic of Muhammed Din'.

The selection of short stories in this volume is drawn entirely
from magazines and books held in the British Library. I have tried
to avoid including too many well-known writers in order to allow
readers to discover new stories and authors. The works included
range from Home Front stories to a soldier's story by "Sapper"
and nursing tales such as Mary Borden's field hospital sketch,
'Paraphernalia'. They also show that short stories about the First
World War could be comic as well as tragic, which is perhaps under-
standable; the reading public were unlikely to want unremitting

gloom in fiction as well as in real life. The final two stories in the volume, Stacy Aumonier's 'Armistice Day' and Francis Brett Young's 'Armistice', take us beyond 1918 and give us a glimpse of how people remembered the war when its events were still fresh in the memory.

The volume is split into three sections—Home, Abroad, and Aftermath—each of which is organized in roughly chronological order by date of publication. I hope you enjoy the journey of discovery on which these stories will take you.

ANN-MARIE EINHAUS
Senior Lecturer in Modern and Contemporary Literature
Northumbria University

Home

A PRISONER OF WAR

P. G. Wodehouse

published in the *Strand Magazine*, vol. 49 (March 1915)

Unfit on medical grounds to serve in the armed forces, Wodehouse (1881–1975) was living in the USA when the war broke out, and remained there throughout the conflict. He made his living as a prolific contributor to various magazines and as a Broadway lyricist. Even on the far side of the Atlantic, he found himself confronted with the consequences of war on public and cultural life. The opening of his post-war story 'The Man Who Married An Hotel', which appeared in the *Strand Magazine* in March 1920, reflects his exasperation with wartime displays of patriotic fervour and his relief at the end of the war: "Peace had come at last. The Great War, with all its horrors,—its spy plays, its war novels, its articles by our military expert, and its revues with patriotic finales—had passed away like a dark cloud." 'A Prisoner of War' is one of the few Wodehouse stories in which the war makes a more than passing appearance. Even so it is not strictly speaking a war story, but rather a tale about a man who is cured of arrogance and unkindness during his enforced absence from home. The war is simply a convenient plot device to locate the American protagonist in Britain.

M RS. LORA DELANE PORTER, THAT GREAT WOMAN, WAS condescending to argue with Herbert Nixon, a mere menial. The points under discussion were three:—

(*a*) Why had Herbert been absent from duty between the hours of 3 p.m. and midnight on the previous day?

(*b*) Why had he returned singing?

(*c*) Why had he divested himself of his upper garments and stood for twenty minutes before the front door, daring the Kaiser to come out and have his head knocked off?

Those were the main counts in Mrs. Porter's indictment, and she urged them with the skill of one who for many years had been in the forefront of America's Feminist movement. A trained orator and logician, she made mincemeat of Mr. Nixon.

Herbert's official position was that of odd-job man to the house which Mrs. Porter had taken for the summer in England. He had gone with the place as a sort of bonus.

"You don't understand, ma'am," he said, pityingly. "Being a female, you wouldn't understand. It's polerticks. This 'ere country 'as 'ad to go to war—"

"And so you had to go and stupefy the few brains you possess at the village inn? I don't see the connection."

"I can't *argue* with you, ma'am," said Mr. Nixon, patiently. "My 'ead don't seem just right this morning. All I know is—"

"All *I* know is that you can go right away now and look for another job."

"'Ave it your own way, ma'am, 'ave it your own way. If you don't want me, there's others that'll be glad to 'ave me."

"Don't let me keep you from them," said Mrs. Porter. "Good morning."

Herbert vanished, and Mrs. Porter, dipping her pen in the ink, resumed the chapter of "Woman in the New Era" which his entry had interrupted.

Sybil Bannister came into the room. She was small and fluffy. Mrs. Porter greeted her with an indulgent smile. Ruthless towards the Herbert Nixons, she unbent with Sybil. Sybil was her disciple. She regarded her as a gardener regards some promising young plant.

Six months before Sybil had been what Mrs. Porter called undeveloped. That is to say, she had been content to live a peaceful life in her New York home, worshipping her husband, Mrs. Porter's nephew Hailey. The spectacle of a woman worshipping any man annoyed Mrs. Porter. To see one worshipping Hailey, for whom she entertained the contempt which only strong-minded aunts can feel for their nephews, stirred her to her depths.

Hailey, it is true, had not been a perfect husband. He was a rather pompous young man, dictatorial, and inclined to consider that the machinery of the universe should run with his personal comfort as its guiding motive. But Sybil had not noticed these things till Mrs. Porter pointed them out to her. Until Mrs. Porter urged her to assert her rights, she had not thought the matter out sufficiently to understand that she had any.

That determined woman took the situation strongly in hand. Before Hailey knew what had struck him the home was a battlefield, and when the time arrived for Mrs. Porter to go to England things came to a head. She invited Sybil to accompany her. Hailey forbade her to go. Sybil went. That is the whole campaign in a nutshell.

"I have just dismissed Nixon," said Mrs. Porter. "I have no objection to England going to war, but I will not have my odd-job man singing patriotic songs in the garden at midnight."

From the beginning of hostilities Mrs. Porter's attitude towards the European War had been clearly defined. It could continue, provided it did not bother her. If it bothered her it must stop.

Sybil looked uncomfortable.

"Aunt Lora, don't you think—I've been thinking—I believe I ought to go home."

"Ridiculous! You are perfectly safe here."

"I wasn't thinking so much about myself. I—I believe Hailey will be worried about me."

Mrs. Porter directed at her shrinking *protégée* one of the severe stares which had done so much to unman Mr. Nixon at their recent interview. This was backsliding, and must be checked.

"So much the better. It is just what Hailey wants—to have to worry about somebody except himself. The trouble with Hailey has always been that things have been made too comfortable for him. He has never had proper discipline. When Hailey was a child I once spanked him with a clothes-brush. The effects, while they lasted, were extremely gratifying. Unfortunately, immediately after the incident I ceased to be on speaking terms with his father, so was not able to follow up the good work."

Sybil shifted uneasily. She looked mutinous.

"He's my husband," she said.

"It's too late to worry about that."

"He was always very kind to me."

"Nonsense, child! He treated you like a door-mat. When he was in a bad temper he snarled at you; when he was in a good temper he patronized you."

"He's very fond of me."

"Then why doesn't he try to get you back? Has he written you a single letter, asking you to go home, in the last two months?"

"You don't understand Hailey, Aunt Lora. He's so proud."

"Tchah!"

When Mrs. Porter said "Tchah!" it was final. There was nothing ill-tempered or violent about the ejaculation: it was simply final. Sybil withdrew.

It was Mrs. Porter's daily practice, when she had made her simple breakfast and given her household staff its instructions, to walk briskly out of her garden-gate, proceed for a mile down the high road, then, turning, to walk back and begin work on her current book. The procedure had two advantages. It cleared her brain, and it afforded mild exercise to Mike, her Irish terrier.

On the morning after the rout of Herbert Nixon, she had just emerged from the garden, when she was aware of a ragged figure coming towards her down the straight white road. She called to the dog, who was sniffing at an attractive-smelling dead bird which he had located under the hedge.

"Mike!"

Lora Delane Porter was not afraid of tramps; but it is no sign of fear to mobilize your forces; it is merely a sensible precaution in case of accidents. She mobilized Mike. He left the bird, on which he had intended to roll, with a back-glance of regret, and came trotting to her side.

"To heel!" said Mrs. Porter.

The tramp was a typical ruffian of his species. He was unkempt and grimy; he wore a soiled hat, a grey suit of clothes picked out with splashes of brown and green, and there was no collar round his neck. He walked as if he had been partially hamstrung by a bungling amateur who had made a bad job of it.

As she drew level with him he looked at her, stopped, and said: "Aunt Lora!"

Mrs. Porter made it a rule to pass the ordinary tramp without a glance; but tramps who addressed her as "Aunt Lora" merited inspection. She accorded this inspection to the man before her, and gave a little gasp. His face was obscured by dust and perspiration, and he had a scrubby beard; but she recognized him.

"Hailey!"

To preserve a perfect poise in the face of all of life's untoward happenings was part of Mrs. Porter's religion. Though, for all her stern force of character, she was now inwardly a flame with curiosity, she did not show it in her manner.

"What are *you* doing here, Hailey?" she inquired, calmly.

He passed the ruins of a silk handkerchief over his grimy face and groaned. He was a shocking spectacle.

"I've had an awful time!"

"You look it."

"I've walked every step of the way from Southampton."

"Why?"

"Why! Because I had to. Do I look as if I were doing this for my health?"

"It's an excellent thing for your health. You always did shirk exercise."

Hailey drew himself up and fixed his aunt with a gaze which was a little too bloodshot to be really dignified.

"Aunt Lora, do not misunderstand me. I have not come to you for sympathy. I have not come to you for assistance. I have not—"

"You look like a walking ploughed field."

"I have merely come—"

"Have you been sleeping in those clothes?"

Hailey's hauteur changed to a human irritation.

"Yes, I *have* been sleeping in these clothes, and I wish you wouldn't look at me as if I were a kind of freak."

"But you are."

"Aunt Lora, I have not come to you for sym—"

"Bless the boy, don't tell me all the things you have not come to me for. What *have* you come for? In the first place, why are you in England at all? Have you come to try and get Sybil to go home?"

"I have not. If Sybil is to return home, she must do so of her own free will. I shall not attempt to persuade her. I am here because, on the declaration of war, I was obliged to leave Paris, where I was spending a vacation. When I reached Southampton and tried to get a boat back to New York I found it impossible. My traveller's cheques and my letter of credit were valueless, and I was without a penny. I had lost all my baggage. I set out to walk to you because you were the only person who could tell me where Professor Tupper-Smith lived."

"Professor Tupper-Smith?"

"Certainly. Professor Tupper-Smith. The English bore you planted on me when he visited New York last year."

Hailey spoke bitterly. Over the unconscious head of this same Professor Tupper-Smith there had raged one of the most serious of the battles which had shattered his domestic peace. The professor was a well-known English writer on sociology, who had come to New York with a letter of introduction to Mrs. Porter. Mrs. Porter, wishing to house him more comfortably than he was being housed at his hotel, had taken him to Sybil. Hailey was out of town at the time, and the thing had been done in his absence. He and Sybil had

had one of their first quarrels about it. In the end the professor had stayed on, and incidentally nearly driven Hailey mad.

Now, if a man had nearly driven you mad in New York, bursting with your meat the while, the least he can do, when you call on him, destitute, in England, is to honour your note-of-hand for a few hundred dollars.

That was how Hailey had argued, and that was what had driven him to his aunt. She knew the location of this human El Dorado; he did not.

"Why do you want to see Professor Tupper-Smith?"

Hailey kicked the hard road in his emotion.

"I want to ask him for his photograph. That's all. Of course, I entertain no idea of getting him to lend me money so that I can get back to New York. As he is the only man I know in England, naturally that had not occurred to me."

Mrs. Porter was a grim woman, sparing with her smiles, but at these words she laughed heartily.

"Why, of course! Do you know, Hailey, I think I must be getting stupid. I never realized till now what a complete fix you were in."

"Will you tell me that man's address?"

"No. At least, not for a long time. But I'll do something else. I'll give you a job."

"What do you mean?"

"Hailey, you always were an undisciplined child. I often told your father so—when we were on speaking terms. Rich men's sons are always like that. I was saying to Sybil only yesterday that what you needed was discipline. Discipline and honest work! They may make something of you yet. My odd-job man left me yesterday—you shall take his place. You know what an odd-job man is, I presume? He does odd jobs about the house and garden. For instance"—she looked past him—"he washes the dog. I see that Mike is rolling again. He cannot understand that we don't like it. You had better catch him and wash him at once, Hailey. Take care he does not bite you. Irish terriers are quick-tempered."

"Aunt Lora, do you imagine for a moment that I am going to—"

"You won't find out where Professor Tupper-Smith lives if you don't."

Hailey's unshaven jaw fell. There was a silence broken only by the pleased snortings of Mike.

"Aunt Lora, if it is your wish to humiliate me—"

"Don't be absurd, child. Humiliate you, indeed! You talk as if you were a prince of the blood. I am doing you a great kindness. This will be the making of you. You have been spoiled since you were a boy. You treated Sybil as if you were a Sultan. You were a mass of conceit. A month or two of this will—"

"A month or two!"

"Or three," said Mrs. Porter. "Well, make up your mind quickly. You have a perfectly free choice. If you prefer to go on tramping through England, by all means do so."

A minute later Mike, busy with his bird, felt his collar grasped. He gazed up into a set, scrubby-bearded face. It was the face of a man with a hidden sorrow.

"Under the tap in the stable-yard is the best place," said Mrs. Porter.

Of the two principals in the ablutions of Mike, the bather and the bathed, it would have been hard for an impartial spectator to have said which looked the unhappier. Mike's views on total immersion were peculiar. To plunge into any river, pond, or other sheet of water was one of his chief pleasures. In a tub, with soap playing a part in the proceedings, he became a tortured martyr.

Nor did Hailey approach the operation in a more rollicking spirit. He had never washed a dog before. When his dog in New York required washing, some underling below-stairs did it. The thought crossed his mind, as he wrought upon Mike, that whatever that underling's wages were, they were not enough.

He was concentrating tensely upon his task when Sybil entered the yard.

Sybil was in the grip of a number of emotions. When Mrs. Porter had informed her of Hailey's miraculous appearance, joy had predominated. When she learned of his misfortunes, it had been succeeded by pity. Then the curious fact came home to her that, though Hailey was apparently there, he had not yet appeared before her. And when this mystery was explained by the information that he was washing the dog in the stable-yard, her astonishment grew. Finally, when she had grasped the whole position of affairs a great dismay came upon her. She knew Hailey so well—his pride, his sensitive fastidiousness, his aloofness from all that was rough and undignified in the world. This was terrible. She pleaded with Mrs. Porter, but Mrs. Porter remained resolute.

Then she sped to the stable-yard, to witness the horror for herself.

Hailey looked up.

Silence reigned in the stable-yard. Hailey looked at Sybil. Sybil stood there without a word. Mike shivered miserably, as one on the brink of the tomb.

"Well?" said Hailey, at length.

"Oh, Hailey!"

"Well?"

"Oh, Hailey, it *is* nice seeing you again!"

"*Is* it?"

Sybil's mouth quivered, and her eyes grew large and plaintive. Hailey did not soften. Sybil, he reminded himself, was in Mrs. Porter's camp, and it was Mrs. Porter who had inflicted this beast of a dog on him.

He removed Mike from the tub and enveloped him in the towel.

"Hailey, dear, don't be cross."

"Cross?"

It is difficult for a man conscious of a four days' beard and perhaps a quarter of an inch of English soil on all the exposed parts of his person to raise his eyes with chilly dignity, but Hailey did it. He did it twice.

"Cross?"

"I begged Aunt Lora not to—"

"Not to what?"

"Not to—to make you do this. I begged her to ask you to—to stay with us."

"I am staying with you."

"I mean as a guest."

A third time Hailey raised those dusty eyebrows.

"Do you imagine for a moment that I would accept my aunt's hospitality?"

There was a pause.

Hailey released Mike, who shot out of the yard like a torpedo.

"Why did you come to England, Hailey?"

"I was on a vacation in France, and had to leave."

"You didn't come to—to see me?"

"No."

"Hailey, you don't seem very fond of me."

Hailey picked up the towel and folded it.

"If Aunt Lora tells you where Mr. Tupper-Smith lives, I suppose you will go back to New York again?"

"If Mr. Tupper-Smith will lend me the money, I shall go by the first boat."

He lifted the tub with an air of finality, and emptied it down the drain. Sybil paused irresolutely for a moment, then walked slowly away.

The days which followed did nothing to relieve Hailey's depression. Indeed, they deepened it. He had not imagined that he could ever feel sorrier for himself than he had felt by bedtime that first night, but he discovered that he had merely, so to speak, scratched the surface of gloom.

On the second day he sought audience of his aunt.

"Aunt Lora, this cannot continue."

"Why? Have you decided to become a tramp again?"

"You are taking an unjustifiable advantage of my misfortune in being helpless to resent it to—"

"When you were a small boy, Hailey, you came to visit me once, and behaved like a perfect little devil. I took advantage of your misfortune in being helpless to resent it to spank you with a clothes-brush. My mistake was that I stopped the treatment before I had cured you. The treatment has now begun again, and will continue till you are out of danger."

"Aunt Lora, you cannot realize the humiliation of my position."

"Nonsense! Use your imagination. Try to think you're a pioneer out in the West."

"I have no ambition to be a pioneer out in the West."

"Your real trouble, Hailey, is that you think the society beneath you."

"I am not accustomed to hob-nob with cooks."

"It is exceedingly good of my cook to let you hob-nob with her. She knows you came here without a reference, after having been a tramp. It shows she is not a snob."

Hailey returned to his hewing of wood and drawing of water.

For a rather excessively fastidious young man with an extremely high opinion of himself there are more congenial walks in life than that of odd-job man in a country house.

The duties of an odd-job man are extensive and peculiar. He is seldom idle. If the cook does not require him to chop wood, the gardener commandeers him for potato-digging. He cleans the knives; he cleans the shoes; he cleans the windows; he cleans the dog. In a way his is an altruistic life, for his primary mission is to scatter sweetness and light, and to bestow on others benefits in which he himself cannot share; but it is not an easy one.

Hailey did all these things and others besides. His work began at an hour which in happier days he had looked on as part of the night, and it ended when sheer mental fatigue made it impossible for those in command over him to think up anything else for him to do. When this happened, he would light his pipe and stroll moodily in the garden. It was one small count in his case against Fate that he, once known for his nice taste in cigars, should be reduced to a cheap wooden pipe and the sort of tobacco they sell in English villages.

His was not a nature that adapted itself readily to deviations from habit, particularly when such deviations involved manual labour. There were men of his acquaintance in New York who would have treated his predicament in a spirit of humorous adventure. But then they were men whose idea of enjoyment was to camp out in lonely woods with a guide and a fishing-rod. Newport was the wildest life that Hailey had ever known. He hated discomfort; he hated manual labour; he hated being under orders; and he hated the society of his social inferiors. To treat his present life in a whimsically adventurous spirit was beyond him.

Of all its disagreeable features, possibly that which he resented most was the sense of inferiority which it brought with it. In the real fundamentals of existence, he now perceived, such as reducing unwieldy blocks of wood to neat faggots and putting a polish on a shoe, he was useless. He, Hailey Bannister, respected in Wall Street as a coming man, was continually falling short of even the modest standard of efficiency set up by his predecessor, Mr. Nixon. The opinion below-stairs was that Herbert had been pretty bad, but that Hailey was unspeakable. They were nice about it—but impatient, distinctly impatient; and it wounded Hailey. He tried to tell himself that the good opinion of the masses was not worth having, but he could not bring himself to believe it. For the first time in his life he found himself humble, even apologetic. It is galling for a young man's self-esteem to be in Rome and fail through sheer incompetence to do as the Romans do. There were moments when a word of praise from the cook would have given Hailey more satisfaction than two successful deals in Wall Street.

It was by chance rather than design that Sybil chose the psychological moment for re-entering his life. His moods since his arrival had alternated between a wild yearning for her and positive dislike. But one night, as he stood smoking in the stable-yard, he was longing for her with a sentimental fervour of which in the days of his freedom he had never been capable. It had been a particularly hard day, and, as he stood poisoning the summer night with his tobacco, a great loneliness and remorse filled him. He had treated Sybil badly, he told himself. He went over in his mind episodes of their life together in New York, and shuddered at the picture he conjured up of himself. No wonder she shunned him.

And as he stood there, she came to him.

"Hailey!"

She was nervous, and he did not wonder at it. A girl coming to speak to the sort of man he had just been contemplating might have been excused if she had called out the police reserves as an escort.

"Yes?"

He was horrified at the gruffness of his voice. He had meant to speak with tender softness. It was this bad tobacco.

"Hailey, dear. I've brought you this."

Wonderful intuition of Woman! It was the one thing he desired—a fat cigar, and as his trained senses told him, a cigar of quality. He took it in a silence too deep for words.

"We were calling on some people. The man's study-door was open, and I saw the box—I hadn't time to take more than one—I thought you would like it."

Hailey could not speak. He was overcome. He kissed her.

He was conscious of a curious dizziness.

In the old days kissing Sybil had always been one of his daily acts. He had done it first thing in the morning, last thing at night. It had not made him dizzy then. He had never even derived any particular pleasure from it, especially in the morning, when he was a little late, and the car was waiting to take him to business and the butler standing by with his hat and cane. Then it had some-times been almost a nuisance, and only his rigid conscientiousness had made him do it. But now, in the scented dusk of this summer night—well, it was different. It was intensely different.

"I must go back," she said, quickly. "Aunt Lora is waiting for me."

Reluctantly he released her, and the night swallowed her up. It was a full minute before he moved.

He became aware of something in his right hand. It was the broken remnants of a crushed cigar.

They fell into the habit of meeting in the garden after dark. All day he looked forward to these moments. Somehow they seemed to supply something which had always been lacking in his life. He had wooed Sybil in the days before their marriage in ballrooms and drawing-rooms. It had seemed quite satisfactory to him at the time; but this—this stealthy coming together in the darkness, these whispered conversations under the stars—this was what he had always been starving for. He realized it now.

His outlook on life seemed to change. He saw things with different eyes. Quite suddenly it was borne in upon him how amazingly fit he felt. In New York he had been exacting in the matter of food, critical, and hard to please. Now, if supper was a trifle behind time, he had to exercise restraint to keep himself from raiding the larder. Hitherto unsuspected virtues in cold mutton were revealed to him. It might be humiliating for a young man highly respected in Wall Street and in the clubs of New York to chop wood, sweep leaves, and dig potatoes, but these things certainly made for health.

Nor had his views on the society in which he moved remained unaltered. The cook—what a good, motherly soul, always ready with a glass of beer when the heat of the day made work oppressive. The gardener—what a sterling conversationalist! The parlour-maid—what a military expert! That night at supper, when the parlour-maid exposed Germany's entire plan of campaign, while the cook said that she never did hold with war and the gardener told the story of his uncle who had lost a leg in the Indian Mutiny, was one of the most enjoyable that Hailey had ever spent.

One portion of Hailey's varied duties was to walk a mile down the road and post letters at the village post-office. He generally was not required to do this till late in the evening, but occasionally there would be an important letter for the morning post, for Mrs. Porter was a voluminous correspondent.

One morning, as he was turning in at the gate on his way back from the village, a voice addressed him, and he was aware of a man in a black suit, seated upon a tricycle.

This in itself would have been enough to rivet his interest, for he had never in his life seen a man on a tricycle. But it was not only the tricycle that excited him. The voice seemed familiar. It aroused vaguely unpleasant memories.

"My good man—why, Mr. Bannister! Bless my soul! I had no idea you were in England. I am delighted to see you. I never tire of telling my friends of your kindness to me in New York."

The landscape reeled before Hailey's blinking eyes. Speech was wiped from his lips. It was Professor Tupper-Smith.

"I must not offer to shake hands, Mr. Bannister. I have no doubt there is still risk of infection. How *is* the patient?"

"Eh?" said Hailey.

"Mumps is a painful, distressing malady, but happily not dangerous."

"Mumps?"

"Mrs. Porter told me that there was mumps in the house. I trust all is now well? That is what has kept me away. Mrs. Porter knows how apprehensive I am of all infectious ailments, and expressly forbade me to call. Previously I had been a daily visitor. It has been a great deprivation to me, I can assure you, Mr. Bannister. A woman of wonderful intelligence!"

"Do you mean to tell me—do you live *near* here?"

"That house you see through the trees is mine."

Hailey drew a deep breath.

"Could I speak to you," he said, "on a matter of importance?"

In the stable-yard, which their meetings had hallowed for him, Hailey stood waiting that night. There had been rain earlier in the evening, and the air was soft and mild, and heavy with the scent of flowers. But Hailey was beyond the soothing influence of cool air and sweet scents. He felt bruised.

She had been amusing herself with him, playing with him. There could be no other explanation. She had known all the time that this man Tupper-Smith was living at their very gates, and she had kept it from him. She had known what it meant to him to find the man, and she had kept it from him. He waited grimly.

"Hailey!"

There was a glimmer of white against the shadows.

"Here I am."

She came to him, her face raised, but he drew back.

"Sybil," he said, "I never asked you before. Can *you* tell me where this man Tupper-Smith lives?"

She started. He could only see her dimly, but he sensed it.

"N-no."

He smiled bitterly. She had the grace to hesitate. That, he supposed, must be put to her credit.

"Strange," he said. "He lives in that red house down the road. Curious your not knowing, when he used to come here so often."

When Sybil spoke, her voice was a whisper.

"I was afraid it would happen."

"Yes; I'm sorry I have not been able to amuse you longer. But it must have been delightful while it lasted. You certainly fooled me. I didn't even think it worth while asking you if you knew his address. I took it for granted that, if you had known, you would have told me. And you were laughing the whole time! Well, I suppose I ought not to blame you. I can see now that I used to treat you badly in New York, and you can't be blamed for getting even. Well, I'm afraid the joke's over now. I met him this morning."

"Hailey, you don't understand."

"Surely it couldn't be much plainer?"

"I couldn't tell you. I—I couldn't."

"Of course not. It would have spoiled everything."

"You know it was not that. It was because—do you remember the day you came here? You told me then that, directly you found him, you would go back to America."

"Well?"

"Well, I didn't want you to go. And afterwards, when we began to meet like this, I—still more didn't want you to go."

A bird rustled in the trees behind them. The rustling ceased. In the distance a corncrake was calling monotonously. The sound came faintly over the meadows, emphasizing the stillness.

"Don't you understand? You must understand. I was awfully sorry for you, but I was selfish, I wanted to keep you. It has all been so different here. Over in New York we never seemed to be together. We used to quarrel. Everything seemed to go wrong. But here it has been perfect. It was like being together on a desert island. I couldn't end it. I hated to see you unhappy, and I wanted it to go on for ever. So—"

Groping at a venture, he found her arm, and held it.

"Sybil! Sybil, dear, I'm going back to-morrow; going home. Will you come with me?"

"I thought you had given me up. I thought you never wanted me back. You said—"

"Forget what I said. When you left New York I was a fool. I was a brute. I'm different now. Listen, Sybil. Tupper-Smith—I always liked that man—lent me fifty pounds this morning. In gold! He tricycled five miles to get it. That's the sort of man he is. I hired a car, went to Southampton, and fixed things up with the skipper of an American tramp. She sails to-morrow night. Sybil, will you come? There's acres of room, and you'll like the skipper. He chews tobacco. A corking chap! Will you come?"

He could hear her crying. He caught her to him in the darkness.

"Will you?"

"Oh, my dear!"

"It isn't a floating palace, you know. It's just an old, rusty tramp-ship. We may make New York in three weeks, or we may not. There won't be much to eat except corned beef and crackers. And, Sybil—er—do you object to a slight smell of pigs? The last cargo was pigs, and you can still notice it a little."

"I *love* the smell of pigs, Hailey, dear," said Sybil.

In the drawing-room Lora Delane Porter, that great woman, relaxed her powerful mind with a selected volume of Spinoza's "Ethics." She looked up as Sybil entered.

"You've been crying, child."

"I've been talking to Hailey."

Mrs. Porter dropped Spinoza and stiffened militantly in her chair.

"If that boy Hailey has been bullying you, he shall wash Mike *now*."

"Aunt Lora, I want to go home to-morrow, please."

"What!"

"Hailey has met Mr. Tupper-Smith, and he lent him fifty pounds, and he motored into Southampton—"

"Mr. Tupper-Smith?"

"No; Hailey."

"*That's* where he was all the afternoon! No wonder they couldn't find him to dig the potatoes."

"And he has bought accommodation for me and himself on a tramp-steamer which has been carrying pigs. We shall live on corned beef and crackers, and we may get to New York some time or we may not. And Hailey say's the captain is such a nice man, who chews tobacco."

Mrs. Porter started.

"Sybil, do you mean to tell me that Hailey proposes to sail to New York on a tramp-steamer that smells of pigs, and live on corned beef and crackers? And that he *likes* a man who chews tobacco?"

"He said he was a corking chap."

Mrs. Porter picked up her Spinoza.

"Well, well," she said. "I failed with the clothes-brush, but I seem to have worked wonders with the simple-life treatment."

THE PRISONER'S DEFENCE

Arthur Conan Doyle

published in the *Strand Magazine*, vol. 51 (February 1916)

Conan Doyle (1859–1930) is best known for his fictional detective Sherlock Holmes and his trusty side-kick, Dr Watson. Both of these characters were revived for a one-off special in the *Strand Magazine* and *Collier's Weekly* in September 1917. That Sherlock Holmes tale, titled 'His Last Bow', shows Holmes as a private counter-espionage agent who takes down a dangerous German agent just before the war. However, Holmes's one-off reappearance was not Conan Doyle's only contribution to the war effort. He was one of twenty-five prominent British authors invited by the War Propaganda Bureau at Wellington House to write in aid of the British war effort in September 1914. Conan Doyle rose to the challenge by producing a range of texts that sought to boost morale and convince the world of the justness of the Allied cause. 'The Prisoner's Defence' contributed to a wider campaign of vilification of the German enemy by showing readers the unscrupulousness of the fictional spy. The story also questions how far a patriotic Englishman may have to go to serve his country; the hero shows himself willing to sacrifice his lover, his career and potentially his life.

T HE CIRCUMSTANCES, SO FAR AS THEY WERE KNOWN TO THE public, concerning the death of the beautiful Miss Ena Garnier, and the fact that Captain John Fowler, the accused officer, had refused to defend himself on the occasion of the proceedings at the police-court, had roused very general interest. This was increased by the statement that, though he withheld his defence, it would be found to be of a very novel and convincing character. The assertion of the prisoner's lawyer at the police-court, to the effect that the answer to the charge was such that it could not yet be given, but would be available before the Assizes, also caused much speculation. A final touch was given to the curiosity of the public when it was learned that the prisoner had refused all offers of legal assistance from counsel and was determined to conduct his own defence. The case for the Crown was ably presented, and was generally considered to be a very damning one, since it showed very clearly that the accused was subject to fits of jealousy, and that he had already been guilty of some violence owing to this cause. The prisoner listened to the evidence without emotion, and neither interrupted nor cross-questioned the witnesses. Finally, on being informed that the time had come when he might address the jury, he stepped to the front of the dock. He was a man of striking appearance, swarthy, black-moustached, nervous, and virile, with a quietly confident manner. Taking a paper from his pocket he read the following statement, which made the deepest impression upon the crowded court:—

I would wish to say, in the first place, gentlemen of the jury, that, owing to the generosity of my brother officers—for my own means are limited—I might have been defended to-day by the first talent of the Bar. The reason I have declined their assistance and have determined to fight my own case is not that I have any confidence in my own abilities or eloquence, but it is because I am convinced that a plain, straightforward tale, coming direct from the man who has been the tragic actor in this dreadful affair, will impress you more than any indirect statement could do. If I had felt that I were guilty I should have asked for help. Since, in my own heart, I believe that I am innocent, I am pleading my own cause, feeling that my plain words of truth and reason will have more weight with you than the most learned and eloquent advocate. By the indulgence of the Court I have been permitted to put my remarks upon paper, so that I may reproduce certain conversations and be assured of saying neither more nor less than I mean.

It will be remembered that at the trial at the police-court two months ago I refused to defend myself. This has been referred to to-day as a proof of my guilt. I said that it would be some days before I could open my mouth. This was taken at the time as a subterfuge. Well, the days are over, and I am now able to make clear to you not only what took place, but also why it was impossible for me to give any explanation. I will tell you now exactly what I did and why it was that I did it. If you, my fellow-countrymen, think that I did wrong, I will make no complaint, but will suffer in silence any penalty which you may impose upon me.

I am a soldier of fifteen years' standing, a captain in the Second Breconshire Battalion. I have served in the South African Campaign and was mentioned in despatches after the battle of Diamond Hill. When the war broke out with Germany I was seconded from my

regiment, and I was appointed as adjutant to the First Scottish
Scouts, newly raised. The regiment was quartered at Radchurch,
in Essex, where the men were placed partly in huts and were partly
billeted upon the inhabitants. All the officers were billeted out, and
my quarters were with Mr. Murreyfield, the local squire. It was
there that I first met Miss Ena Garnier.

It may not seem proper at such a time and place as this that I
should describe that lady. And yet her personality is the very essence
of my case. Let me only say that I cannot believe that Nature ever
put into female form a more exquisite combination of beauty and
intelligence. She was twenty-five years of age, blonde and tall,
with a peculiar delicacy of features and of expression. I have read
of people falling in love at first sight, and had always looked upon
it as an expression of the novelist. And yet from the moment that
I saw Ena Garnier life held for me but the one ambition—that she
should be mine. I had never dreamed before of the possibilities of
passion that were within me. I will not enlarge upon the subject, but
to make you understand my action—for I wish you to comprehend
it, however much you may condemn it—you must realize that I
was in the grip of a frantic elementary passion which made, for a
time, the world and all that was in it seem a small thing if I could
but gain the love of this one girl. And yet, in justice to myself, I will
say that there was always one thing which I placed above her. That
was my honour as a soldier and a gentleman. You will find it hard
to believe this when I tell you what occurred, and yet—though for
one moment I forgot myself—my whole legal offence consists in
my desperate endeavour to retrieve what I had done.

I soon found that the lady was not insensible to the advances
which I made to her. Her position in the household was a curious
one. She had come a year before from Montpellier, in the South

of France, in answer to an advertisement from the Murreyfields in order to teach French to their three young children. She was, however, unpaid, so that she was rather a friendly guest than an *employée*. She had always, as I gathered, been fond of the English and desirous to live in England, but the outbreak of the war had quickened her feelings into passionate attachment, for the ruling emotion of her soul was her hatred of the Germans. Her grandfather, as she told me, had been killed under very tragic circumstances in the campaign of 1870, and her two brothers were both in the French army. Her voice vibrated with passion when she spoke of the infamies of Belgium, and more than once I have seen her kissing my sword and my revolver because she hoped they would be used upon the enemy. With such feelings in her heart it can be imagined that my wooing was not a difficult one. I should have been glad to marry her at once, but to this she would not consent. Everything was to come after the war, for it was necessary, she said, that I should go to Montpellier and meet her people, so that the French proprieties should be properly observed.

She had one accomplishment which was rare for a lady; she was a skilled motor-cyclist. She had been fond of long, solitary rides, but after our engagement I was occasionally allowed to accompany her. She was a woman, however, of strange moods and fancies, which added in my feelings to the charm of her character. She could be tenderness itself, and she could be aloof and even harsh in her manner. More than once she had refused my company with no reason given, and with a quick, angry flash of her eyes when I asked for one. Then, perhaps, her mood would change and she would make up for this unkindness by some exquisite attention which would in an instant soothe all my ruffled feelings. It was the same in the house. My military duties were so exacting that it was only in the evenings that I could hope to see her, and yet very often she remained in the little study which was used during the day for the children's lessons, and would tell me plainly that she wished to be alone. Then, when she saw that I was hurt by her caprice, she would laugh and apologize so sweetly for her rudeness that I was more her slave than ever.

Mention has been made of my jealous disposition, and it has been asserted at the trial that there were scenes owing to my jealousy, and that once Mrs. Murreyfield had to interfere. I admit that I was jealous. When a man loves with the whole strength of his soul it is impossible, I think, that he should be clear of jealousy. The girl was of a very independent spirit. I found that she knew many officers at Chelmsford and Colchester. She would disappear for hours together upon her motor-cycle. There were questions about her past life which she would only answer with a smile unless they were closely pressed. Then the smile would become a frown. Is it any wonder that I, with my whole nature vibrating with passionate, whole-hearted love, was often torn by jealousy when I came upon those closed doors of her life which she was so determined not to open? Reason came at times and whispered how foolish it was that I should stake my whole life and soul upon one of whom I really knew nothing. Then came a wave of passion once more and reason was submerged.

I have spoken of the closed doors of her life. I was aware that a young, unmarried Frenchwoman has usually less liberty than her English sister. And yet in the case of this lady it continually came out in her conversation that she had seen and known much of the world. It was the more distressing to me as whenever she had made an observation which pointed to this she would afterwards, as I could plainly see, be annoyed by her own indiscretion, and endeavour to remove the impression by every means in her power. We had several small quarrels on this account, when I asked questions to which I could get no answers, but they have been exaggerated in the address for the prosecution. Too much has been made also of the intervention of Mrs. Murreyfield, though I admit that the quarrel was more serious upon that occasion. It arose from my finding the photograph of a man upon her table, and her evident confusion when I asked her for some particulars about him. The name "H. Vardin" was written underneath—evidently an autograph. I was worried by the fact that this photograph had the frayed appearance of one which has been carried secretly about, as a girl might conceal the picture of her lover in her dress. She absolutely refused to give me any information about him, save to make a statement which I found incredible, that it was a man whom she had never seen in her life. It was then that I forgot myself. I raised my voice and declared that I should know more about her life or that I should break with her, even if my own heart should be broken in the parting. I was not violent, but Mrs. Murreyfield heard me from the passage, and came into the room to remonstrate. She was a kind, motherly person who took a sympathetic interest in our romance, and I remember that on this occasion she reproved me for my jealousy and finally persuaded me that I had been unreasonable, so that we became reconciled once more. Ena was so madly fascinating and I so hopelessly her slave that she could always draw me back, however much prudence and reason warned me to escape from her control. I tried again and again to find out about this man Vardin, but was always met by the same assurance, which she repeated with every kind of solemn oath, that she had never seen the man in her life. Why she should carry about the photograph of a man—a young, somewhat sinister man, for I had observed him closely before she snatched the picture from my hand—was what she either could not, or would not, explain.

Then came the time for my leaving Radchurch. I had been appointed to a junior but very responsible post at the War Office, which, of course, entailed my living in London. Even my week-ends found me engrossed with my work, but at last I had a few days' leave of absence. It is those few days which have ruined my life, which have brought me the most horrible experience that ever a man had to undergo, and have finally placed me here in the dock, pleading as I plead to-day for my life and my honour.

It is nearly five miles from the station to Radchurch. She was there to meet me. It was the first time that we had been reunited since I had put all my heart and my soul upon her. I cannot enlarge upon these matters, gentlemen. You will either be able to sympathize with and understand the emotions which overbalance a man at such a time, or you will not. If you have imagination, you will. If you have not, I can never hope to make you see more than the bare fact. That bare fact, placed in the baldest language, is that during this drive from Radchurch Junction to the village I was led into the greatest indiscretion—the greatest dishonour, if you will—of my life. I told the woman a secret, an enormously important secret, which might affect the fate of the war and the lives of many thousands of men.

It was done before I knew it—before I grasped the way in which her quick brain could place various scattered hints together and weave them into one idea. She was wailing, almost weeping, over the fact that the allied armies were held up by the iron line of the Germans. I explained that it was more correct to say that our iron line was holding them up, since they were the invaders. "But is France, is Belgium, *never* to be rid of them?" she cried. "Are we simply to sit in front of their trenches and be content to let them do what they will with ten provinces of France? Oh, Jack, Jack, for God's sake, say something to bring a little hope to my heart, for sometimes I think that it is breaking! You English are stolid. You can bear these things. But we others, we have more nerve, more soul! It is death to us. Tell me! Do tell me that there is hope! And yet it is foolish of me to ask, for, of course, you are only a subordinate at the War Office, and how should you know what is in the mind of your chiefs?"

"Well, as it happens, I know a good deal," I answered. "Don't fret, for we shall certainly get a move on soon."

"Soon! Next year may seem soon to some people."

"It's not next year."

"Must we wait another month?"

"Not even that."

She squeezed my hand in hers. "Oh, my darling boy, you have brought such joy to my heart! What suspense I shall live in now! I think a week of it would kill me."

"Well, perhaps it won't even be a week."

"And tell me," she went on, in her coaxing voice, "tell me just one thing, Jack. Just one, and I will trouble you no more. Is it our brave French soldiers who advance? Or is it your splendid Tommies? With whom will the honour lie?"

"With both."

"Glorious!" she cried. "I see it all. The attack will be at the point where the French and British lines join. Together they will rush forward in one glorious advance."

"No," I said. "They will not be together."

"But I understood you to say—of course, women know nothing of such matters, but I understood you to say that it would be a joint advance."

"Well, if the French advanced, we will say, at Verdun, and the British advanced at Ypres, even if they were hundreds of miles apart it would still be a joint advance."

"Ah, I see," she cried, clapping her hands with delight. "They would advance at both ends of the line, so that the Boches would not know which way to send their reserves."

"That is exactly the idea—a real advance at Verdun, and an enormous feint at Ypres."

Then suddenly a chill of doubt seized me. I can remember how I sprang back from her and looked hard into her face. "I've told you too much!" I cried. "Can I trust you? I have been mad to say so much."

She was bitterly hurt by my words. That I should for a moment doubt her was more than she could bear. "I would cut my tongue out, Jack, before I would tell any human being one word of what you have said." So earnest was she that my fears died away. I felt that I could trust her utterly. Before we had reached Radchurch I had put the matter from my mind, and we were lost in our joy of the present and in our plans for the future.

I had a business message to deliver to Colonel Worral, who commanded a small camp at Pedley-Woodrow. I went there and was away for about two hours. When I returned I inquired for Miss Garnier, and was told by the maid that she had gone to her bedroom, and that she had asked the groom to bring her motor-bicycle to the door. It seemed to me strange that she should arrange to go out alone when my visit was such a short one. I had gone into her little study to seek her, and here it was that I waited, for it opened on to the hall passage, and she could not pass without my seeing her.

There was a small table in the window of this room at which she used to write. I had seated myself beside this when my eyes fell upon a name written in her large, bold handwriting. It was a reversed impression upon the blotting-paper which she had used, but there could be no difficulty in reading it. The name was Hubert Vardin. Apparently it was part of the address of an envelope, for underneath I was able to distinguish the initials S.W., referring to a postal division of London, though the actual name of the street had not been clearly reproduced.

Then I knew for the first time that she was actually corresponding with this man whose vile, voluptuous face I had seen in the photograph with the frayed edges. She had clearly lied to me, too, for was it conceivable that she should correspond with a man whom she had never seen? I don't desire to condone my conduct. Put yourself in my place. Imagine that you had my desperately fervid and jealous nature. You would have done what I did, for you could have done nothing else. A wave of fury passed over me. I laid my hands upon the wooden writing-desk. If it had been an iron safe I should have opened it. As it was, it literally flew to pieces before me. There lay the letter itself, placed under lock and key for safety, while the writer prepared to take it from the house. I had no hesitation or scruple. I tore it open. Dishonourable, you will say, but when a man is frenzied with jealousy he hardly knows what he does. This woman, for whom I was ready to give everything, was either faithful to me or she was not. At any cost I would know which.

A thrill of joy passed through me as my eyes fell upon the first words. I had wronged her. "Cher Monsieur Vardin." So the letter began. It was clearly a business letter, nothing else. I was about to replace it in the envelope with a thousand regrets in my mind for my want of faith when a single word at the bottom of the page caught my eyes, and I started as if I had been stung by an adder. "Verdun"— that was the word. I looked again. "Ypres" was immediately below it. I sat down, horror-stricken, by the broken desk, and I read this letter, a translation of which I have in my hand:—

MURREYFIELD HOUSE, RADCHURCH.

DEAR M. VARDIN,—Stringer has told me that he has kept you sufficiently informed as to Chelmsford and Colchester, so I have not troubled to write. They have moved the Midland Territorial Brigade and the heavy guns towards the coast near Cromer, but only for a time. It is for training, not embarkation.

And now for my great news, which I have straight from the War Office itself. Within a week there is to be a very severe attack from Verdun, which is to be supported by a holding attack at Ypres. It is all on a very large scale, and you must send off a special Dutch messenger to Von Starmer by the first boat. I hope to get the exact date and some further particulars from my informant to-night, but meanwhile you must act with energy.

I dare not post this here—you know what village postmasters are, so I am taking it into Colchester, where Stringer will include it with his own report which goes by hand.— Yours faithfully, SOPHIA HEFFNER.

I was stunned at first as I read this letter, and then a kind of cold, concentrated rage came over me. So this woman was a German and a spy! I thought of her hypocrisy and her treachery towards me, but, above all, I thought of the danger to the Army and the State. A great defeat, the death of thousands of men, might spring from my misplaced confidence. There was still time, by judgment and energy, to stop this frightful evil. I heard her step upon the stairs outside, and an instant later she had come through the doorway.

She started, and her face was bloodless as she saw me seated there with the open letter in my hand.

"How did you get that?" she gasped. "How dare you break my desk and steal my letter?"

I said nothing. I simply sat and looked at her and pondered what I should do. She suddenly sprang forward and tried to snatch the letter. I caught her wrist and pushed her down on to the sofa, where she lay, collapsed. Then I rang the bell, and told the maid that I must see Mr. Murreyfield at once.

He was a genial, elderly man, who had treated this woman with as much kindness as if she were his daughter. He was horrified at what I said. I could not show him the letter on account of the secret that it contained, but I made him understand that it was of desperate importance.

"What are we to do?" he asked. "I never could have imagined anything so dreadful. What would you advise us to do?"

"There is only one thing that we can do," I answered. "This woman must be arrested, and in the meanwhile we must so arrange matters that she cannot possibly communicate with any one. For all we know, she has confederates in this very village. Can you undertake to hold her securely while I go to Colonel Worral at Pedley and get a warrant and a guard?"

"We can lock her in her bedroom."

"You need not trouble," said she. "I give you my word that I will stay where I am. I advise you to be careful, Captain Fowler. You've shown once before that you are liable to do things before you have thought of the consequence. If I am arrested all the world will know that you have given away the secrets that were confided to you. There is an end of your career, my friend. You can punish me, no doubt. What about yourself?"

"I think," said I, "you had best take her to her bedroom."

"Very good, if you wish it," said she, and followed us to the door. When we reached the hall she suddenly broke away, dashed through the entrance, and made for her motor-bicycle, which was standing there. Before she could start we had both seized her. She stooped and made her teeth meet in Murreyfield's hand. With flashing eyes and tearing fingers she was as fierce as a wild cat at bay. It was with some difficulty that we mastered her, and dragged her—almost carried her—up the stairs. We thrust her into her room and turned the key, while she screamed out abuse and beat upon the door inside.

"It's a forty-foot drop into the garden," said Murreyfield, tying up his bleeding hand. "I'll wait here till you come back. I think we have the lady fairly safe."

"I have a revolver here," said I. "You should be armed." I slipped a couple of cartridges into it and held it out to him. "We can't afford to take chances. How do you know what friends she may have?"

"Thank you," said he. "I have a stick here, and the gardener is within call. Do you hurry off for the guard, and I will answer for the prisoner."

Having taken, as it seemed to me, every possible precaution, I ran to give the alarm. It was two miles to Pedley, and the colonel was out, which occasioned some delay. Then there were formalities and a magistrate's signature to be obtained. A policeman was to serve the warrant, but a military escort was to be sent in to bring back the prisoner. I was so filled with anxiety and impatience that I could not wait, but I hurried back alone with the promise that they would follow.

The Pedley-Woodrow Road opens into the high-road to Colchester at a point about half a mile from the village of

Radchurch. It was evening now and the light was such that one could not see more than twenty or thirty yards ahead. I had proceeded only a very short way from the point of junction when I heard, coming towards me, the roar of a motor-cycle being ridden at a furious pace. It was without lights, and close upon me. I sprang aside in order to avoid being ridden down, and in that instant, as the machine flashed by, I saw clearly the face of the rider. It was she—the woman whom I had loved. She was hatless, her hair streaming in the wind, her face glimmering white in the twilight, flying through the night like one of the Valkyries of her native land. She was past me like a flash and tore on down the Colchester Road. In that instant I saw all that it would mean if she could reach the town. If she once was allowed to see her agent we might arrest him or her, but it would be too late. The news would have been passed on. The victory of the Allies and the lives of thousands of our soldiers were at stake. Next instant I had pulled out the loaded revolver and fired two shots after the vanishing figure, already only a dark blur in the dusk. I heard a scream, the crashing of the breaking cycle, and all was still.

I need not tell you more, gentlemen. You know the rest. When I ran forward I found her lying in the ditch. Both of my bullets had struck her. One of them had penetrated her brain. I was still standing beside her body when Murreyfield arrived, running breathlessly down the road. She had, it seemed, with great courage and activity scrambled down the ivy of the wall; only when he heard the whirr of the cycle did he realize what had occurred. He was explaining it to my dazed brain when the police and soldiers arrived to arrest her. By the irony of fate it was me whom they arrested instead.

It was urged at the trial in the police-court that jealousy was the cause of the crime. I did not deny it, nor did I put forward any witnesses to deny it. It was my desire that they should believe it. The hour of the French advance had not yet come, and I could not defend myself without producing the letter which would reveal it. But now it is over—gloriously over—and so my lips are unsealed at last. I confess my fault—my very grievous fault. But it is not that for which you are trying me. It is for murder. I should have thought myself the murderer of my own countrymen if I had let the woman pass.

These are the facts, gentlemen. I leave my future in your hands. If you should absolve me I may say that I have hopes of serving my country in a fashion which will atone for this one great indiscretion, and will also, as I hope, end for ever those terrible recollections which weigh me down. If you condemn me, I am ready to face whatever you may think fit to inflict.

THE SAFE

H. B. Marriott Watson

published in the *Strand Magazine*, vol. 52 (September 1916)

Born in Australia and raised in New Zealand, Watson (1863–1921) wrote a large number of plays, novels and short stories besides working as a journalist and editor. His only son was killed during the German spring offensive of 1918. Having previously lost his wife Rosamund in 1911, Watson survived his son by only three years. Watson's work was versatile and ranged from historical romance to ghost and adventure fiction. The basic ingredients of his 1916 tale 'The Safe' are common in wartime short fiction: a dastardly spy, a gullible young woman with her heart in the right place, and a plot that ensures that the evil-doer meets his final comeuppance.

I T WAS AT LADY RUDGWICK'S HOUSE THAT PROFESSOR GRETTON first met the Count Boloski. Gretton was a man of sixty, very deliberate in manner, rather abstracted, and abominably deaf. He was clean-shaven, had silver hair, and carried with him an air of distinction. It was partly because of this that he was in social request, but partly also because of his great chemical attainments. He was entitled to append many letters to his name, including "F.R.S." It could not be said that he was overfond of social gaiety, though he did not object to an occasional plunge into London *salons*. He went out a good deal because his wife enjoyed it. She was much younger than he; nearly thirty years divided them, and she had a passion for movement, excitement, exhilaration. Her husband's position opened doors for him into various circles to which she would have had no access otherwise; but she had a feverish craving for "more," and did not realize that Gretton, as it was, made many personal sacrifices to meet her wishes.

Lady Rudgwick was sister-in-law to a prominent Minister, and Helen Gretton was glad to be at her reception. It was unusually crowded and full of fine uniforms and expensive dresses. All the Allies were represented in that room, and Mrs. Gretton's heart beat fast with satisfaction and pleasure. She had already fallen across some acquaintances, and had enjoyed herself in conversation; and now coming straight towards her, with the obvious intention of reaching a goal, she saw her hostess and a very striking man. This was Count Boloski, who was introduced by Lady Rudgwick.

"Count Boloski, my dear Mrs. Gretton, whose country has been so ravaged, you know, under those dreadful Huns. He can tell you lots of interesting things."

The introduction thus abruptly made, she left the two together— the man with a bow hardly yet finished, the woman palpitating with a sense of adventure. Count Boloski sat down beside her. He was a tall, dark man, with fine eyes and a spruce, military bearing, some- thing over forty, and carrying an air of one who knows the world.

"You are interested in Poland, Mrs. Gretton?" he asked, in English which was almost without foreign accent.

"Yes," she said, eagerly. "I don't know much about your country, Count, but I know enough to be very sorry."

"Ah!" he said, softly. "She will come to her own—now. The Czar has promised—but you know that. It only remains to rid ourselves of the invaders. It will be done, but it will be difficult. At last we have hope—after a century—hope to see ourselves once more a nation. You can understand what that means, Mrs. Gretton."

"I can," she said.

His voice was exquisitely tempered, and his restrained glances sought her face with deference and admiration. She was arresting to the eyes. She had a slender face, paper white even to the verge of her lips, and two great blue eyes rolled and melted in it. There was something in her personality that made an instantaneous appeal to the man. She was uncharacteristically English. He talked of Poland and she listened, but all the time her thoughts were fluttering about him. He had asked Lady Rudgwick to introduce him. He must, therefore, have been interested in her. It was pleasant to her vanity; it was stimulating. His talk drifted insensibly from affairs to other matters, and began to fascinate her. She had little to say herself, but was charmed by his evident interest in her, and presently, when she saw her husband approaching, she rose. Professor Gretton had come with the suggestion that they should leave.

"Edward," she said, "this is Count Boloski, who has been telling me most interesting things about Poland."

Gretton gravely acknowledged the introduction, and said something complimentary to the country. Boloski replied, and was interrupted.

"My husband is rather deaf, Count."

He continued his reply, raising his voice. "We have all heard of you, Professor—all who are interested in science. Your name stands very high in my country."

Gretton was human enough to be susceptible to flattery, and he smiled deprecatingly.

"I am only a beginner," he said. "I have learnt enough to know that."

"But your discovery of the L 2 telluride salts?" protested the Count.

Gretton looked at him more interestedly. "You have studied chemistry?" he asked.

Boloski shrugged his shoulders. "A little as an amateur. It is very fascinating."

As Helen Gretton turned to leave with her husband she said, pleasantly:—

"You must come and see us, Count—25, Raymond Gardens."

"Delighted!" he murmured, with a repetition of his ceremonious bow.

He called three days later. Gretton was out, but his wife was at home, and there were others present. This woman had interested him in a peculiar way, and though he talked amiably he felt impatient at the presence of others. He left, however, before them, and expressed his disappointment at not seeing Professor Gretton. Upon this, Mrs. Gretton hoped he would call again, adding, by way of explanation for her husband's absence:—

"He is very much engaged just now—Government work, you know."

Count Boloski, it appeared, was aware of this. "I remember you have a Scientific Committee to advise the Government—a very wise proceeding, and Professor Gretton's help would be invaluable."

Nevertheless, when he called again, Gretton was away. Boloski, while appearing to regret this, was in reality quite satisfied with the situation. The woman exercised on him a curious fascination. That pallid face provoked him, and the indications he thought he detected of a latent passionate nature stimulated him. He was more than usually entertaining, and even ventured on more familiar ground than had been reached previously in his more formal politeness. Helen Gretton talked of their house in Kent, of the great labora-tory, of the gardens.

"But it is rather dull sometimes," she said, interrupting her note of satisfaction. "One misses town life. Things are so stuffy in the country."

"Stuffy!" he repeated, unable to follow this piece of English colloquialism. "Ah, *triste*. I understand. Yes, I am a metropolitan like yourself. I enjoy London, I enjoy Paris. I would enjoy Moscow if—when it is really ours."

Mrs. Gretton gently sympathized. She looked upon him as an exile from a land overrun with brutish barbarians and laid waste. He spoke about his estates.

"A German general lives in my *château*, and drinks my wine, and tramples my gardens underfoot. But Time holds the balance, and the scales will dip."

On his third call he was fortunate enough to see the Professor, who received him amiably. There was some little chemical talk, and Gretton received several delicate compliments. But it tried the Pole to have to shout into ears things that should of their very nature be conveyed with subtle intonation. It was like using a megaphone for a violin.

During the next few weeks the Count dropped in fairly often, and sometimes found his hostess alone. On one or two occasions he met Gretton, and there was more chemical talk. The savant was agreeably surprised by the extent and resources of the Count's knowledge, and showed himself very friendly. Meanwhile Mrs. Gretton had become so much involved in interest with her new and distinguished acquaintance that when the time arrived for their departure into Kent she was quite dismayed. Then she had an impulse.

"You like Count Boloski, Edward. Shall we ask him down for a few days? He is very agreeable company."

Gretton assented. "Yes, he's intelligent. If you would like to, why, certainly. But I've no doubt he's booked up."

It was approaching the end of July, but the Count was not booked up; and a little later he went down to Felhurst for a few days. He went for a few days, but he stayed for more than a week, and this narrative explains how his stay came to an end.

Professor Gretton was busier in Kent than he had been in London, but the business that engrossed him was rather different. At Felhurst he had his great laboratory, and he always retired to the quiet country to devote himself to any important piece of work. Of course he had his laboratory at the college, which he used in town, but he preferred his own. It was really a fine and a finely-equipped extension of the rather ugly square house. The utilitarian laboratory broke the unified stolidity of its aspect, and even imported into the atmosphere a suggestion of picturesqueness, of romance. Yet within the chambers of the living house, and along the passages, there was no footfall of romance. The Grettons lived an amiable life of pedestrian conjugality. But there was come now an irruption on the calm domesticity in the person of this fascinating Pole. Gretton was content to leave his wife to her own devices, and his guest to her. He was a shrewd man when he turned his attention to anything, but the trouble was that he thought so few things worth attention. In the domain of politics he was a stranger; he adventured docilely, as has been explained, into social affairs, but his one passion was chemistry.

There were some interesting views and walks in the neighbourhood of Felhurst, and it seemed that the Count was interested in historical traditions. Mrs. Gretton was his cicerone, and he was a delightful companion, with a respectful admiration flashing from his fine eyes on occasion. The dead white of Mrs. Gretton's face fascinated him. He had speculated often as to her story. How came she to marry this dryasdust? The dryasdust was little in the way. In his veins no real blood ran, and the Count considered himself excused for philandering on that account, if on no other. As a matter of fact, he recognized no bounds to his actions save those which might occur to him as useful or advisable. On one occasion, which marked a stage in this development, they were all three upon an expedition. It was a beautiful evening, and Professor Gretton, who had been hard at work for days, was induced to accompany them to a Roman earthwork in the neighbourhood. Professor Gretton was interested in antiquities, and knew a good deal about them, so that he was able to entertain his guest, who was quick to express his appreciation. Returning towards dusk, they were walking in a narrow lane, sunken as if it had been a Devon lane, and, as it chanced, the Count was a little behind with Mrs. Gretton. Professor Gretton had seemingly fallen into a muse, and walked with his hands behind him, gazing upon the ground. A motor-car came suddenly flying along the lane, and Mrs. Gretton and her companion stepped aside on the noise of its approach. The Professor was in the centre of the road, and the horn of the oncoming car, driven rather recklessly, hooted loudly. But he did not move. It hooted more loudly still, and the driver made no attempt to alter his course, as it was obvious that no one who was not stone-deaf could avoid hearing it. Unfortunately, though not stone-deaf, Professor Gretton was very deaf, and his mental abstraction completed his inattention to the warning. Mrs. Gretton screamed, and the Count, taking in the situation, jumped agilely forward and, with an abrupt movement of his hands, whirled the imperilled man away. The car shot by them so closely as to brush his arm.

Gretton looked up bewildered, and then understood.

"That was a shave," he said. "I owe you many thanks, Count. If I had my way I'd send ruffians like that to prison every time. Many thanks," he repeated, as he stooped to pick up his hat, that had been knocked off. Mrs. Gretton's thanks also gushed out.

"How dreadful! If Edward had— It was only your action saved him—so prompt. I don't know how we can thank you, Count."

"By recovering our equilibrium," said he, smiling.

But, though the equilibrium was recovered, the gratitude endured. It was pleasant to have a beautiful woman grateful, and the Count allowed himself to press his advantage. The tie between husband and wife was an unheroic tie, and he had no doubt as to the possibility of its disintegration. He had hardly before been aware of the extent of the Professor's deafness. But now it interested him.

His conversation with Mrs. Gretton never reached Gretton's ears. With his general abstraction added he lived aloof even at table, and very swiftly Boloski fell into small familiarities with his hostess. Seizing a chance which had started in a compliment, he called her Guinevere, and she did not resent it. It was done delicately, even charmingly, and Mrs. Gretton had fallen so under the influence of this cosmopolitan that she was even gratified.

Count Boloski had welcomed the incident of the motor-car for two reasons, and he was justified in both his expectations. He had engaged Mrs. Gretton's sympathies deeply, and he had crossed the gap which he had sensibly felt to yawn between him and Gretton. The Professor, recognizing what he owed, sloughed his temperamental reserve by an effort. He talked chemistry when it was required of him, and found an intelligent listener. Boloski it was who drew the conversation towards explosives. He knew something about explosives in an amateur way, he said, modestly.

"The romance of explosives may seem an odd phrase, but there is really something in it. Think of the procession from crude black powder onwards to guncotton, cordite, lyddite, T.N.T."

Gretton nodded. He was evidently interested—if only in his own thoughts.

"And why should T.N.T. be the end?" pursued the Count. "There is no last word in discovery."

"No," said Gretton, and smiled a little. "There is no reason to suppose it is the end."

He was obliging enough that same afternoon to invite his guest to an inspection of his laboratory, an invitation eagerly accepted. There was a good deal to explain in the experiments in progress there, and the explanation fell on understanding ears.

"And this?" inquired the Count at last, indicating a number of retorts, glasses, acids, and other apparatus upon a table.

The Professor smiled. "It is concerned with certain researches I have just completed."

He rather abruptly brought the inspection to a close, and the Count went out to join his hostess. He had so far advanced in her favour now that he had dropped many of his precautions. What was he there for? he asked himself more than once. It had been better that his purpose should be single. As it was he was divided. Across the table and elsewhere in Gretton's presence he talked to the woman almost without reserve, and she had thrills and tremors at his audacity. The Professor's deafness was an adequate protection for him.

Once, when he had come in from a walk and found his hostess at tea alone, he referred to his visit to the laboratory, and to Gretton's great reputation.

"I suppose," he said, lightly, "that the Professor has many discoveries which he is too unworldly to put to commercial use?"

Mrs. Gretton didn't know anything definite about his discoveries.

"He is always at work," she said. "His services are greatly valued. Of course, he registers all his experiments. He has a huge safe in which he keeps everything of that sort."

"In his laboratory, of course?"

"No; it's in his study, the room off the laboratory. It's a big thing, specially made for him. He has all his private papers and other things there. More tea, Count?"

The Count would have some more tea, and he pursued the conversation, idly, disinterestedly.

"Oh, Edward is really very careful—as careful as he is over his experiments. No one is allowed to touch his safe. He keeps the keys on his watch-chain. There are three locks—what do you call them? I forget the name."

Count Boloski could not suggest a name. That night they had a very pleasant dinner, with the squire and his wife and daughter, and one or two others. The Count seemed struck by the beauty of Miss Allinson, and paid her much polite attention. Mrs. Gretton was at first pleased by the reflected distinction of her guest, then bewildered, and finally irritated. She had been used to his devoted homage. Was it now to go to Miss Allinson, whom she considered insipid?

When the Professor had temporarily retired to his laboratory later the Count made amends.

"A charming girl, but—"

She hung on the "but." He shrugged his shoulders.

"Do you like veal, Mrs. Gretton?"

She laughed happily. "It happens to be the one thing I can't eat."

"Nor can I," he said, with a look from under his heavily-bushed eyes. "I like nothing immature."

"And I am going to give you lamb and green peas to-morrow. At least, the cook is."

He waved aside with an expressive hand all thoughts of food, and began on "Guinevere." He knew passages of Tennyson by heart, and he focused his talents on her. Mrs. Gretton experienced once more the curious thrill which was now familiar, but which was nevertheless always alarming—and delightful.

Count Boloski had come to the conclusion that the time was nearly ripe. If he had gone on quoting Tennyson he might have added:—

And Modred said, "The time is near at hand."

Mrs. Gretton exercised an unaccountable fascination for him but that, of course, was a secondary matter. He was used to a sexual triumph. There was more difficult work before him.

The study, into which the Count had never been invited, was a room off the laboratory, with a door giving on a little lawn and the garden beyond. He saw it for the first time one day when Gretton was paying a visit to town, entered it quietly, and took in its features. There was in reality little of the study about it. It was sparely furnished with writing bureau and chairs, bookshelves on three walls, and a commercial file for correspondence. But the most prominent feature in the room was a huge safe, which occupied almost the whole of one side and stood at least six feet high. This drew his eyes after he had discarded the files. What he wanted was securely held within the safe.

This is not a story of intrigue, but the story of an incident. Professor Gretton, one of the foremost chemists of the day, had discovered a new explosive mixture, and vague rumours of it had gone about. It was, of course, a profound secret, and the Government had bought it up. It was the evening after the Count had had a cursory glance at the study that Mrs. Gretton's emotional defences were battered down, as it had been by a much greater explosive.

He held her hand, called upon Heaven to witness, talked of affinity, and the right of living one's own life. She was shattered and shaken, and spent a miserable night, a day thereafter with intermittent moods and thrills. What did it all mean?

He left her in no doubt later. He had been out most of the day making certain preparations, and he had gone as far as Masling, a town ten miles away, where he had given instructions to the proprietor of a garage. At dinner he was a spirited companion, and made handsome recognition of the hospitality shown him. "But I have trespassed too grossly on your indulgence," he said. "The charm of Felhurst has made a bore of me. I shall always be deeply in your debt, and can never repay the principal, though I hope always to be ready with my interest."

It appeared that he must leave for town on the morrow, and though he civilly expressed regret Professor Gretton was obviously not disturbed by the news. He withdrew himself later to his laboratory, and the Count was left with Mrs. Gretton.

"I am going to-morrow," he said, advancing swiftly towards her. "But I am not going alone. I am going back to Poland, to my unhappy country, but I'm not going alone. You understand?"

She avoided his burning eyes, and faltered. "No—no," she said.

"Listen. I shall have a car here at the gates at four o'clock in the dawn. You must join me there. I shall be in the study. We can leave by the door upon the lawn."

He was gone before she could answer, but he left her in the full confidence of her passive obedience. He had had considerable experience of women.

The household had retired early, and it was only just eleven when Professor Gretton left his laboratory and went upstairs with his keys. Upon a table near his bed was a decanter containing whisky, a glass, and a siphon of soda. They stood in readiness for his nightcap, which was his invariable practice. He slowly made the mixture, disposed of it as deliberately, and undressed, throwing his clothes over a chair. He slept soon, and his sleep was as deliberate as all other processes in his life.

Shortly after one o'clock, when a few stars reigned in the sky, Count Boloski stole from his room, where he had been busy with preparations, and listened at the door. He was in a lounge suit, and he carried in his hand a small electric torch. He listened to the unbroken silence of the sleeping house. Then he passed noise-lessly along the corridor till he had reached the door of Professor Gretton's room. This he opened softly, and stayed to listen once more. Silence enwrapped everything and darkness enfolded all. He switched on his torch and the light sprayed the contents of the room. At the farther end it illuminated dimly a bed, and towards this Boloski made his furtive way. Professor Gretton lay sleeping like a child, and the Count looked down on him with a smile.

"He wouldn't hear if I fell over the fire-irons," he said, almost with a sneer.

Then he turned his attention to the discarded clothes on the chair—to the watch and chain, and all that was attached to it on the dressing-table. He made up his mind quickly about the keys, but, as there were several, to save time he took the bunch. Moreover, it was well to be on the safe side. He passed out of the room as noiselessly as he had entered, closed the door, and descended the staircase.

Outside the door of the laboratory he paused to find the key. It turned in the lock, and he entered. The same key opened the study, and then he switched on the electric light of the room in order to inspect the great safe more narrowly.

From the look of the locks, which were of a special make, he had already determined the keys, and he now applied them. The door swung open readily; it was hung perfectly, and answered to a touch. Boloski peered in. The safe was divided into two parts—one full of shelves in which documents and files of all kinds were col-lected; but the other half was clear and fitted with a small project-ing shelf, on which rested a packet. He switched off the room light and entered, and with the light of his own torch examined this. It rendered him nothing of interest. He thereupon gave his atten-tion to the files which were stowed in pigeonholes, and diligently searched for letters which might cover the object of his inquiry. He was quite half an hour in these investigations before he reached what seemed to be what he wanted.

Professor Gretton, with a somewhat uneasy sense of a light on his face, woke up and stared into perfect darkness. He closed his eyes again, but unfortunately a problem in chemistry which had worried him in the laboratory re-entered his mind and worried him again. The formula was wrong. He was sure of that. It pursued and persecuted him. Sleep fled as a mist disperses before the risen sun. He got up, switched on the light, threw on his dressing-gown, and got into his slippers. He would look through the formula again; the reaction had been wrong.

He went downstairs and found his laboratory door ajar, which made no impression on his engaged mind. That the study door also was open reinforced something in his subconsciousness, and made him vaguely uneasy. But at the sight of his desk this was only transient. He slipped into his chair, found his papers, and began a reconsideration of them.

Count Boloski, inside the safe, had heard the approaching footsteps and had swung the heavy door lightly to, till but a crack was open. He put out his torch and waited in suspense. The man at the desk stirred in his chair, rustled his papers, and his pen scratched as he made alterations in his notes. Boloski pushed the noiseless door open and peered out. Professor Gretton sat with his back to him, humped up in his dressing-gown, and the light flooded the room. Gretton stirred, shifted in his chair, and rose. As he did so the Pole softly pulled the door to its previous position.

Gretton stood for a moment in thought. Things were running through his head. He was tempted to go into the laboratory to try the other acid. He turned towards the safe, where so many of his registers were kept, looked at the door, and remembered that he had not brought his keys. But the laboratory and the study were open!

This fact flashed upon him for the first time, and left him puzzled. He approached the safe and examined it with a frown. How could he have left the doors open? He was in physical contact with the steel doors now, and there was a little click. He was deaf and did not hear.

He withdrew and went out into the laboratory, switching on the light. Then he went to his jars and retorts at the farther end.

After half an hour's work he returned to the study, took his seat at the table, and resumed his notes. He had got what he wanted. He sat for twenty minutes, and then there came to his inner senses an impression of disturbance. He glanced up involuntarily, and listened. There was a sound somewhere. It must come from without. He redirected his attention to his paper, and went on with his notes.

The great heavy steel door of the safe had clicked into its place under the slight pressure of Gretton's touch. For a moment or two Boloski waited in silence in his cramped position within, and then he ventured to put forth a hand and explore. He felt the door, and pushed it. It stood firm and unyielding, and after he had made several attempts he abandoned them in despair. Then he turned on his torch and examined his surroundings. On all sides of him was the terrible prison of steel. He shuddered, switched off the light in order not to waste it, and began a dispassionate review of his situation. Release was impossible except from without. He would have to wait until Mrs. Gretton arrived, attract her attention by knocking, and so be liberated. He was a man of iron resolution, or he would not have been what he was—one of the ablest spies ever employed by the Germans; and he made himself as comfortable as was possible in the cramped space at his command. Presently, however, he became conscious of an oppression, which seemed to increase. There was a choking sensation in his throat, and he drew breath in a laboured way. The feeling disconcerted him, and as he set his wits to work to discover the reason it came upon him with a startling flash that the safe was air-tight, and that his supply of atmosphere was confined to the contents of the safe. The thought penetrated to his inmost being with a terrible chill. If he could not manage to get the door open he would die of suffocation. How long—how long? As he drew in a shuddering inspiration of the vitiated air he flung himself on the steel wall and began to hammer with his torch. He hammered and he cried aloud. His voice came back to him from the wall. He cried out louder—he screamed. Someone must hear him—it mattered not who it was. He was blind to all thought of detection and capture. He wanted to be detected. Suffocation! He could have faced death in other forms, but this slow strangulation— He dashed upon the steel and screamed.

Professor Gretton turned in his chair. There was a noise some-where. But he was deaf, and he could make out neither its quality nor its direction. He opened the door to the lawn, and listened. It was a rumble only that reached his deaf ears.

"Probably an aeroplane," he reflected, and then, with a little touch of alarm, "A Zeppelin!" He looked up into the clear sky, and shook his head. "No, not on a night like this."

He went back into the study, cleared up his papers, yawned, and, passing into the laboratory, locked the door. Something was still drubbing in his head, but he had given it up. Perhaps it was the guns at the camp.

On his way to his room he paused outside his wife's door and, seeing a light under it, went in. Mrs. Gretton, who was seated in a chair near the bed, rose with a little cry. She had taken off her frock and thrown a dressing-gown over her déshabillé. Her husband did not notice this.

"My dear," he said, "did you hear any noises? Is that why you are up? I think it must be either the guns at Wayford Camp or aeroplanes."

"No," she said, rather tremulously. "I heard nothing."

"Ah, well; it may have been traction engines or motor-lorries on the road." He became aware that it was odd for her to be up at that time of night. "Couldn't you sleep?"

"No, I have rather a headache."

"I'm sorry, my dear. Better get to bed. It will pass off. Our guest will be off early, so you must get some sleep. I'm—" he paused, "I'm rather glad he's going. He's a persistent man, but agreeable—agreeable."

"I shall be glad when he's gone," said Mrs. Gretton, hoarsely.

He put his hand lightly on her arm, and she took it in hers.

"Good night, Edward."

When he had gone she stared at the wall, unseeing. In an hour's time or so Count Boloski would be waiting for her in the study—his car at the end of the avenue. She rose, went to the door, and turned the key. Then she undressed and went slowly to bed. Noises! There was only the noise in her own mind, which drummed loudly. She closed her eyes, and waited. It was four o'clock when she passed off into troubled sleep.

AS IT IS WRITTEN: A STRANGE STORY

"Tetroul" (identity unknown)

published in *"Carry On": The Armstrong Munition Workers' Christmas Magazine*
(Newcastle-upon-Tyne: Armstrong Whitworth, December 1916)

'As It Is Written', published under a pseudonym in December 1916,
puts the enemy at the heart of the British war effort. Its setting
would have been intimately familiar to its original readership,
given that it was published in a magazine for munition workers:
the story is set in a British munitions factory during a blackout
triggered by a German Zeppelin raid. London was the target of
repeated Zeppelin attacks throughout the war, as Germany sought
to damage or destroy Woolwich Arsenal, but such airship attacks
also occurred all over the country including Tyneside, where the
story is set. The enemy in this story is not so much Germany as
Prussia and, like other atrocity tales of the period, the narrative
takes care to highlight rifts and conflicts within Germany to convince readers of the vulnerability of the enemy war effort. In 1916
Britons faced their third Christmas of the war, and the first following
the devastating losses of the first Battle of the Somme. With no
end to the hostilities in sight, there was clearly a need for morale-
boosting propaganda. "Tetroul" offers reassurance on a number of
fronts, from stressing the superior quality of British armaments
and equipment to outlining the internal divisions eating away at
German morale. The story also offers a sympathetic portrayal of
life in a munitions factory and emphasizes the crucial role played
by munition workers in the war effort.

"The first to speak was a man. He growled something in gruff German. With a thrill I realized it was Von Darwitzon. Then a woman. At first I could not hear very well, and then— Mother of Heaven! I recognized the voice. It was Greta."

HE WAS KNOWN IN L.M. SHOP AS A "PROGRESS MAN." IN THE vernacular of the shop, it really meant that he was the man who helped to cater for the ever-hungry machines. If you ever ran short of steel, brass, or aluminium, and things on your section were looking dicky, "Progress" would pop up, wave his wand, and immediately get you supplied with the necessary fodder. You would always see him stalking through the shop just before breakfast, and then he would disappear to reappear at five. His ways were mysterious. He was rarely to be seen, yet always on the spot when you wanted him. What he did with his spare time no one ever knew. Someone once said he used to sit behind some forgotten scrap-heap on the banks of the river, writing poetry. However, that may be, but "Progress" was a bit of a mystery. No one knew whence he came, or where he disappeared to at 6-30 when "L.M." heaved a sigh and disgorged her tired thousands.

Now to create an air of mystery about yourself in a munition factory is a very silly thing, and it often leads to complications.

Of course many were the suggestions as to the identity of "Progress." Someone said he was a spy, but that was absurd. The fitters were sure he had an eye for other things, but the girls pooh-poohed the suggestion and built Garvice-like romances round him.

It was more or less by accident that I came to know his story. It was the third night of my week on night-shift. It had been a very hot day, and when I entered the shop at five the place felt like an oven. Outside, the sky was heavy and sullen, inside the day-shift were just gasping to get into the air, such as it was. Things got away fairly well under the circumstances, but just after supper an electric tremor ran through the shop. There were "Zepps" about. The girls, the first alarm over, set about to make themselves comfortable for some hours if need be.

I was kept busy for half-an-hour putting things as "shop shape" as possible.

At length things began to settle down, so I betook myself to a little corner I knew of to await further developments.

Feeling my way round the corner of a large "auto" I bumped into a tall figure.

"Hullo!" I said, "who's that?"

"Platt," came back a quiet voice. It was "Progress."

After a few uncomplimentary remarks on the expected Zepps, I asked him where he was making to. He told me he was seeking a place to rest.

"Come with me" I said, and I steered him to my corner.

We had been talking on various and general topics for a few minutes when he suddenly said, "I hear that I am a bit of a mystery." I replied that our curiosity *had* been aroused.

I don't know whether it was because we had been thrown together in a bond of common danger, or what, but presently he broke in, "look here, I'll tell you my story. I am going to surprise you. I am a German." He rapped the last sentence out quickly, and then was silent awaiting my reply. For a moment I sat amazed. "Progress" a German! Then he must be a spy after all. But that couldn't be. How had he got into the shop? I had a hundred questions on my lips at once, but the man beside me seemed to divine my state of mind, and answered my unspoken thoughts the next minute. "Yes, what I have said is true.

"Let me tell you, both my parents were German. They had two children, my sister Greta and myself. My father met my mother when a young beautiful girl, at Baden, many years before, and immediately fell in love. It was a case of love at first sight. After a short engagement they married, my father having obtained a professorship at the Liege University. It was in Liege that Greta, my little sister, and I were born. It was under the shadow of the grey old University that she and I spent our childhood. Those were happy days. It all comes back to me when I tell you the story, and I thank God that the time draws near—ah, very near."

For a moment he was silent, and I sat and wondered.

"There was an old-world garden at the back of the house," he said, picking up the threads of his story again, "and often in the after glow of an autumn day we would sit under the golden apple trees at the bottom of the garden—my father and mother, Greta and I, and the old couple would plan out the future. I was to be an engineer, and of course do great things for the Fatherland. Greta would some day meet *the* man, and have a home of her own. At this latter thought my old mother would look at my little sister and tears would fill her eyes.

"So the years sped on. I finished my schooling and went to serve my time to be an engineer. Greta meanwhile had grown into a beautiful girl. Ah! man; the iron bites deep into my soul when I think of her at twenty-one. Her eyes were like the twin stars that used to shine over the spires of the University in the early summer mornings; her voice like the croon of a summer sea. Her lips were like a crushed rose petal; her hair, a wayward sunbeam, wilful and uncontrolled.

"But I get too sentimental. No! it is not sentiment. See! I have opened my heart to you and painted with feeble words a little picture of my dear sister. Of admirers she had many—but none had her heart.

"At last one day, a cloud, no bigger than a man's hand, came across our sky. From across the border in Germany came news of great preparations. The air was full of rumours and alarms of a long prepared-for war. My father, a quiet, peaceful and unassuming man, had all his life, since his student days, been a member of a German Socialist Party against war. Let me explain that the party was not of a Radical type. The members merely preached quietly and calmly the gospel of the great brotherhood of man. Naturally their doctrine was not altogether popular in a country which for forty years had as its aim the domination and overrunning of Europe.

"Then the thundercloud burst, and as you know, Europe was plunged in the greatest horror of all time. Our people had laid their preparations well. My father hurriedly made arrangements to leave Belgium and return to Germany, but at the last minute we received instructions to wait. As an engineer, I was not for the army but for the munition factory, so received a special message to remain in Liege, and guard the interests of the Fatherland."

At this point Platt gave a short bitter laugh, and was silent. He continued a minute later.

"Our army, as you well know, made rapid strides, and after a few hammer-like strokes, was soon at the gates of Liege. I shall never forget those early days. Even though at the time the Belgians were my enemies I was filled with awe and admiration at the way they defended their beautiful town. However, it was only a question of time, for the preparations of years told in the end, and our troops took the City.

"Germany once in possession, we were again at liberty to come and go as we pleased. The Military Authorities took charge of the engineering factory in which I had worked and turned it into a munition factory. I was sent back to my trade, but instead of Belgians, I had my fellow-countrymen as work mates.

"Life soon dropped back into its old swing, our army having advanced across the fair fields of Belgium into France. As the University had closed its doors on the outbreak of war, my father was given a post in the Hospital, which was filled with our wounded. Here also, Greta worked, ministering to the needs of the suffering. Meanwhile my life was filled with my new work. We were working at a break-neck speed, as guns were always needed. It was while working on the new pattern of an anti-aircraft gun sight, that I first caught a glimpse of an idea which sent a thrill through me. I had suddenly tumbled across a way to make a new sight for the guns. It was a simple enough idea, and when perfected, would, I was sure, revolutionize warfare in the air.

"It was shortly after this, the first of a series of incidents which were to change the whole course of my life occurred. While at her work in the Hospital, Greta had met a Captain Von Darwitzon, a tall imposing Prussian, who was the assistant Provost Marshal of the City. He had come to the Hospital in quest of some of his men and met her. From what I subsequently heard, it appeared that Von Darwitzon was impressed by Greta and at once began to urge his suit. It commenced in the old, old way. There were presents of flowers, invitations to dinner, and in fact the hundred and one outward signs of the amorous swain. Greta from the first was repelled by the man. She did not like him, nor the manner in which he treated his men, who hated him. At length things became worse, and Greta was annoyed at the persistence of the man whom she had many times snubbed. Then one evening matters reached a climax.

"The Captain, on some pretext or other, had come to the house, and incidentally made himself quite at home. During the earlier part of the evening his manner had been somewhat overbearing, and as time went on, he became more and more offensive. Greta, without being unduly rude, had shown in a decided manner more than once that she disliked his attentions. This, as you will guess, nettled the Prussian, and all the worst in the man asserted itself. At length, after he had thoroughly disgusted us, he took his departure. As is the custom, Greta, who was acting as hostess, my mother being ill at the time, accompanied our visitor to the door.

"My memory plays me tricks as to what subsequently happened, but I remember hearing a scream. Rushing to the front door I found Greta struggling in the embrace of Von Darwitzon, who was making clumsy attempts to kiss her. I then, as you English say, saw red, and catching the man by the throat I pulled him away, and struck him good and strong between the eyes. He went down heavily. For a minute he was stunned, then he rose, and spitting blood from his lips he said in a voice of deadly hatred 'So!—It will be *my* turn next.' Without a further word I closed the door in his face, and putting my arm around Greta, comforted her.

"There was not the slightest doubt that we had made a dangerous enemy, and one who would do all in his power to hurt me and mine. It was some days before the blow fell; I was surprised that Von Darwitzon had not taken action at once. However, his plan was subtle. It happened exactly a week after I had ejected him from the house. We were at breakfast at the time, when there came a sharp rat-tat-tat at the door. A maid rushed in with the news that soldiers were at the door and a minute later the Captain strode into the room, followed by a squad of his men.

"Walking up to my father, he said with a horrible smile on his face, 'Professor, I arrest you. You are a traitor. I believe there are some nice little papers in this house referring to a Peace Brotherhood Society? Dangerous documents to have when the Fatherland is at war, eh?—perhaps Greta is sorry now for her rudeness,' he said, leering at my sister. 'Meanwhile, *dear* Professor, come with me—*the Fatherland wants you.*'

"I was dumbfounded at the turn of events. I had not expected this. I could do nothing. I was helpless. As the soldiers formed round to march him away, my mother and Greta cried out and attempted to hold him; I also pushed up to the Captain. Rough hands thrust me back, and a minute later my father had disappeared and we were left alone."

Platt now began to speak hurriedly, as if anxious to get the whole story told quickly. His voice and manner suggested that he wished to try and forget. "For three days," he continued, "we heard nothing. Then once again the Captain appeared. This time he was alone. Approaching my mother, he said, 'Madame, I have a letter for you.' My mother glanced at the contents and then gave a low stricken moan, and sank to the ground. Guessing its purport, I snatched the document from her hand, and there, in cold official print was the statement—'Carl Stern, Professor. Shot last night at sundown, and buried in the Laang Platz this morning. Crime:—Conspiring against the Arms of the Fatherland. (signed) Fritz Von Darwitzon, Captain, Assistant Provost Marshal, Liege.'

"Then I seemed to go mad and I made a jump at the villain who had been responsible. However, he anticipated me, gave a sharp command, and a company of men who must have been waiting outside, rushed into the room. 'Arrest these people,' said the Captain, pointing to my mother and me, and looking round he said, 'But there is another. The fair lady of my heart—where is she?' He referred to Greta, who earlier in the day had gone into the town on a message. Bidding his men watch over us, he searched the house. He was not successful, and returning ordered us to be marched down to the prison.

"'Ah, there is plenty of time,' he whispered in my ear just before we were placed in the cell, 'I can find my lady—later.'

"My friend, words fail me when I try to tell you of all that happened during the awful time which followed. All night I sat beside my mother and tried to comfort her, but she was inconsolable. Her husband had been treacherously put to death, her daughter at the mercy of an unscrupulous villain. Once or twice she lost possession of herself and screamed to God to help her. The end came quite unexpectedly. It was during one of these paroxysms that she suddenly clutched at her heart in agony. With a great cry of sorrow I rushed to her side, but it was of no avail. At last, just when her eyes were dimming, she looked up at me. 'Son, I know I am dying, but there is one thing. Swear to me that you will be revenged. Swear to me that you will be revenged. Kill,' she said weakly raising herself up, 'Kill, kill Von Darwitzon. He murdered your father. Kill, kill—kill everything that stands for the Prussian military system—kill.'

"She sank back exhausted. A minute later she again opened her eyes and a smile broke over her poor tired face. 'Ah! son of mine, it is when things are darkest that we see them bright. Somewhere I can hear the birds sweetly singing as they used to do at nesting time in the orchard, when you and Greta were children—oh, happy days. Son! son! I can see him. Ah! Carl, I come.' Then with a little sigh she slipped away, and I was alone.

"Yes! alone, and the chill of tragedy settled round me like a cloak. How I kept my sanity during the hours which followed, God only knows. There were times when I must have been very nearly mad. One thing remains stamped on my memory. It was in the dim light of that room, which was both mortuary and prison cell, that I determined to fulfil the solemn oath my mother had whispered ere she died. Yes! I would kill Von Darwitzon. My poor dead father had always been right. The gospel of hate and arrogance preached by the Prussians he had said would bring about the downfall of the Fatherland. Now I saw how right he had been. It was the great Juggernaut which would ultimately run amok and take with it to destruction the German race.

"Prussianism for generations to come would be remembered as a foul-smelling sore which had to be cut out, but in the process of which a great nation was destroyed.

"I don't know how long I sat fondling the dear dead hands, but at last I fell asleep from sheer exhaustion. The next thing I remember was being roughly shaken by the shoulder and told to prepare for a journey. The dawn was breaking, but my gaolers must have entered earlier as my mother's body had disappeared—I never saw her again. After a scanty meal I was hurried with others to the station, where we were all placed in a train.

"I was returning to Germany in a manner I had little expected. I was leaving behind in the shell-shattered Belgian city, one living relation in all the world—my sister. My tortured thoughts cried out to God above to watch over and protect her. I could do nothing. We were heavily guarded and the chance of escape was remote.

"We left the station just at noon, and slipping smoothly along were soon well on our way to the frontier. Everywhere the Prussian system had left its mark. When last I made the journey the country lay smiling under the peaceful autumn sunshine. The farmlands with their little red-roofed houses lay stretched out in all the golden glory of the harvest time. Here and there, where the smoke drifted lazily up to the blue sky, were patches of red and a spire marking a sleepy little village, where the good dame sang softly as she prepared the evening meal. In the distance came the whisper of a convent bell calling the humble to vesper; across the fields the lowing cattle were slowly going to the milking.

"On this day it was all changed. The awful blight of war had fallen. Just a heap of stones marked what had once been a peaceful village. The golden harvest fields gone, trampled underfoot; in the little ruined convent lay a broken crucifix—on the steps of the shattered altar the dead body of a nun. The very air stank. This was the Prussian system. It had caught *me* in its claws aud crushed me—what must it have done to these quiet peaceful people, whom Prussia had labelled—'enemy.'

"Ah!" said Platt, and I could feel him turn closer to me, "it was awful!—I can hardly describe it. But I am wandering from my story. We had been on our journey two hours when the next card was played. The train was running slowly through flat country, when, for some reason or other, I looked up, and saw in the distant sky three aeroplanes. For a moment I thought they were German machines on their way to Liege, but I was mistaken. As they came nearer I could make them out, they were of the famous Morane type which I had once seen flying at an air meeting in Southern Belgium. They must have seen us, for the next minute the French raiders swung round and swooped toward us. Instantly the train was in a tumult, but for us there was no escape. As the monoplanes came round there were three white puffs, and three bombs dropped ahead, just missing the train. Swinging into line again, the end Morane hovered for a second high above us. Again I saw the puff—then a thundering flash and oblivion.

"It was dusk when I awoke. I discovered I was lying in a ditch some distance from what had once been a railway train. I staggered giddily to my feet, only to fall again. One side of my face was sticky with blood. I found I'd a nasty wound on the head, but the bleeding had stopped. Beyond this I was unhurt, and realized that I'd had a wonderful escape, and what was more, was, for the time being, a free man. My chief thought, now that I was free, was to get back to Liege, settle with Von Darwitzon, and rescue Greta. I lay until I had recovered sufficiently to crawl down to a stream near by. Here I washed my wound, bathed, and ate a ration of black bread given before leaving."

"You were lucky," I broke in, "only one in a thousand would have been as fortunate."

"Yes," he said, "it seemed as if the way had been opened for me.

"Anyhow a little later I was able to start on my journey back to Liege. I won't dwell on the incidents that happened on the way, but, it is sufficient to say that by midnight I had reached the city. I determined to go straight to Von Darwitzon's house. The house, I must explain, stood on a large piece of ground on the outskirts. Under cover of darkness I escaped detection, and clambering over a wall, was soon in the garden. Lights came from some of the windows, but beyond this there was little to indicate that, apart from the servants, anyone else was at home. However, I was wrong. I crawled up to a large French window which opened on to a lawn, and listened. I'd only to wait a minute, and then I heard voices. The first to speak was a man.

"He growled something in gruff German. With a thrill I realized it was Von Darwitzon. Then I heard a woman. At first I could not hear very well, and, then, Mother of Heaven! I recognized the voice. It was Greta. Even as I realized that she was there, I heard her give a pitiful cry and say, 'No! no! not *that!*—I'll shoot.' Two shots rang out in quick succession. The whole incident had only been a matter of seconds. Smashing the door open with a kick, I rushed into the room.

"My heart gave a bound, seemed to stand still, and then turn to ice. There, near the door, with a revolver by her side, lay Greta. Near the fireplace was Von Darwitzon, with a shattered leg, and groaning horribly. I rushed to Greta and gathered her in my arms. She smiled bravely up at me.

"'Paul, you've come. I knew you would,' she murmured. 'You are just in time, Paul—just in time. I am going on a long journey, Paul. Say good-bye to Mother and Father. Tell them… tell them… that the Captain brought me here by force. We… we were alone… he wanted to rob me… rob me of my honour. But I still have… have that Paul. I sh… shot at him… I thought I'd missed… so there was only… only one thing left… it was horrible pulling the trigger… and oh, the steel was *so* cold.' She stopped, and seemed to breathe more easily, then………

"Then my pent-up hate broke all bounds. In a hell fury I rushed at the man I'd sworn to kill. All the devils in hell and on earth were screaming in my brain. He must have seen murder in my eyes, for he gave a yell of terror. But it was of no avail. I clutched at his throat and slowly squeezed it until his face grew livid. Tighter and tighter I pressed, and with each effort I remember saying, 'Ah! my father, that for my father, that for my mother, and *this* and *this* and *this* for Greta. When I released my fingers from his throat, Von Darwitzon had gone to a place where there will be many Prussians to keep him company."

During this recital, Platt's voice had almost reached a whisper. But it was the voice of a man who had settled some great debt. There had been no malice in it, just a plain calm statement of fact. Nevertheless, I gave a shiver.

"So I redeemed my pledge," he continued. "Killed him. Whilst making sure that Von Darwitzon was quite dead, I heard voices in the distance, someone was approaching the house. Going over to where Greta lay, I passionately kissed her cold lips, took a last look at her dear form, and swiftly and silently went my way. It was no use trying to get her body away from the place. Her spirit had gone to where there was no war—no Prussia.

"After three days of great hardships and many perils, I managed to get across the border into Holland by persuading the Dutch guards I was a Belgian and had escaped from the Germans. The deception was easy, and after a while I was enabled to get to England.

"My knowledge of engineering secured me a position in this shop. *Now*! perhaps I may tell you something else. During the time I've been here I've worked many, many hours on my invention, which I told you about earlier in my story. The idea I'd so carelessly stumbled across in the factory at Liege has now been improved, and I think I've produced the perfect sight. The authorities have accepted my design, and they are now on all English guns."

Then, by way of conclusion, and with ever such a tiny note of triumph in his voice, he said, "So I may be able to *repay* Prussia."

Hardly had the words left his mouth when a dull thud smote my ears. There was not a sound in the shop;—the girls and men had also heard the sound and were—listening. Then again, this time three distinct thuds, but nearer.

Accompanied by Platt I at once went round stations and gave the necessary orders. The girls meanwhile were behaving wonderfully. It was really a little pale-faced girl with yellow hair who saved the situation. In a thin but clear voice which wavered a little at first, she commenced to sing what the girls had jokingly called their "Hymn of Hate".

> "If the Zeppelins come to 'L.M.'
>   Never mind,
> If the Zeppelins come to 'L.M.'
>   Never mind.
> We are making shot and shell
> And we'll blow them all to—
> If the Zeppelins come to 'L.M.'
>   Never mind."

It was only a music-hall ditty, but it had a haunting refrain. In a minute the tune was taken up by the rest and the sound rose and fell, the voices in harmony. I secretly thanked God for putting the words of the song into the mouth of the little girl with yellow hair.

The noise had died down a little when Platt and I were able to sneak out of the bottom of the shop into the yard. He naturally was in a high state of excitement. Up to now we had not heard the wail of our anti-aircraft guns. We stood outside the door and looked skywards. There was nothing to be seen at first. Then suddenly, one, two, three long beams of light, like long skinny fingers, slit the darkness and searched the sky. They seemed to do their work methodically and ever so slowly. Inch by inch they crept over the star-studded floor. Their method was merciless. My attention had been attracted for a second when Platt gave a gulp. One of our searchlights had picked up a long cigar-shaped form. Another searchlight came to its assistance. The Zepp. made frantic efforts to escape and dropped three bombs. Then an anti-aircraft gun chipped in from amid the darkness lower down. With a rocket-like "shoosh" the shell rushed skywards. We held our breath. Platt gave a shout as the stern of the Zepp. dropped a little. Meanwhile frantic flashings further west showed that a second Zepp. had been ferreted out; so there were two of them. Well! Platt's sights would be put to the test. Two bombs dropped from the new-comer, then again we heard our "Antis." There was no doubt this time. The shell appeared to catch the ship fair and square just above the front gondola. She went up in a mass of flames. Platt just about went mad with excitement at this. Rushing into the yard he raised his hands above his head and shouted hoarsely, half in English, half in German, "Greta, Greta, this is for you, and father and mother, see I have avenged you."

I called to him to come under cover but he stood watching the remaining Zepp. It dropped no further bombs; the air seemed terribly still. Only the rattle of its engines every now and then. This way and that it twisted in its endeavour to escape.

The Zepp., after further frantic manœuvering slowed for less than a minute, and then the gun spoke for the third time. God! the sights must have been perfect. The next second the raider seemed to crumple up. There was a great roar as the whole structure blew up with a tremendous explosion.

Just then, one of the girls rushed into the yard. Platt, Who had been standing transfixed, then seemed to realize his danger and that of the girl. With a great bound he rushed towards her and pulled her to the ground, at the same time covering her body with his own, and just in time.

When willing hands were able to go to their assistance the girl was found to be unhurt, but poor Platt had reached the end of his long journey of sorrow.

So I come to the end of my tale. It has been a tragedy; but do we not live in a tragic age? To-day, a cot in one of our great Hospitals is called *"Outside Progress."* The girls of "L.M." gave it. Sometimes strangers see the name and ask what it means, but very few people can tell them. The girls at "L.M." still talk about him, and wonder who and what he was.

This is his history,—as it is written.

WAR WORKERS

May Edginton

published in the *Strand Magazine*, vol. 54 (1917)

Edginton (1883–1957) was a successful novelist and playwright. Several of her works were adapted for the screen in the 1920s. She also contributed regularly to popular magazines of her day, including the *Strand Magazine*. Her particular strengths were romance and gentle comedy, and 'War Workers' combines both of these. Like many contemporary war stories, 'War Workers' shows the impact of the First World War on the Home Front, particularly as regards women's voluntary work, but it also reminds us that life carried on despite the war and that readers at home still liked a laugh.

"**A**ND NOW," SAID MRS. BROWN-PERKINS, "TO OPEN THE parcel so kindly sent to us from my friend Lady Tubbs!"

Lightly as Mrs. Brown-Perkins spoke, there was a thrill in her voice. It was like a *tremolo* straying by accident into a trumpet-call. As the other ladies of the Burtonbury War Relief Fund Committee crowded round her with appropriate curiosity her firm hand shook a little.

"Dear Lady Tubbs!" said she; "so ever thoughtful, so always kind! Amid all her activities in the great world she does not forget little me in my small sphere down here. Scissors—or a penknife, I think."

One being handed to her by Miss Caroline Vestal and the other by Miss Virginia Crombie—the two leading unmarried lady residents of Burtonbury—the president of the War Relief Fund Committee cut the string and disclosed the contents.

During the subsequent shock of horror, preceding a chill silence, Mrs. Brown-Perkins essayed an unsuccessful smile.

"These are, no doubt, from Lady Tubbs's own wardrobe," said Mrs. Tombs, in a cold voice.

"I had gathered from you, dear Mrs. Perkins," remarked Mrs. Baker, "an impression of *quite* a different type of woman."

Other ladies present voicing similar thoughts, Mrs. Brown-Perkins, murmuring something about an explanation, sought for and found a folded note.

"My dear Mrs. Brown-Perkins," she read, "I send you a little consignment which I hope you will be able to sell for the good of your cause. They were sent to me by a prominent actress, lately widowed, who, while, of course, wearing the usual black outwardly, feels that she must at least be mauve throughout underneath. It is a feeling which does her credit, I think. The garments appear to me to be of considerable value and should be easily disposed of."

"I suppose," said Mrs. Tombs, stretching out a finger and thumb, "that this is *not* a—a dress?"

"It is certainly not," Miss Vestal replied, laying both hands upon it with a touch of avidity.

"And what is this?" Miss Crombie asked.

"And this?" said Mrs. Baker.

"And this?"

"And these?"

As each lady sat with a butterfly garment spread upon her knee, and a look of horror and disapprobation petrified upon her face, a well-known silhouette passed by the windows of the parish meeting-room, in the direction of the door.

Every lady, starting, exclaimed, with unanimous inflection, "Professor Ruby!"

"That saintly man!" said Mrs. Baker, crumpling an offensive nightgown into a ball and dashing it into the box again. "Do not let him catch even a glimpse of these things!"

"With his wonderful standard of womanhood—" began Miss Vestal, tremulously, flinging away a lapful.

"True," said Mrs. Brown-Perkins, "most true. I would not offend the dear Professor's fastidiousness for the world. As you observe, dearest Miss Vestal, his standard is the highest one. It is set in the clouds. What he would think of pink and yellow—"

"Though, being a bachelor, he would not know what they are," said Miss Crombie, bringing relief.

"Neither would my husband know, my dear, though we have been married for twenty-five years," said Mrs. Baker. "If he were even to see me looking at underclothes like that, he would say to me, 'Bessie,' he would say—"

"Put the lid on quickly!" exclaimed Mrs. Tombs, in a voice of authority, as there entered the parish room the wonderful man who, though not of the cloth itself, yet, by reason of his high friendship with Burtonbury's absent rector—now C.F.—had taken upon himself all parish duties possible to one of the laity, and even closely assimilated the manner and habits of his revered associate.

"Good afternoon, ladies," said he, laughing readily. "What have we here? What a really fine—what a magnificent collection for the jumble sale! What kind friend sent us that splendid centre-piece for a table? Really! Really! it is very little broken, too. Wonderful! wonderful! I suspect Mrs. Brown-Perkins has had a strong hand in this! And I'm sure she has had able lieutenants in Mrs. Baker and Mrs. Tombs, and I expect that Mrs. Hargraves and Mrs. Slater are conspiring brilliantly as usual in good works; while as for Miss Vestal and Miss Crombie, dear Mrs. Brown-Perkins, can you not persuade these indefatigable ladies to take a little rest? War is war, of course. We all know that, alas! Aha! aha! aha! I feel perfectly certain—a little *bird* told me—that we are going to have a fine day."

"Ever the optimist!" murmured Miss Crombie, with upturned eyes, praising the ascetic and great scholar.

"You always bring cheer," said Miss Vestal, casting down her lashes.

Mrs. Baker rose from her seat and, standing with her back against the box on the table, formed an ample screen.

"Aha! aha!" said the Professor, laughing after the most favoured rectorial manner. "I must see the whole collection. What have we in this box?"

"It is only something for sale," replied Mrs. Baker, while the other ladies clustered round, intent on saving their most distinguished neighbour's finer feelings.

"Ha! ha! ha!" said Professor Ruby, laughing, "something for sale! Let me be your first bidder."

A mingled "Oh!" went up, and Miss Crombie with upturned eyes exclaimed, "You are always generous, but—" while Mrs. Brown-Perkins issued an explanation discreetly.

"It is merely apparel, dear Professor Ruby."

"Indeed!" said the Professor, becoming extremely grave. "In-deed! How very, very kind of someone to send us some apparel! Well, well. This is splendid."

"We ordered three dozen bottles for the War Time Fruit-Bottling Club," said Mrs. Tombs, turning the conversation with a nimble wit.

"Really! really!" cried the Professor, laughing again in safety. "Three dozen! Ha! ha! ha! I must be getting home or I shall be late for tea." Continuing to laugh until he was out of the parish room, he then ceased, and walked quite naturally down the street.

"I didn't know where to look," said Miss Vestal, with a girlish shyness, the retention of which did credit to the pertinacity of her character.

"We must sell these extraordinary and deplorable clothes outside Burtonbury," said Mrs. Brown-Perkins, clasping Lady Tubbs's letter still in her hand. "I shall send them to a London wardrobe-dealer, a Mrs. Tizza, in Petticoat Lane, and they will be out of our hands. I will pack them up and send them off to-night."

Amid the congratulations of the other matrons on so satisfactory a solution, Miss Vestal and Miss Crombie took their departure.

The figure of the Professor was proceeding distantly down the High Street. He was lifting his hat and laughing at frequent intervals.

"How popular the dear man is!" said Miss Crombie.

"He is wonderful!" replied Miss Vestal.

"Walk home with me, dear," said Miss Crombie, "and have tea. The air is so fresh that I thought we might make a round and go down the Green Lane."

They walked on together.

Then, "That *lingerie!*" exclaimed Miss Crombie, pronouncing the word boldly.

"Did you really look at it closely?" said Miss Vestal, with some hesitation.

Miss Crombie replied: "Not closely. I had no desire to look closely."

"Nor I."

"But the sewing was very nicely done."

"So I thought, dear."

"If everything had been rather lower and higher, and broader—"

"If there had been more of everything, in fact—"

"And had the material been different—"

"Thicker—"

"Exactly, dear. Then one might have admired the fine sewing. I am not narrow; and given all those things, I would have expressed admiration of the work."

"It was merely the colour which made me look at them at all. Yellow—"

"The pink attracted me. I thought it a pretty shade."

"Hush!" said Miss Vestal.

The Green Lane ran by the walls of the Cloistered Hall, and the Professor himself was approaching his gates.

"Fancy meeting him!" Miss Crombie exclaimed.

"How well he walks!" Miss Vestal murmured.

Miss Crombie said, "I always admire that restrained, reticent expression of his when one is not looking. When one looks it vanishes and he laughs that beautiful hearty laugh. He might be own brother to our rector. But I often wonder of what he is thinking."

"These reserved looks cover a great deal," said Miss Vestal. "I do admire a reserved man. Professor Ruby has such high ideals; that is why he has never married. He replied to Mrs. Baker once, when she told him that a wife would be such a help in his position, that he was afraid of meeting with a great disappointment."

"Dear man!" murmured Miss Crombie.

"May his dreams come true!" said Miss Vestal, with holy fervour.

Each lady looked at the other a little askance.

"By the way, dear," said Miss Crombie, "what was the name of that wardrobe-dealer? Not that it matters. All I was wondering was if she was quite honest."

"Tizza, Petticoat Lane, I believe," said Miss Vestal, with a perfect nonchalance. "I jotted it down. But hush!"

The Professor drew level with them. He lifted his hat very courtly.

"Indefatigable!" he cried, with laughter. "Indefatigable!"

He passed, laughing, through his gate.

The ladies continued their way, well rewarded for the *détour*.

When the scholar attained his own door he became pensive again. The high-thinking expression so revered and discussed by the ladies of Burtonbury sat in his eye. It was part an inspiration, part a dream, part a quest. Thus it had been dissected, and thus it was. Professor Ruby went through life seeking the ideal; and still he sought her.

What manner of woman was she? Where to be found? How should she attain that wonderful standard which such a man rightly asked?

Many ladies of the most upright character and impeccable manners would have cared to know.

The Professor found tea prepared in his study.

Seated at his desk, he helped himself from the lonely tray. He thought. His brow furrowed. Once or twice it cleared as at a vision, but furrowed again, and he shook his head. There was no laughter in him.

"When?" he inquired of himself; "when, oh, when?"

By nature he was not cold. He wished to marry. None was readier than he to tread the path assigned to man. But he had an ideal; and where to find her? How to be sure, quite, quite sure?

Seated thus lonely, the thoughtful man opened a drawer and took therefrom a picture; obviously he had mounted it himself upon a square of fine cardboard. One may imagine that it had been a labour of sheer love. It was a charming picture of beauty unadorned, and adorned the most.

A fair, smiling girl in the most entrancing—yet limited—of *dessous* gazed from the picture at the Professor. She represented, in fact, the favourite advertisement of the Three Graces Corset Company—an advertisement most familiar and popular with the public, since it occupied a full page of that most exemplary and respected of all family magazines, the *Charing Cross*.

Under such eminent chaperonage, indeed, Professor Ruby had found her, and she was intriguing. Oh, the shoulder-straps!

The fluff and foam! She had bewitched more hearts than this ascetic's.

To-day he was asking himself, as he had often asked before: "Do they really wear these? I fear! I fear!"

A man of such unimpeachable morals, without spot or stain upon the bright lustre of his conscience, has no way of obtaining an answer to such a question, save one.

He can marry.

And then?

Supposing the answer to be in the negative?

And, given such an answer, suppose that someone else might have replied differently?

The bitterness of it!

One cannot wonder that this brilliant man whispered to himself, "I fear! I fear!"

After Professor Ruby had put the picture away again he sat long with his head in his hands, despairing.

Up early the next morning, he beheld Miss Vestal hurrying for the early train. She was going up to London to buy the flannel for the soldiers' hospital shirts, to be made up by the working party. Hardly had the Professor's genial laughter ceased before he saw Miss Crombie out, posting an early letter in time for the postal clearance for London letters. Except for these two pleasant meetings, however, he passed a quietish morning with minor bereavements. When specially occupied with his problem he usually managed this. It was easier, somehow, than wreathing one's face in laughter, to pass into some lowly dwelling, appearing as harassed as one truly felt, and whispering, "The trouble, Mrs. Scraggs, the trouble? How is it to-day? I am about to write a long letter to our rector, and must include *your* news," to leave the visited to do the rest, and to make an ever-enjoyable appearance in high-light melodrama. It will be noted with approbation how conscientiously this layman undertook the parochial duties of Burtonbury, as his part in the Great War. While composed in listening to the exhaustive genealogy of the ulcer, Professor Ruby dreamed some lovely little dreams.

At the end of the day he knew with the rest of Burtonbury that Miss Vestal had returned from London with two parcels, one containing Army flannel; and two days after this he heard, with other local gossip, that an inquiring postman had delivered a torn newspaper-wrapped package at Miss Crombie's door, and was talking about what the postmistress said of the exuding contents; but the learned man was dreaming, and he recked naught.

It was shortly after this that Miss Crombie's maid-of-all-work met Miss Vestal's ditto, and, imparting to her news of curious phenomena, received certain information in return.

When one knows that Miss Vestal's maid was daughter to Mrs. Brown-Perkins's cook, it is scarcely necessary to dilate upon the matter further.

It was, in short, Mrs. Baker who, with her magnificent readiness to enter intimately into the affairs of anyone in the world, undertook to speak to Miss Crombie and Miss Vestal, and this within twelve hours of the conversation already mentioned.

One can readily understand that any evidence other than hearsay is indeed difficult to obtain in a case of this sort. Miss Crombie, on whom the first call was paid, wore, in fact, a suitable blouse of an opaque nature, and with a boned lace collar-band. One may put it that she was properly prepared to keep herself to herself.

"Mrs. Brown-Perkins and myself, and indeed all the other ladies, know everything," said Mrs. Baker, sitting in Miss Crombie's drawing-room, "and to say that we are astonished is not to express

our feelings at all. In fact, we do not wish to express them. We feel
that it is kinder not to do so. We are disgusted, Miss Crombie—
disgusted. That is the word which just hints our sense of what
you and Miss Vestal have done—I may say, of what you are doing.
May I ask, are you wearing them at this very moment—as I sit
talking to you?"

Miss Crombie hardily admitting it, Mrs. Baker hurried on:
"Girls of your age should know better. You were forty-eight last
birthday, and Caroline Vestal is slightly your senior. If your dear
mothers were alive I do not know what would happen. Now, dear,
we do not wish to be unkind, but we ask: Whatever possessed
you to do such a thing? Under what influence have you two girls
fallen? Cannot I be of any help? Will not you be guided by Mrs.
Brown-Perkins, who knows Lady Tubbs intimately? That was poor
Mrs. Brown-Perkins's first thought. 'Oh!' that poor thing said, 'if I
didn't move so much in fashionable society,' she said, 'this would
never have happened. What are we to do about it? They say the
butcher knows.' 'Leave it to me, dear,' I said. 'Let me go round,' I
said, 'and talk to these two girls. I knew their dear mothers.' That
is exactly what I said."

This splendid matron's pleading with Miss Vestal was of similar *genre,* and was similarly received. Something had happened to
these two young ladies, something queer, hitherto inexperienced,
and terribly natural. They had entered into temptation and fallen.
Was it their fault? If Eve had lived in a garden where apple-trees
simply wouldn't grow, she could not have eaten the apple. There
are delicate and great problems in the world.

To Miss Vestal Mrs. Baker put the case urgently: "It is so terrible,
so deceptive, of you to hurry off at once to London and buy—what
you bought. And that Virginia Crombie should write the *very*

next day, without a word to Mrs. Brown-Perkins! Burtonbury will ostracize you. You are washing them at home yourselves so that the laundry may not know, but remember that you both have young girls in your employment. Oh, think! I knew your dear mother. If our absent rector guessed! If Professor Ruby had even the faintest idea! Oh, Caroline! oh! How you will face that sainted man, knowing what you know, is past our comprehension."

"You will not tell him?" said Miss Vestal, breathing a little quicker.

"We *could* not tell him," replied Mrs. Baker, blushing deeply.

Miss Vestal's heart regained its normal beats.

The two young ladies received a request from Mrs. Brown-Perkins not to attend the War Relief Fund Committee again until a decision had been arrived at and further communication made. Meanwhile, would they carefully consider...?

Ostracized from tea-party society, the recipients of stiff bows and cold looks instead of endearing greetings, it is to be expected that they felt drawn to one another as never before. They never walked alone through the town now, but called for each other lovingly and shopped together.

Together, too, they spoke of their divergence from Burtonbury's graces. They began to dress their hair differently, to give their hats a rake, and they shortened their skirts by a full half-inch.

"I don't know what has come to me," said Miss Vestal, as they walked together down the High Street, "but it has come."

"The feeling of being all ninon underneath," said Miss Crombie, "is wonderful. I am taking a different view of sin. You are not shocked, dear?"

"In my own case," whispered Miss Vestal, "I feel it, too. I am dropping into this shop, dear, to buy myself a walking-stick."

They each bought one, and, having ordered the umbrellas they had been carrying to be sent home, swung the sticks fearlessly as they continued down the High Street.

Mrs. Scraggs kept her children away from Miss Crombie's Sunday-school class; Mrs. Brown-Perkins had a long talk with Dr. Hargraves, in which she begged him—delicately, of course—to explain the physical and psychic phenomena of the case; and only Professor Ruby remained oblivious for the space of one week.

At the end of a week Miss Vestal—ever the bolder of the two renegades—went the whole-hogger.

Corruption was festering in her. The seed was sown. The net was spread. The gin was set. Everything, in short, worked propitiously towards the devilish end. She saw Selfrod's advertisement on the front page of the daily paper, and she bought a transparent blouse.

Miss Crombie being a victim to headache that morning, Miss Vestal walked out alone into the High Street, and met Professor Ruby.

He had commenced to laugh, when he saw.

Bemused, he went pale. He said to himself in a daze: "What! Have I lived so near and yet so far from this lovely woman for twenty years? And has she worn them all the time?"

"Allow me to walk with you," he said, very, very softly. "There is nothing I would like better than to accompany you all my life. I dreamed about you last night."

They made a dazzling progress down the High Street. Ladies bowed to him flutteringly, but he did not laugh at all. He could not. He took Miss Vestal away quietly to her home by way of the leafy Green Lane.

"Here," he said, "near my gates, I have so often met you going about your dear little womanly errands. It has been a privilege which I have vastly enjoyed."

In Miss Vestal's drawing-room he sought her hand in marriage very ardently.

With such methods as he was inspired to employ, one need not wonder that he obtained it.

His happiness was intense. When he had to tear himself away to receive, as rector's delegate, a deputation of verger *versus* church-dusters at the Cloistered Hall he was rapturous. Awaiting the deputation, he took from its hiding-place the Three Graces advertisement. With a pair of scissors he snipped the head out neatly, and sought a large photograph of a school-treat group which included Caroline Vestal. He decapitated her, placed her head upon the other shoulders, and gazed at her dreamily. True, she wore a hat; but this did not really detract from the *ensemble*. Her decorum, too, added piquancy. It was something after the best Kirchner style.

While the deputation was raising a grievous discussion, with the Professor as judge and counsel to both parties all at once, as to whether the verger or the lady church-dusters should track the horny spider to his lair, Miss Vestal, flushed, palpitating, and happy, had hurried round to Miss Crombie.

Miss Vestal had changed into a nice satin blouse, and carried a parcel.

She fell upon Miss Crombie's neck and embraced her.

"Dearest!" she said, "dearest! dearest!"

"Dearest!" said Miss Crombie.

"Guess my news!" Miss Vestal panted.

"Oh, Caroline!" said Miss Crombie.

"You are quite right, dear," replied Miss Vestal, "that is it."

It should be placed to Miss Crombie's credit that her generous heart permitted her—after the first few pangs—to display nothing but unbounded enthusiasm. The two girls sat down hand in hand,

and, gazing raptly into each other's eyes, conversed in hushed voices.

"When will it be, dear?" Miss Crombie inquired, tenderly.

"Soon," said Miss Vestal, sighing, "very soon, I am afraid. I fear that Charles will hurry me. You can guess how agitating it all is! He appeared so eager!"

"With you as leader of Burtonbury," said Miss Crombie, "Mrs. Brown-Perkins will have to bow her head."

"Regarding Mrs. Brown-Perkins, dearest," said Miss Vestal, "I feel most strongly now that, about a *certain matter,* she was right. I met her on my way here and told her *the news,* and her first thought was of—you know, dearest. Almost before she had begun to speak, I replied most emphatically, 'Of course I shall! Can you ask?' I said. And here I am, dear, and here they are, including those which I had on this morning when it took place, and which I will rinse out in your bathroom, if I may run up there at once, but I felt that my house was not the place for them for *one moment longer.*"

Here Miss Vestal untied the string and displayed in all their fragile temptations her six sets of yellow ninon lingerie.

"I brought them straight to you, dear," said she; "take them. It is a pleasure. You will understand how I feel about them. Knowing what Charles would suffer, I could not; no, I simply could not. They may not be so unsuitable for an unmarried girl like yourself, but in my future position—I need say no more. How I shuddered this morning! Believe me, I felt hot and cold, and then cold and hot. If Charles had noticed! Oh, Virginia!"

Shivering a little still, Miss Vestal continued: "I had on my new blouse, too—I have put it here, and beg your acceptance of it— and all the while I was thinking, 'Oh, if he sees!' But love is blind, Virginia. Happily it is so."

Miss Crombie was profoundly impressed by the possible catastrophe, only averted, as it were, by the veil of a sweet infirmity.

"You will take them, Virginia?" said Miss Vestal; "indeed, I feel they are your due."

The warm-hearted girl spoke from a sense of that pure justice more often met with in the French exercise-book than in women; thus: "I shall have a husband, but you will have six yellow ninon sets."

She kissed Miss Crombie very tenderly, made an arrangement about the duties of chief bridesmaid, and went away.

Virginia Crombie was a woman; no more, no less.

For awhile she was content to sit dreaming, imaging the yellow; then she went upstairs and fetched the pink.

She wished to envisage the whole luxurious heap.

Glory!

They ranged over the round table in her drawing-room, entirely obscuring Tennyson, some family photographs, and ten books of seaside views.

Miss Crombie then, hastily recalled by her young maid to the duty of morning shopping too long postponed, left all the eleven sets there, put on her hat, and hurried out.

This was the moment which Fate selected for Professor Ruby to call for the purpose of begging Miss Crombie to replace, as church-duster, one of the ladies who, refusing all arbitration, had resigned her responsibility only half an hour before.

The young maid shut him in the drawing-room to wait.

Professor Ruby was a man; no more, no less.

Thanks entirely to the Three Graces advertisement, he was enabled to guess at the nature of what he saw before him. It is needless to say that he was struck, staggered, mute, and tremulous, before, with an effort—for he was not weak—he pulled himself together.

He spent a charming quarter of an hour in idealistic thought before he rang for the young maid.

He took her by the hand, led her up to the table, and she uttered a scream.

"Oh, sir," she said, faintly, "forgive me! Pardon me, sir! I didn't know they was there."

"Mary Scraggs," said the Professor, in a new, strong voice, "answer my questions immediately. Remember who I am and what you are. Anything which I demand of you will be perfectly right and proper. Now, are you ready?"

"Yes, sir," the young girl replied, and closed her eyes.

Professor Ruby retained her wrist in an iron grip, being vastly moved.

"These garments, Mary Scraggs, belong to Miss Caroline Vestal, I believe?"

"Please, sir," the young girl replied, more faintly yet, "the yeller did; but the pink was Miss Crombie's."

Professor Ruby was ruthless and strong, desperate and cunning. In his present mood not even his rector could have foiled him. Pursuing his train of discovery:—

"And now, Mary Scraggs?"

"Please, sir, Miss Vestal brought all hers and gave them to Miss Crombie only this morning."

"How do you know this, Mary Scraggs?"

"Please, sir," the young girl replied, "I was very near the drawing-room door."

"You heard what was said?"

"Please, sir, yes. Miss Vestal won't wear hers no more."

Releasing the maiden's wrist, the Professor caught a bead of perspiration as it trickled down his brow. A faint groaning sound escaped him.

"Go, Mary!" he said, when he could speak naturally.

An idealist is frequently a man of action, and when vision and action meet, what a force we have!

Miss Crombie, returning with her basket, found Professor Ruby in the act of packing a parcel swiftly. He used the brown paper and string brought by Miss Vestal a little earlier, and upon the table Tennyson, the family portraits, and the seaside books had emerged again. As for the Professor, he was singing one of the well-known Indian love-lyrics in a clear voice.

Without a moment's hesitation he took Miss Crombie in his arms and embraced her passionately.

"My dearest girl," said he with an ardour of which she had never dreamed even after the advent of yellow *robes de nuit*, "once I saw through a glass darkly, but now I know. I see I love you. For years you have been my ideal, and searching my heart this morning I know I have no other. Kiss me just one kiss!"

"Oh, Caroline! Caroline!" cried Miss Crombie, wringing her hands as well as she could. "Oh, my poor betrayed friend! Oh, Professor, mine cannot be the hand to smite her!"

Filled with a wonderful exhilaration, Miss Crombie was kissed by the ascetic and high-souled man.

"Leave your conscience to me," he said, more passionately yet. "Let the atonement for man's frailty be my part. I love you. Will you be mine?"

"It will be in all the papers," trembled Miss Crombie. "A breach of promise. It will be terrible… Yes, Charles, I will."

Professor Ruby pressed on. "To-day?"

"Oh, Charles!" murmured Miss Crombie, covering her face. "I cannot. I am not ready. And surely—at a day's notice—"

"If anyone knows how to be married at a day's notice, I do," said Professor Ruby, most firmly. "I will not postpone it for an hour. You are to come now at once, as you are. We are going to fly, and I shall represent to the rector that a special licence—"

"But I must pack. Oh, Charles!"

One knows that the Professor guessed but too well what delay meant.

"I cannot come as I am," said Miss Crombie, thinking; and one knows what she thought.

"Just as you are, in what you stand up in," said he, more and more ardently. "I ask no better. You are looking lovely. As for packing, seeing a few things on the table and presuming them to be yours, my love, I hastily put them together. We will take them. Do not think of to-morrow. Leave all to me. One more kiss, and then—"

It surely suffices to say that he hurried her, breathless yet exalted, away to the station, by way of the Green Lane, "where," he whispered as they went, "I have so often had the privilege of watching you go by on your beautiful womanly errands"; that they caught, by lovers' luck, an immediate train; that Professor and Mrs. Charles Ruby are still at the Cloistered Hall; and that Mrs. Brown-Perkins has bowed her head.

ONE OF THE OLD GUARD

Annie Edith Jameson (J. E. Buckrose)

published in *War-Time in Our Street: The Story of Some Companies Behind the Firing Line* (London: Hodder and Stoughton, 1917)

More or less forgotten today, Jameson (1868–1931) was a prolific writer of fiction and published forty novels and volumes of short stories during her lifetime. Her wartime collection of short stories, *War-Time in Our Street*, focuses on the effects of war on a small rural community. Anxious lovers, parents, grandparents and children strive to "keep their end up" while waiting for loved ones at the front to return—or, tragically, not to return. Jameson's subtitle is particularly telling, and also reflected in this particular story. Her ordinary civilians are part of "companies behind the firing line" because the war touches them closely, irrespective of their distance from the actual fighting, and because they meet the challenges and privations of war just as bravely as any soldier.

TWILIGHT WAS FALLING IN OUR STREET—A TWILIGHT THAT had no beauty at all. Grey, damp fog crept up from the river and penetrated old Mrs. Basset's aching bones as she sat by the fire knitting for the soldiers. The newspaper boy's voice, calling out the news of the war, sounded hoarse with the accumulated colds of many autumn days.

Mrs. Basset put down her knitting for a moment because her rheumatic hands ached so badly.

"Real Flodmouth Fair weather!" she said to herself, peering out into the gloom.

She had lately acquired this habit of talking to herself because there was no one else to talk to, and she was a gay old soul, fond of company. Her unmarried daughter lived at home, and before the war was considered delicate, following closely every new fashion in pills, and always lying down from two to four. It was one of the many miracles of the war to observe this once invalidish lady whisk down our street, and to know that she competently did V.A.D. work with her right hand, canteen work with her left, and packed, as it were, for prisoners of war with her teeth.

Naturally, therefore, old Mrs. Basset sat alone by the fire, and, naturally enough also, she saw in the red coals pictures of past fair-times, when her life was almost too crowded with people and talk and love and joy and care—the whole hurly-burly of being urgently wanted by husband and children and sisters and brothers, as well as by the old people at home.

Now—she saw this as she sat thinking—now she was one of the old people herself, and not really needed by anybody. Those loving attentions which she had lavished on a delicate daughter were happily not wanted. "Happily"—yet it is so sweet to be wanted that Mrs. Basset sighed, though she would not have had those invalidish days back for the world.

As it grew darker Mrs. Basset rose and sat near the window, peering wistfully out into the grey air and the twilight. Perhaps somebody might chance to see her sitting alone there and pop in to see her for a few minutes...

Brisk footsteps sounded down the street. She leaned forward, her face close to the window-pane, and saw it was the widow who lived opposite. How nice if she should come in, with her pleasant voice and her way of making chilly old people feel the world was a warm and jolly place after all. Mrs. Basset longed for that reassuring presence like a starved child for a fire.

The brisk footsteps went past without pausing, and Mrs. Basset leaned back with a sense of disappointment which only old and lonely people can quite understand. Others went by. Some glanced in and nodded; some did not see her at all; some passed on the further side of the street. But every one passed by.

Then the newspaper boy again, bawling: "Local casualty list!" And the bitterness of war swept over Mrs. Basset in a great wave, almost overwhelming her. She fought against it, and went back to her place by the fire. She must not take it like this, when there was so much real suffering about which other women bore so heroically.

Some echo from the old days of Flodmouth Fair coming back to her, she seized her sock again, despite her aching fingers, and began to sing defiantly in a high, cracked treble, a comic song which was then a sign of rollicking merriment: "Tommy Make Room for Your Uncle!"

The maid came in while she was thus engaged, and said patronizingly: "Singing a bit of a hymn-tune to yourself, are you'm? Quite right. We want all the religion we can get these days."

Old Mrs. Basset murmured a guilty assent, and the maid proceeded to draw down the blinds, remarking as she left the room: "It's my night for washing-up at the Canteen, you know'm. I suppose you'll be all right?"

"Certainly. It is very good of you to give up your night for that purpose, Mary."

"Oh, we all like to do our bit," responded Mary, with conscious rectitude.

Soon the front door banged, and Mrs. Basset was left quite alone.

After a little while, the bread and milk which Mary had placed on the table was sufficiently cool to eat; she therefore drew up her chair and began her supper. But after a couple of mouthfuls she was obliged to put the spoon down; Mary, in her haste, had burnt the milk.

To a young, well person, such an occurrence is nothing; but to an elderly invalid alone in a house at the end of a long, dreary day, it is a sort of tragedy.

For a moment or two Mrs. Basset's brave spirit entirely failed her. Then she gave herself a shake, and muttering: "Disgraceful! When you think of what they put up with in the trenches!" she gulped down the burnt bread and milk to the end.

After that she returned to the fire, sitting with idle hands before her. At last she muttered:

"I'm no use. I can't do anything." And she felt behind her eyes that miserable pressure of tears that cannot come which old people endure.

Then, suddenly—everyone knows how who has ever heard such voices—these words seemed to speak themselves aloud from the empty air:

"Let us pray!"

She glanced round, a little startled at first; then she knew it was but the sound of the wind getting up outside which had taken her back through the years to the little windy church on the wolds where she was christened and married. Some hidden string of memory had been pulled, and the old parson with his big spectacles stood in his reading desk before her. She even saw the pattern of her own lavender muslin gown as she had sat listening, and picked with a sort of wonder at the black stuff she now wore.

"Knitting and prayers! That's all an old woman like me can do. What's knitting and prayers?"

For she did so want to be out among all the rest, working, helping, striving, taking part in this splendid adventure of the women of England.

But after a while she drowsed a little, and awoke to an uneasy sense of something left undone. To her simple mind it now almost seemed as if she had received a command to pray—only it seemed such an odd thing to kneel down in a sitting-room in the middle of the evening. At last, however, she got down on her knees—clumsily on account of her stiffness, and with her back to the fire—and burying her face in her hands she asked God to take care of all our dear soldiers that night.

And as she prayed—it was the sweetest and yet most natural thing—the darkness made by her closed eyelids and knotted hands was filled by the faces of weatherworn lads such as she had seen during the day in the illustrated papers, and they were all smiling at her.

Very soon she rose, because her knees began to hurt intolerably, but she was comforted; and she slept in her chair until the sound of her daughter's footstep on the little garden path awakened her. Then she sat up, suddenly alert, filled with joy and eagerness; almost like a young girl at the approach of her lover. Young people will think this cannot be, but lonely old mothers everywhere—they know.

The front door opened and Miss Basset came briskly into the house, bringing stir, motion, outside life—all Mrs. Basset craved—into the little heated room.

"Well, mother! How are you? Got on all right?" she said, throwing off her cloak. And she continued without waiting for an answer: "Several new cases to-day. Most awfully interesting. But that idiotic Nurse Stephens…" And here followed a long and intricate story—not really unkind, but only very human—about various members of the devoted company who fortunately did not cease to be human when they earned the right to be regarded as angels.

Miss Basset tore herself away from this entrancing subject finally with an effort, and asked:

"Anyone been?"

"No."

"Selfish pigs! Why didn't somebody come?"

"Everyone is so busy, dear," said Mrs. Basset. "I had my knitting. I was all right."

"Then you were not lonely?"

"Not a bit!" said Mrs. Basset heartily.

But her conscience troubled her a little afterwards because she had "told a story" at her time of life. She had not the least idea, either then or later, that she was a member of the Old Guard who serve England all unconsciously and recognized by neither press nor public. No badge or medal will ever be bestowed on any one of them, but the glorious words "For valour" are being written, I believe, across their tired souls.

TRUTH'S WELCOME HOME

Edward Garnett

published in *The English Review*, vol. 26 (June 1918)

Garnett (1868–1937) was a critic, literary editor and writer who moved in thoroughly literary circles all his life: his father was a librarian and also a writer, his wife Constance a celebrated literary translator, and his son David a well-known novelist. Garnett was, moreover, friends with many literary notables of his day, including John Galsworthy, Joseph Conrad, and D. H. Lawrence, whose career he furthered by securing publication of Lawrence's novel *Sons and Lovers* (1913). 'Truth's Welcome Home' is an allegorical story that expresses Garnett's reservations about the way in which war affected free speech and culture, a concern which he shared with a number of his literary friends, not least Lawrence.

WHEN PEACE FLED AWAY FROM THE HEARTS OF THE WAR-ring nations the Virtues met together in hurried council. It was imperative that Humanity should not be left to struggle alone in the clutch of Murder, Rapine, Hatred, Lust, and Devastation. But it was a slight shock to everybody when, looking round the Assembly Hall, the Virtues saw themselves all arrayed in khaki! All but Justice, who, with his stern brow and meditative eyes, wore as of old his colourless mantle. And where was Truth? Was that her clear voice raised in notes outside the door? A voice gradually drowned in yells of savage laughter? Justice rose and strode to the entrance, and there he saw a woman on the steps, struggling in the hands of a mob of angry citizens striving to lynch her. "Fellow citizens, leave her to me! I am Justice!" rang out the Virtue's voice like a clarion. And the mob shrank sullenly from his eyes as he lifted Truth and drew her back with him over the threshold.

The speeches in the conclave, as befitted war-time, were brief and, for the Virtues, strangely unanimous. All the chief Virtues must go to the front; Courage, Honour and Duty, Self-sacrifice, Faith and Hope must lead and sustain the soldiers amid the horrors of the battlefield, and inspire their souls with belief in the ultimate triumph of Right.

Only Justice sat silent, staring before him as each fresh speech showed in turn how even more necessary to War than to Peace were the Virtues.

Then Truth's voice was heard, asking, "Will you work on all the fronts, with all the armies?"

"Naturally! We cannot desert the soldiers anywhere!" cried the other Virtues, staring at her.

"In that case you will be fighting with men against yourselves and inspiring all the aggressors," objected Truth.

But the Virtues pooh-poohed her objection. History showed it had always been like that. And how could the Virtues hang in the rear? And the meeting broke up on the high ringing note of hope and inflexible endeavour.

"Come and dine with me, Truth," begged Justice, and his stern eyes shone with the undying passion he ever cherished to make her his own. He put Truth in a taxi, amid the cheers of the patriotic crowd when it saw all the khaki-clad Virtues emerge from the hall; and he drove her to a little Soho restaurant, where the patron hastened to find them a quiet corner. Never had Justice shown himself more ardent. "We have time for ourselves now," he urged. "You will see that while War will accomplish his designs in our name, we sha'n't be listened to for a long while. Come away with me, Truth, to the mountains. There we can strengthen ourselves in the irradiant ether, in the pure sunlight, like the great eagles. Together we will trace the source of the lakes upwards to the eternal glaciers that have never been defiled by man. Come with me, Truth! Your eyes are the loveliest thing to me in the wide universe."

Was it the wine had loosened Justice's tongue? or the thought of her pure body when he lifted her to his breast and bore her away from the crowd? But Truth shook her head. His passion stirred her strangely, but how could she seclude herself with him when all the world would be clamouring for her to show her face, and then spitting on it in rage when it did not reflect men's desires?

"I love you, Justice, but as a sister," she said softly, gazing at him with her luminous eyes. "I shall always raise my cry to men on your behalf."

"Take my advice, Truth," he begged her. "Go everywhere, and see everything, as before, but don't cry aloud in war-time. Even in peace people dislike listening to you, but now they will howl you down if you open your lips. It is the day of the Lies. Don't you hear their leathery wings flapping round you?"

"I always hear them," said Truth.

The other Virtues departed for the Front, and served in the trenches, loyally and faithfully, never murmuring, animating the score of millions of men in the armies by day and night. It was gratifying that War welcomed them as his oldest friends, consulted them at every turn, sought their advice, and consulted their wishes wherever possible. It seemed strange at first, but the great armies were indeed the abode of the Virtues! They were cheered, heartened, immensely uplifted by the deference shown to them from the privates to the Higher Command, but the more the Armies relied on their aid the more disgustingly familiar grew the Vices. Formerly wherever Love went Murder would shrink away from him, muttering; but now she would sidle up to him, with her bony face and glittering eyes, chuckling, "Kiss poor Murder, Ducky! Ain't we comrades?" Formerly Faith and Honour had kept Outrage and Cruelty at a distance, but now the two Vices would swagger up to the delicate girls, seize them, press their breasts, cover their faces with hot reeking kisses, and call them their War-brides! and even the soldiers, under their orders, would stand looking on, yelling hoarse laughter. During the battles, too, and for days and nights afterwards, the Vices, with Torture and Madness, would hold high carnival. They would dance round their victims shot to pieces, dreadfully mimicking their voices as they besought mercy, lying in the shell-holes, begging to be put out of their torment. Mercy would plead with Death to visit them, but often he shook off her grasp and turned away. He had so much to do!

"Eh! my friend, remember you came here to kill!" mimicked Malice, leering at the moaning man. "Think! You have served this sauce to your fellows!" And then Malice would yell derisively across the battlefield, "Glory! Duty! Here's another of your recruits!"

And month after month and year after year Courage and Duty and Honour led millions of men to pile up hecatombs of their fellows mountains high, while Slaughter and Sin stood by, grinning. Who could complain? The Virtues supervised everything on all the fronts, and penetrated everywhere, saluted respectfully by the men they led forward to-day and read prayers over to-morrow. What would you have? It was war-time.

Meanwhile what splendid new openings the stay-at-home Vices found for themselves. "Patriotism!" and "Our country first!" was their cry, and under its cover they took possession of the souls of the caballing politicians, who, struggling for rank and power, gathered round them swarms of greedy placemen. The steady honest people saw themselves jockeyed and elbowed aside by the brazen-tongued adventurers who could pull the wires of self-advancement and make good terms with the Vested Interests. All the fat Profiteers, bustling about and advertising their services, seized the occasion to come in on the ground floor. Jacks-in-office swarmed, clambering upon the car of officialdom and helping their relatives to snug places. Every intriguing Vice took on a brand new official face, with a knife up his sleeve for his colleague whose place he coveted. And behind the Press the Dictator, like a gigantic cuttle-fish, lurked, squirting his cloud of poisonous ink on the men who disputed his will, on the Ministers, soldiers, sailors he had marked to pull down. And behind the inner doors of Power what whisperings of corrupt Ministers with hooded, obscure journalists! The stay-at-home Vices rubbed their fat-fingered hands and trafficked in the War, while the prosperous mob day by day howled at poor little Peace and hunted her through the streets.

At last the stay-at-home Virtues grew alarmed at the brazen way the Vices swaggered about in the public places and eyed all men insolently through the eye-holes of Power and Patriotism. "The Vices are getting everything into their hands at home while you are doing the bidding of War at the Front," was the message they sent to the Virtues in khaki. Who knows if it ever reached them? Then the stay-at-home Virtues hunted about for Truth. Everybody spoke of her, but nobody had heard her voice for ages! At last they found out that she had disguised herself as a stretcher-bearer and was always with the dying soldiers. Then they got a letter out to her.

The night after the letter reached her Truth was on the battle-field, helping to collect the wounded, when a man with a shattered spine opened his eyes as she looked into his face. "How many went over the top with me?" he asked. "Twenty thousand," she said. "How many came back alive?" "Four thousand," she replied. "Tell them at home," he said, and closed his eyes.

One morning, just before it grew light, Truth was lying at the door of a dug-out, looking up at the pale stars, when she saw sinister shapes emerging from the obscurity. Furtively and warily they dragged themselves forward, and soon there were a dozen figures squatting in a half-circle round her, looking hungrily towards her. She knew them—they were the great Sins. Foremost among them sat Murder, Treachery, and Cruelty staring gloomily before them. But how changed were they! They looked mere skeletons, burnt out by War's rapine.

"Yes, look well at us, Truth!" they growled. "We are so burnt out that we can scarcely drag ourselves farther. War has utterly consumed us!" Truth examined their haggard faces, their emaciated limbs, their cavernous eyes. Then they muttered hoarsely: "Let the world know, Truth, that it is your lovely Sisters, not we who are destroying the nations! War had satiated himself long ago but for their insistence. Hope and Faith are still pressing the millions forward into the pit of slaughter. Ah! your Virtues butcher a hundred men for one we kill!" And the great sins shambled off, holding on to one another, so weak were they in their weariness.

Truth came back to the peoples at home, and as soon as she began to speak of the battlefields the people struck her in the face and bade her be silent. "Go away!" they cried angrily. "This isn't the moment for Truth." She went to the editors, and her narrative froze their blood. When the editors had eviscerated her narrative and the Censor had censored what remained, every citizen read it aloud at breakfast. "Truth's Message." "Why We Are Winning." She went to the Ministers, to the M.P.s to the clergy, to the publicists, and they repulsed her with horror.

"Gag her!" they cried.

"No! Cut her tongue out! It's safer!"

It was done.

"Cut her hands off!" "She can write," urged anxious Patriotism.

It was done.

"Put her eyes out! Make her deaf!" urged National Gain and Greed, leering into her bleeding face.

"No!" said the politicians. "We shall make use of her later on. Put a placard on her breast, 'A Woman Mutilated by the Enemy,' and let her walk about the streets."

Truth sat down by the roadside, and everyone who heard her moans crossed themselves in horror.

"Oh, poor woman! This is what the enemy has done to you!" and they heaped charity on her. But when she opened her mouth and waggled the stump of her tongue they felt troubled and complained to the Authorities.

The Authorities considered the matter. "It's really a mental case! The poor woman should be in an asylum. It's kinder to her," they agreed. So they took Truth to a hospital for the insane. But when they undressed her they found she was a man, with his name and Red Cross number hanging round his neck.

"Why, it's an R.A.M.C. orderly, wounded by shell fire!" said the doctor, and they transferred her to a Hospital for Incurable Soldiers.

There she lay among the soldiers with shattered spines, without faces and without legs and arms, with nothing left to them but mutilated life. She lay there among them, staring up at the ceiling, now and then making queer signs with her mutilated arms to the nurses and the doctors, who were puzzled to know what she meant.

But the soldiers knew right enough. "It's Truth," they repeated. "She's telling people about the War."

But no one paid them attention.

It was War-time.

Abroad

THE DESPATCH-RIDER

Edgar Wallace

published in the *Strand Magazine*, vol. 48 (1914)

Best known today as a prolific writer of crime thrillers, Edgar Wallace (1875–1932) was also a journalist and scriptwriter, whose final work was the script for *King Kong* (1933). He enlisted in the infantry as a young man and served in South Africa for a few years. Following his stint in the army he covered the South African war as a war correspondent, and as a regular reporter for the *Daily Mail* once he returned to England. His career as a fiction writer began in earnest only after he was dismissed from the *Mail* following a number of libel cases, although he still took on journalistic commissions to make ends meet, as he was chronically in debt. The First World War did not put Wallace off his stride, as his usual detective and spy stories were perfectly suited to being adapted to wartime. 'The Despatch-Rider' is not a typical detective story, however, and shows Wallace's versatility as a popular magazine writer. It picks up on early concerns over women's role in the war effort, and although it hardly supports radical new freedoms for women, it shows how at least one spirited young woman can hold her own under pressure.

I

LADY GALLIGAY WAS ALWAYS STARTING THINGS; OTHER people usually carried them on, complaining bitterly the while that they had ever been born to assume the responsibilities which Lady Galligay created. For the "things" that she started with such zest invariably ended and finished without any assistance whatsoever. They faded away without violence and without noise. In January all Tadminster would be talking of Lady Galligay's newest project; there would be drawing-room meetings innumerable. They might even develop shape as a "cause," and attain to the dignity of a public meeting, recorded in large type in the *Tadminster Times*. But by April, so feeble would the flame of interest flicker, that it was a case of "By the way, what happened to that great scheme of Lady Gally's?" when men and women met.

"The Tadminster Mounted Nurse and Despatch-Rider Corps" was one of this feather-brained little lady's most brilliant inventions. She was forty, and vague, and rich, and immensely energetic, and if she lacked stamina it was not to be expected that all the virtues of organization should dwell in one small body. It was after her "Cottage and Pigsty" for the democracy had been rejected by the same democracy, although two cottages were built and a whole drove of pigs had been mobilized, that Lady Galligay had planned her Mounted Nurses' Corps. It was an idea—even George Mestrell agreed that it was an idea, but, of course, he never dreamt that Jo would take up with the beastly thing. If the truth be told, Jo was rather aghast at finding herself enrolled, but Lady Gally was so awfully plausible, and—well, there it was; George must take the situation as he found it, or leave it.

George, full of good spirits, came down from Aldershot one Saturday in spring, bringing, so to speak, the good news from Aix, for there had been an unexpected resignation and he had got his company. It made all the difference in the world, because matrimony was not encouraged amongst subaltern officers. He was entirely full of his good news, and sat on the edge of the settee in the dinky little drawing-room of Nearminster House, and Jo Gresham, demure and beautiful, her tender grey eyes smiling approval of her soldier lover and his enthusiasm, waited to impart her own news.

She broke it obliquely, with a fine pretence of unconcern. Instinctively she felt, or half felt, that there was something in Lady Galligay's latest which was not quite—

"I suppose you've heard of Lady Gally's corps?" she asked, carelessly.

He had a trick of smiling with his eyes which ordinarily was very pleasing. For the first time in their acquaintance it failed to warm her. Rather it sent her heart sinking down and down.

"Why do you smile?"

"I read something about it in the papers," he laughed. "What a dear, funny old bird she is! Not a bad idea, but imagine a corps of attractive young women gallivanting over a modern battlefield!"

"In the sacred cause of humanity," she said. She knew she was being horribly trite, and felt no sweeter in consequence.

He stared up at her solemnly, for she had risen and stood, a slim, heroic figure, her rebellious chin tilted up, her fine brows set in menace.

"You are a soldier and you are biased," she went on, slowly. "You don't realize how women's positions have changed, how their capacities have enlarged. You don't understand."

Now the curious thing was, as she admitted to herself, that she herself had thought the corps a little ridiculous, and on the first "parade" she had felt so self-conscious as to vow a vow never again to appear in public so arrayed. But now, encountering a half-anticipated opposition, her attitude of mind had changed, and she indulged herself in a veritable orgy of inconsistency. She was unreasonably angry with him.

"Wait!" she commanded, suddenly, and whisked out of the room.

He waited, frowning his bewilderment, a neat, cleanly soldier man. How like Jo to jump down his throat for nothing at all! She was the dearest and sweetest and most perverse and obstinate of girls, and why on earth she should champion Gally the Lord only knew. So he thought, and, thinking, wondered why she had left him so dramatically. After ten minutes' wait, ten minutes in the course of which he was by turn angry, amused, alarmed—suppose she was crying over something he had said?—and resigned, he heard her footsteps on the parquet of the hall, and rose as she entered. He had had no intention of rising, because George's manners were deplorable, as everybody in Tadminster knows, but he rose—and gasped.

She came into the room, closing the door behind her, and stood, a little flushed, a little defiant, confronting him. Upon her pretty head was a wide sombrero hat, which was fastened under her chin by a strap. She wore a tight-fitting tunic blouse of blue cloth, with two rows of silver buttons; a skirt of serge braided in scarlet, which reached only so far as midway between knee and ankle; patent leather riding boots; and a suggestion of dark blue riding breeches went with snow-white haversack, military cross-belt, and riding gauntlets to complete the picture.

For a moment there was silence; then he spoke.

"Fancy dress or something?"

She pressed her lips tightly together and shook her head. There was a light in her eyes which should have warned him.

"What *is* the joke?" he asked, earnestly. "Is it private theatricals?"

She withered him with one glance.

"This is the uniform," she said.

"The uniform?"

"Lady Galligay's Mounted Nurses and Messengers," she explained, with unnatural patience.

He looked at her from head to toe, and in his scrutiny there was to Jo something unpardonably offensive.

"But," he said, slowly, "you're not rowing in that galley, dearie—dash it all, I mean you're not one of those infernally sill— I mean one of those—" He blundered himself to a standstill.

"Go on, please," she encouraged him, though her eyes were very moist and she was biting her very red lips with unnecessary vehemence.

"But, my girlie, it's so dashed absurd!" He blurted out the truth in his despair, this tall young man (something of a strategist in another field).

"Absurd?"

"I mean," he floundered, "it's so jolly theatrical, and the girls look such guys, and—"

"Thank you."

"But don't you see," he protested, "you can do nothing—you can't gallop about on a battlefield, darling; it isn't done. What *can* you do? You can't carry wounded soldiers about on horseback;

and, as for despatch-riding, who the dickens is going to take orders from you?"

"I can—we can do many things," she said, firmly and coldly; "but it would be foolish of me to argue the matter—I think you are just horrid, and I hate you!"

He stood in the centre of the room after she had flounced out, and for exactly three minutes he was penitent. Then he became annoyed, and when a tight-lipped and wholly antagonistic maid had informed him curtly that Miss Josephine was not to be seen, he was very angry indeed, and went back to town by the next train.

And that was the beginning of a tactless correspondence between two young people, a correspondence in which the effect of a certain scrappy tenderness was utterly annihilated by the indiscriminate use of notes of exclamation.

Jo resigned her membership of the Flying Nurses, gave her uniform to the gardener—an unimaginative man who saw possibilities for little boys' breeches in the voluminous riding-skirt—and she went abroad on the long-planned motor tour through South-Western France, previously despatching a half-hoop of diamonds with a curt note to "Lieutenant G. Mestrell, 1st Southamptonshire Regiment, Talavera Barracks, Aldershot." And this though George had explained to her the highly important fact that he had secured his captaincy.

Of her adventures, her spasms of remorse, of letters reproachful and letters affectionate and letters completely penitent which she wrote and tore up, it is not necessary to tell. She lost her girl companion at a little town between Paris and Orleans.

There were rumours of war in the air, but that was no unusual experience in France. Bertha Mansell, however, was nervous, and must go home, and Jo was left with her little two-seater to decide whether she should take the Paris-Amiens road, or whether she should continue northward to the old-world town of Senlis. Here in the heart of the country an aunt had a little château. Jo decided on the second course, and came to the Château Verte to find herself its sole occupant, Aunt Martha having been bitten by the war scare and having left in a hurry for England.

It suited Jo, this month of absolute rest after the strenuous days of motoring. She sketched and slept and listened with amusement to the wild stories of war which an ancient French servitor and his no more youthful spouse regaled her with.

Then one day she awoke with a shock to learn the truth. There was war. Motoring out towards Beauvais, she had seen French soldiers marching northward. Belgium had been invaded, Liége was in their hands—even Brussels, they said, but that was unbelievable. Yes, it was possible to get to Ostend, but she must hurry.

The English were also at war, they told her, but only on the sea. She felt a sudden lightening of heart at this—hugged the obviously unlikely story to her heart, though reason told her that one Service could not be engaged without the other.

She hurried back to the château, packed her traps, and strapped them to the rear of her little car. The servitor and his wife had already made preparations for departure.

"Take the road through Maubeuge, and branch off to Condé, mademoiselle," said the man; "but"—his face was troubled—"it would be better to go to Calais; that is only five hours away."

She shook her head.

It was a perfectly absurd consideration, but she had come to the Continent by way of Ostend, and had her return ticket by that route. Moreover, there was a rebate to be claimed at the frontier; a rebate of the provisional duty she had paid on her car.

Besides, she might see something of the fighting—an exhilarating and joyous thought. She set her car at the hill which led from the château to the plateau above Senlis with a sense of glorious anticipation.

II

Over by Condé the guns were sobbing fitfully. You had to listen with your ears strained to catch the insistent note. If you climbed to the high belfry of St. Peter's you saw, through good glasses, little woolly balls of smoke appearing in the air, saw the shapeless drift of it as it thinned, and, listening with all your nerves tense, you might identify one of the far-off sobs with that lazy smoke spume.

"I think mademoiselle had better go quickly." The old priest, his cassock white with the dust of the roads, was hollow-eyed and weary. His shoes were hard and burnt and grimy, and there was a two-days' stubble of beard on his chin. He stood by the side of the girl in the belfry, plucking at his lip thoughtfully, his anxious eyes divided between the northern horizon and the slim girl by his side.

Jo was young and immensely pretty—not the rose and cream prettiness of England, but the old-ivory beauty of the South. The eyes were big and grey and wide set, her mouth small but full—parted now in her excitement. The rough tweed dress, the short skirt, and puttied ankles suggested a bicycle, but it was a little two-seater "Mombo" that stood by the porch of the old church, a worn trunk strapped to the carrier. Altogether, thought Father Pierre, an incongruous figure in this area of horrible war. Her trim hat appeared grey—it had once been a most uncompromising black, but the roads of Southern Belgium in July are inclined to revolutionize the intentions of the *modiste*.

"They are returning this way," said the priest, after a while, and fidgeted nervously. "Mademoiselle must abandon her idea of crossing Belgium—her way lies through Lille to the coast. She will be safe, for the English hold—"

"The English?" she gasped. "Are there English here?"

He nodded and smiled.

"There is a great division—there." He pointed towards Condé. "Also there are others in the rear."

"But they told me— Are you sure, father?"

He nodded again.

He was very sure, for had he not seen the yellow coats go swaying past through Rheims—yellow coats open to show grey-blue shirts and bare brown throats?

"The regiments?" He shook his head regretfully in answer to her question.

"No, I do not know the regiments. They wore badges—here, on the collar. Some had tigers in brass, one had a sphinx in white metal, some wore little grenades, and one had a bronze fox—"

"A bronze fox!" she gasped.

There is only one regiment in the British Army that wears the "red fox," and that is the Southamptonshire Regiment—that famous fox which they won in the Nepalese War. It took her a second to decide. Somewhere over there where the guns were going "glang!" "glang!" was George—George unreconciled—in danger.

She must see him. She must tell him she was sorry. It was the maddest of ideas. She knew how absurd it was even as she went stumbling down the belfry steps, followed by the startled *curé*.

"No, mademoiselle!" he cried, in apprehension, as she turned the car to the northern road; "not that way—not that way!"

But with a cheery wave of her hand she put the little car to the long, straight road which led towards those dreadful guns.

She passed soldiers busily entrenching, French cavalry stealing along the side of the road. Once she slowed down before a cottage where a bare-armed surgeon was busy with the wreck of a man that lay stretched on a big kitchen table. They glanced at her curiously, but did not stop her. Then there was a clearer stretch of road, and she let out the little Mombo to its top licks. The guns were nearer now, their "boom-boom" was incessant, there was a horrible sound in the air—a whining, whistling, shrieking sound, and once she saw a white house far away to her right burst into flames and crumble slowly to pieces.

She passed through a tiny village which was still blazing. Men and horses lay by the side of the road in curious, unreal attitudes. They had been dragged to the side to allow a battery of artillery to pass. Later she was to see the shattered limber of one of these guns in a ditch with the feet and legs of a French soldier protruding from the wreck. It was as though he had crawled underneath to investigate the cause of the trouble—only he was so terribly still, and the girl went white and felt deadly sick.

She recovered herself with an effort, stiffened her back till she sat bolt upright, and grasped the wheel more firmly.

Then she came suddenly upon more soldiers lying by the side of the road, and occupying the centre of the broad roadway, at a place where it topped the hill before dipping again to the valley, a group of mounted men. She knew it for the general staff of a French division. They were pointing to the left, and two of the officers were looking through their glasses.

The girl stopped the car behind them. Here the roads branched off. A cross-road to the left led to Mons, as she knew; the one to the right would take her to Charleroi. But she realized she had reached the end of her journey. Here was Authority, which would send her back the way she had come. For the moment the staff were too occupied to notice her.

The dapper little general with the gold-laced *képi* was talking sharply, impatiently, to his chief of staff.

"Send a messenger at once to withdraw that company," he rapped. "*Mon Dieu*, it will be annihilated! The English have retired also. It is madness."

"I think they have—" began the other, when he was interrupted.

A group of soldiers were reclining by the side of the road. One had a small telephone receiver to his ear, and a trailing wire from a post above led down to him.

As the staff officer spoke one of the group rose and came towards the general with a slip of paper in his hand. He reached up the slip, saluting, and the general scanned the message.

"Cannot communicate with a company of the Southamptonshire Regiment on my right," he read. "Can you reach Captain Mestrell and order him to retire?"

For a moment the girl in the car swayed backward and forward; for that space of time the rush and roar of battle faded into a faraway buzz.

"Send a cyclist—it is risky." She heard the general speaking. "Tell the Englishman to take the road back to the hills by the stone cross. There's a way out for him."

She saw a young officer leap into the seat of his dirty motorcycle, heard the pat-pat-pat of the engine, and watched him like one in a dream as he streaked down the hill to the right.

She watched him fascinated, gradually receding from view, then suddenly the cycle swayed left and right as though the driver were trying to evade some invisible obstacle. With one final lurch, cycle and rider went crashing to the ground, and the messenger did not rise.

"Send another man."

The curt tone of the general came to her.

Again an officer mounted and went whizzing down the hill. He reached the bottom before, without warning, he went tumbling over and over till at last he lay an inert little bundle of humanity under his broken machine.

The girl heard the impatient click of lips.

"I can't risk another man. The road is swept by rifle fire."

They were going to leave him—to leave George and his men! Her eyes opened wide in horror at the thought. Yet she knew that the general was just.

"He will stay there till he is cut up," said the staff officer's voice, very slowly and deliberately. He had a solemn, mournful voice, she noted mechanically. She wondered in a numb, cold-blooded way if he were married. He spoke like a father of a family. A stout man, who sat his horse ungracefully. And George was to be left—to be—cut up.

The car still purred and trembled under her. The wheel on which her hand rested shivered at intervals, as though it was part of a living, reasoning organism, dreading the ordeal ahead. She did what she did without thought. She gently pressed her foot downward, and the car moved.

"Stop! Who are you, madam?"

It was the general, swinging round on his restive horse.

She could not speak; she could only point to the road that led to Mons.

She heard a warning shout, a cry of command, but they were too late to stop her.

Gathering momentum with every turn of its wheels, the little Mombo leapt down the hill. Her eyes were fixed on the road ahead. The first dead man she could pass without difficulty. She must slow to the next and go round him, and that was the danger point. She flew past the first obstacle, caught a fleeting glimpse of a doubled-up figure and a white face that stared up to the blue heaven, then the glass wind-shield smashed into a thousand pieces, and her lap was filled with splinters of glass. But she was not hit; only one flying splinter had drawn blood from her gloved hand. She was cool now, steadied the car for the man who lay in the middle of the road, and breathed a sigh of relief when she found that she had misjudged the space. There was room enough to pass. One sorrowful glance she gave to the pitiful thing which a few minutes before had been a living, breathing man, and then she began the ascent of a stiff little hill. And all the time she heard the smack, smack of bullets as they struck her car. She saw the off-side lamp jump up and fall, and once there was a sensation as though somebody had breathed a sharp, cold breath before her face.

On the crest of the hill she had immunity from danger. She ran through a cutting for half a mile, then the road turned suddenly, and she saw at the foot a rugged line of men retiring by short, sharp rushes from cover to cover. She heard the shrill whistle of an officer, and the line came with a run over the stubble field to the deep road.

At full speed she sent the car forward, laughing and crying, for she had distinguished the tall young man in command, had indeed picked him out five hundred yards away. Captain George Mestrell, unshaven and grimy, heard the wheels of the car and turned as the tiny two-seater jarred to a standstill.

"My God!" he breathed. "Jo!"

She was still laughing, though her face was wet with tears.

"There is a road behind you," she cried, shrilly, "in the wood by the stone cross, and you've got to retire at once. The general says so."

"Jo!" he repeated, and pressed his hands before his eyes.

"The road by the stone cross," she said. "Look, look! there it is; I'll show you."

She ran the car farther along the road till she came to the stone cross. There was little sign of road, only an opening in the thick bush which apparently led to the hill above, but she turned the car, and turned again, and struck a smooth track which wound between the densely-planted trees round the base of the hill on the left. She looked behind her. The men were following, and George, limping painfully, was with them.

"It is very wonderful," admitted a wholly mystified young officer a little later when a French surgeon had finished dressing an ugly bullet wound in his leg. "Can you tell me in what capacity you are serving?"

She smiled mysteriously.

"Lady Galligay's corps has been mobilized," she answered, untruthfully. And George winced.

THE DEATH GRIP

"Sapper" (H. C. McNeile)

collected in *Men, Women and Guns* (London: Hodder & Stoughton, 1916)

"Sapper" (1868–1937) was a professional soldier, and his pen name derived from the fact that he served with the Royal Engineers and, as a soldier on active duty, was not permitted to publish under his real name. Best known today for his recurring character "Bulldog Drummond", an ex-officer turned investigator and adventurer after the war, "Sapper" was already writing prolifically during the First World War. His stories provided readers of the *Daily Mail* with a fairly hard-hitting insight into the realities of modern combat. They were so popular that Hodder & Stoughton released them in several collections during and after the war, including the complete edition, *Sapper's War Stories*, in 1930. 'The Death Grip' is notable because it looks at the potential effect of war on the men who serve, and portrays a man dramatically changed by his war service. Although the hero of this story suffers physical injury (he is shot in the head), his symptoms seem to be largely psychological, and it could be argued that "Sapper" is responding at least in part to the phenomenon of shell shock (what we would now call post-traumatic stress disorder), which was still a poorly understood condition in 1916.

TWO REASONS HAVE IMPELLED ME TO TELL THE STORY OF Hugh Latimer, and both I think are good and sufficient. First I was his best friend, and second I know more about the tragedy than anyone else—even including his wife. I saw the beginning and the end; she—poor broken-hearted girl—saw only the end.

There have been many tragedies since this war started; there will be many more before Finis is written,—and each, I suppose, to its own particular sufferers seems the worst. But, somehow, to my mind Hugh's case is without parallel, unique—the devil's arch of cruelty. I will give you the story—and you shall judge for yourself.

Let us lift the curtain and present a dug-out in a support trench somewhere near Givenchy. A candle gutters in a bottle, the grease running down like a miniature stalactite congeals on an upturned packing-case. On another packing-case the remnants of a tongue, some sardines, and a goodly array of bottles with some tin mugs and plates completes the furniture—or almost. I must not omit the handsome coloured pictures—three in all—of ladies of great beauty and charm, clad in—well, clad in something at any rate. The occupants of this palatial abode were Hugh Latimer and myself; at the rise of the curtain both lying in corners, on piles of straw.

Outside, a musician was coaxing noises from a mouth-organ; occasional snatches of song came through the open entrance, intermingled with bursts of laughter. One man, I remember, was telling an interminable story which seemed to be the history of

a gentleman called Nobby Clark, who had dallied awhile with a
lady in an estaminet at Bethune, and had ultimately received a
knock-out blow with a frying-pan over the right eye, for being too
rapid in his attentions. Just the usual dull, strange, haunting trench
life—which varies not from day's end to day's end.

At intervals a battery of our own let drive, the blast of the
explosion catching one through the open door; at intervals a big
German shell moaned its way through the air overhead—an express
bound for somewhere. Had you looked out to the front, you would
have seen the bright green flares lobbing monotonously up into
the night, all along the line. War—modern war; boring, incredible
when viewed in cold blood…

"Hullo, Hugh." A voice at the door roused us both from our
doze, and the Adjutant came in. "Will you put your watches right
by mine? We are making a small local attack to-morrow morning,
and the battalion is to leave the trenches at 6.35 exactly."

"Rather sudden, isn't it?" queried Hugh, setting his watch.

"Just come through from Brigade Headquarters. Bombs
are being brought up to H.15. Further orders sent round later.
Bye-bye."

He was gone, and once more we sat thinking to the same
old accompaniment of trench noises; but in rather a different
frame of mind. To-morrow morning at 6.35 peace would cease;
we should be out and running over the top of the ground; we
should be…

"Will they use gas, I wonder?" Hugh broke the silence.

"Wind too fitful," I answered; "and I suppose it's only a small
show."

"I wonder what it's for. I wish one knew more about these
affairs; I suppose one can't, but it would make it more interesting."

The mouth-organ stopped; there were vigorous demands for an encore.

"Poor devils," he went on after a moment. "I wonder how many?—I wonder how many?"

"A new development for you, Hugh." I grinned at him. "Merry and bright, old son—your usual motto, isn't it?"

He laughed. "Dash it, Ginger—you can't always be merry and bright. I don't know why—perhaps it's second sight—but I feel a sort of presentiment of impending disaster to-night. I had the feeling before Clements came in."

"Rot, old man," I answered cheerfully. "You'll probably win a V.C., and the greatest event of the war will be when it is presented to your cheeild."

Which prophecy was destined to prove the cruellest mixture of truth and fiction the mind of man could well conceive…

"Good Lord!" he said irritably, taking me seriously for a moment; "we're a bit too old soldiers to be guyed by palaver about V.C.s." Then he recovered his good temper. "No, Ginger, old thing, there's big things happening to-morrow. Hugh Latimer's life is going into the melting-pot. I'm as certain of it as—as that I'm going to have a whisky and soda." He laughed, and delved into a packing-case for the seltzogene.

"How's the son and heir?" I asked after a while.

"Going strong," he answered. "Going strong, the little devil."

And then we fell silent, as men will at such a time. The trench outside was quiet; the musician, having obliged with his encore, no longer rendered the night hideous—even the guns were still. What would it be to-morrow night? Should I still be…? I shook myself and started to scribble a letter; I was getting afraid of inactivity—afraid of my thoughts.

"I'm going along the trenches," said Hugh suddenly, breaking the long silence. "I want to see the Sergeant-Major and give some orders."

He was gone, and I was alone. In spite of myself my thoughts would drift back to what he had been saying, and from there to his wife and the son and heir. My mind, overwrought, seemed crowded with pictures: they jumbled through my brains like a film on a cinematograph.

I saw his marriage, the bridal arch of officers' swords, the sweet-faced, radiant girl. And then his house came on to the screen—the house where I had spent many a pleasant week-end while we trained and sweated to learn the job in England. He was a man of some wealth was Hugh Latimer, and his house showed it; showed moreover his perfect, unerring taste. Bits of stuff, curios, knick-knacks from all over the world met one in odd corners; prints, books, all of the very best, seemed to fit into the scheme as if they'd grown there. Never did a single thing seem to whisper as you passed. "I'm really very rare and beautiful, but I've been dragged into the wrong place, and now I know I'm merely vulgar."

There are houses I wot of where those clamorous whispers drown the nightingales. But if you can pass through rooms full of bric-à-brac—silent bric-à-brac: bric-à-brac conscious of its rectitude and needing no self apology, you may be certain that the owner will not give you port that is improved by a cigarette.

Then came the son, and Hugh's joy was complete. A bit of a dreamer, a bit of a poet, a bit of a philosopher, but with a virility all his own; a big man—a man in a thousand, a man I was proud to call Friend. And he—at the dictates of "Kultur"—was to-morrow at 6.35 going to expose himself to the risk of death, in order to wrest from the Hun a small portion of unprepossessing ground. Truly, humour is not dead in the world!...

A step outside broke the reel of pictures, and the Sapper Officer looked in. "I hear a whisper of activity in the dark and stilly morn," he remarked brightly. "Won't it be nice?"

"Very," I said sarcastically. "Are you coming?"

"No, dear one. That's why I thought it would be so nice. My opposite number and tireless companion and helper to-morrow morning will prance over the greensward with you, leading his merry crowd of minions, bristling with bowie knives, sandbags, and other impedimenta."

"Oh! go to Hell," I said crossly. "I want to write a letter."

"Cheer up, Ginger." He dropped his bantering tone. "I'll be up to drink a glass of wine with you to-morrow night in the new trench. Tell Latimer that the wire is all right—it's been thinned out and won't stop him, and that there are ladders for getting out of the trench on each traverse."

"Have you been working?" I asked.

"Four hours, and got caught by shrapnel in the middle. Night-night, and good luck, old man."

He was gone; and when he had, I wished him back again. For the game wasn't new to him—he'd done it before; and I hadn't. It tends to give one confidence...

It was about four I woke up. For a few blissful moments I lay forgetful; then I turned and saw Hugh. There was a new candle in the bottle, and by its flicker I saw the glint in his sombre eyes, the clear-cut line of his profile. And I remembered...

I felt as if something had caught me by the stomach—inside: a sinking feeling, a feeling of nausea: and for a while I lay still. Outside in the darkness the men were rousing themselves; now and again a curse was muttered as someone tripped over a leg he didn't see; and once the Sergeant-Major's voice rang out—"'Ere, strike a light with them breakfasts."

"Awake, Ginger?" Hugh prodded me with his foot. "You'd better get something inside you, and then we'll go round and see that everything is O.K."

"Have you had any sleep, Hugh?"

"No. I've been reading." He put Maeterlinck's "Blue Bird" on the table. With his finger on the title he looked at me musingly, "Shall we find it to-day, I wonder?"

I have lingered perhaps a little long on what is after all only the introduction to my story. But it is mainly for the sake of Hugh's wife that I have written it at all; to show her how he passed the last few hours before—the change came. Of what happened just after 6.35 on that morning I cannot profess to have any very clear idea. We went over the parapet I remember, and forward at the double. For half an hour beforehand a rain of our shells had plastered the German trenches in front of us, and during those eternal thirty minutes we waited tense. Hugh Latimer alone of all the men I saw seemed absolutely unconscious of anything unusual. Some of the men were singing below their breath, and one I remember sucked his teeth with maddening persistency. And one and all watched me curiously, speculatively—or so it seemed to me. Then we were off, and of crossing No-Man's-Land I have no recollection. I remember a man beside me falling with a crash and nearly tripping me up—and then, at last, the Huns. I let drive with my revolver from the range of a few inches into the fat, bloated face of a frightened-looking man in dirty grey, and as he crashed down I remember shouting, "There's the Blue Bird for you, old

dear." Little things like that do stick. But everything else is just
a blurred phantasmagoria in my mind. And after a while it was
over. The trench was full of still grey figures, with here and there
a khaki one beside them. A sapper officer forced his way through
shouting for a working-party. We were the flanking company, and
vital work had to be done and quick. Barricades rigged up, communication trenches which now ran to our Front blocked up, the
trench made to fire the other way. For we knew there would be
a counter-attack, and if you fail to consolidate what you've won
you won't keep it long. It was while I slaved and sweated with
the men shifting sandbags—turning the parados, or back of the
trench into the new parapet, or front—that I got word that Hugh
was dead. I hadn't seen him since the morning, and the rumour
passed along from man to man.

"The Captain's took it. Copped it in the head. Bomb took him
in the napper."

But there was no time to stop and enquire, and with my heart
sick within me I worked on. One thing at any rate; it had only been
a little show, but it had been successful—the dear chap hadn't lost
his life in a failure. Then I saw the doctor for a moment.

"No, he's not dead," he said, "but—he's mighty near it. You
know he practically ran the show single-handed on the left flank."

"What did he do?" I cried.

"Do? Why he kept a Hun bombing-party who were working
up the trench at bay for half an hour by himself, which completely
saved the situation, and then went out into the open, when he was
relieved, and pulled in seven men who'd been caught by a machine-
gun. It was while he was getting the last one that a bomb exploded
almost on his head. Why he wasn't killed on the spot, I simply can't
conceive." And the doctor was gone.

But strange things happen, and the hand of Death is ever capricious. Was it not only the other day that we exploded a mine, and sailing through the air there came a Hun—a whole complete Hun. Stunned and winded he fell on the parapet of our trench, and having been pulled in and revived, at last sat up. "Goot," he murmured; "I hof long vanted to surrender…"

Hugh Latimer was not dead—that was the great outstanding fact; though had I known the writing in the roll of Fate, I would have wished a thousand times that the miracle had not happened. There are worse things than death…

And now I bring the first part of my tragedy to a halt; the beginning as I called it—that part which Hugh's wife did not know. She, with all the world, saw the announcement in the paper, the announcement—bald and official of the deed for which he won his V.C. It was much as the doctor described it to me. She, with all the world, saw his name in the Casualty List as wounded; and on receipt of a telegram from the War Office, she crossed to France in fear and trembling—for the wire did not mince words; his condition was very critical. He did not know her—he was quite unconscious, and had been so for days. That night they were trephining, and there was just a hope…

The next morning Hugh knew his wife.

For the next three months I did not see him. The battalion was still up, and I got no chance of going down to Boulogne. He didn't stay there long, but, following the ordinary routine of the R.A.M.C., went back to England in a hospital ship, and into a home in London. Sir William Cremer, the eminent brain specialist, who had operated on him, and been particularly interested in his case, kept him under his eye for a couple of months, and then he went to his own home to recuperate.

All this and a lot more besides I got in letters from his wife. The King himself had graciously come round and presented him with the cross—and she was simply brimming over with happiness, dear soul. He was ever so much better, and very cheerful; and Sir William was a perfect dear; and he'd actually taken out six ounces of brain during the operation, and wasn't it wonderful. Also the son and heir grew more perfect every day. Which news, needless to say, cheered me immensely.

Then came the first premonition of something wrong. For a fortnight I'd not heard from her, and then I got a letter which wasn't quite so cheerful.

"...Hugh doesn't seem able to sleep." So ran part of it. "He is terribly restless, and at times dreadfully irritable. He doesn't seem to have any pain in his head, which is a comfort. But I'm not quite easy about him, Ginger. The other evening I was sitting opposite to him in the study, and suddenly something compelled me to look at him. I have never seen anything like the look in his eyes. He was staring at the fire, and his right hand was opening and shutting like a bird's talon. I was terrified for a moment, and then I forced myself to speak calmly.

"'Why this ferocious expression, old boy,' I said, with a laugh. For a moment he did not answer, but his eyes left the fire, and travelled slowly round till they met mine. I never knew what that phrase meant till then; it always struck me as a sort of author's license. But that evening I felt them coming, and I could have screamed. He gazed at me in silence and then at last he spoke.

"'Have you ever heard of the Death Grip? Some day I'll tell you about it.' Then he looked away, and I made an excuse to go out of the room, for I was shaking with fright. It was so utterly unlike Hugh to make a silly remark like that. When I came back later, he was perfectly calm and his own self again. Moreover, he seemed to have completely forgotten the incident, because he apologized for having been asleep.

"I wanted Sir William to come down and see him; or else for us to go up to town, as I expect Sir William is far too busy. But Hugh wouldn't hear of it, and got quite angry—so I didn't press the matter. But I'm worried, Ginger…"

I read this part of the letter to our doctor. We were having an omelette of huit-œufs, and une bouteille de vin rouge in a little estaminet way back, I remember; and I asked him what he thought.

"My dear fellow," he said, "frankly it's impossible to say. You know what women are; and that letter may give quite a false impression of what really took place. You see what I mean: in her anxiety she may have exaggerated some jocular remark. She's had a very wearing time, and her own nerves are probably a bit on edge. But—" he paused and leaned back. "Encore du vin, s'il vous plaît, mam'selle. But, Ginger, it's no good pretending, there may be a very much more sinister meaning behind it all. The brain is a most complex organization, and even such men as Cremer are only standing on the threshold of knowledge with regard to it. They know a lot—but how much more there is to learn! Latimer, as you know, owes his life practically to a miracle. Not once in a thousand times would a man escape instant death under such circumstances. A great deal of brain matter was exposed, and subsequently removed at Boulogne by Sir William, when he trephined. And it is possible that some radical alteration has taken place in Hugh Latimer's character, soul—whatever you choose to call that part of a man which controls his life—as a result of the operation. If what Mrs. Latimer says is the truth—and when I say that I mean if what she says is to be relied on as a cold, bald statement of what happened—then I am bound to say that I think the matter is very serious indeed."

"God Almighty!" I cried, "do you mean to say that you think there is a chance of Hugh going mad?"

"To be perfectly frank, I do; always granted that that letter is reliable. I consider it vital that whether he wishes to or whether he doesn't, Sir William Cremer should be consulted. And—*at once*." The doctor emphasized his words with his fist on the table.

"Great Scott! Doc," I muttered. "Do you really think there is danger?"

"I don't know enough of the case to say that. But I do know something about the brain, enough to say that there might be not only danger, but hideous danger, to everyone in the house." He was silent for a bit and then rapped out. "Does Mrs. Latimer share the same room as her husband?"

"I really don't know," I answered. "I imagine so."

"Well, I don't know how well you know her; but until Sir William gives a definite opinion, if I knew her well enough, I would strongly advise her to sleep in another room—*and lock the door*."

"Good God! you think…"

"Look here, Ginger, what's the good of beating about the bush. It is possible—I won't say probable—that Hugh Latimer is on the road to becoming a homicidal maniac. And if, by any chance, that assumption is correct, the most hideous tragedy might happen at any moment. Mam'selle, l'addition s'il vous plaît. You're going on leave shortly, aren't you?"

"In two days," I answered.

"Well, go down and see for yourself; it won't require a doctor to notice the symptoms. And if what I fear is correct, track out Cremer in his lair—find him somehow and find him quickly."

We walked up the road together, and my glance fell on the plot of ground on the right, covered so thickly with little wooden crosses. As I looked away the doctor's eyes and mine met. And there was the same thought in both our minds.

Three days later I was in Hugh's house. His wife met me at the station, and before we got into the car my heart sank. I knew something was wrong.

"How is he?" I asked, as we swung out of the gates.

"Oh! Ginger," she said. "I'm frightened—frightened to death."

"What is it, lady," I cried. "Has he been looking at you like that again, the way you described in the letter?"

"Yes—it's getting more frequent. And at nights—oh! my God! it's awful. Poor old Hugh."

She broke down at that, while I noticed that her hands were all trembling, and that dark shadows were round her eyes.

"Tell me about it," I said, "for we must do something."

She pulled herself together, and called through the speaking-tube to the chauffeur. "Go a little way round, Jervis. I don't want to get in till tea-time."

Then she turned to me. "Since his operation I've been using another room." The doctor's words flashed into my mind. "Sir William thought it essential that he should have really long undisturbed nights, and I'm such a light sleeper. For a few weeks everything panned out splendidly. He seemed to get better and stronger, and he was just the same dear old Hugh he's always been. Then gradually the restlessness started; he couldn't sleep, he became irritable,—and the one thing which made him most irritable of all was any suggestion that he wasn't going on all right; or any hint even that he should see a doctor. Then came the incident I wrote to you

about. Since that evening I've often caught the same look in his eye."
She shuddered, and again I noticed the quiver in her hands, but she
quickly controlled herself. "Last night, I woke up suddenly. It must
have been about three, for it was pitch dark, and I think I'd been
asleep some hours. I don't know what woke me; but in an instant I
knew there was someone in the room. I lay trembling with fright,
and suddenly out of the darkness came a hideous chuckle. It was the
most awful, diabolical noise I've ever heard. Then I heard his voice.

"He was muttering, and all I could catch were the words 'Death-
Grip.' I nearly fainted with terror, but forced myself to keep consciousness. How long he stood there I don't know, but after an
eternity it seemed, I heard the door open and shut. I heard him cross
the passage, and go into his own room. Then there was silence. I
forced myself to move; I switched on the light, and locked the door.
And when dawn came in through the windows, I was still sitting
in a chair sobbing, shaking like a terrified child.

"This morning he was perfectly normal, and just as cheerful and
loving as he'd ever been. Oh! Ginger, what am I to do?" She broke
down and cried helplessly.

"You poor kid," I said; "what an awful experience! You must
lock your door to-night, and to-morrow, with or without Hugh's
knowledge, I shall go up to see Cremer."

"You don't think; oh! it couldn't be true that Hugh, my Hugh,
is going—" She wouldn't say the word, but just gazed at me fear-
fully through her tears.

"Hush, my lady," I said quietly. "The brain is a funny thing;
perhaps there is some pressure somewhere which Sir William will
be able to remove."

"Why, of course that's it. I'm tired, stupid—it's made me exag-
gerate things. It will mean another operation, that's all. Wasn't it

splendid about his getting the V.C.; and the King, so gracious, so kind…" She talked bravely on, and I tried to help her.

But suppose there wasn't any pressure; suppose there was nothing to remove; suppose… And in my mind I saw the plot with the little wooden crosses; in my mind I heard the express for somewhere booming sullenly overhead. And I wondered… shuddered.

Hugh met us at the door; dear old Hugh, looking as well as he ever did.

"Splendid, Ginger, old man! So glad you managed the leave all right."

"Not a hitch, Hugh. You're looking very fit."

"I am. Fit as a flea. You ask Elsie what she thinks."

His wife smiled. "You're just wonderful, old boy, except for your sleeplessness at night. I want him to see Sir William Cremer, Ginger, but he doesn't think it worth while."

"I don't," said Hugh shortly. "Damn that old sawbones."

In another man the remark would have passed unnoticed; but the chauffeur was there, and a maid, and his wife—and the expression was quite foreign to Hugh.

But I am bound to say that except for that one trifling thing I noticed absolutely nothing peculiar about him all the evening. At dinner he was perfectly normal; quite charming—his own brilliant self. When he was in the mood, I have seldom heard his equal as a conversationalist, and that night he was at the top of his form. I almost managed to persuade myself that my fears were groundless…

"I want to have a buck with Ginger, dear," he said to his wife after dinner was over. "A talk over the smells and joys of Flanders."

"But I should like to hear," she answered. "It's so hard to get you men to talk."

"I don't think you would like to hear, my dear." His tone was quite normal, but there was a strange note of insistence in it. "It's shop, and will bore you dreadfully." He still stood by the door waiting for her to pass through. After a moment's hesitation she went, and Hugh closed the door after her. What suggested the analogy to my mind I cannot say, but the way in which he performed the simple act of closing the door seemed to be the opening rite of some ceremony. Thus could I picture a morphomaniac shutting himself in from prying gaze, before abandoning himself to his vice; the drunkard, at last alone, returning gloatingly to his bottle. Perhaps my perceptions were quickened, but it seemed to me that Hugh came back to me as if I were his colleague in some guilty secret—as if his wife were alien to his thoughts, and now that she was gone, we could talk... His first words proved I was right.

"Now we can talk, Ginger," he remarked. "These women don't understand." He pushed the port towards me.

"Understand what?" I was watching him closely.

"Life, my boy, *the* life. The life of an eye for an eye and a tooth for a tooth. Gad! it was a great day that, Ginger." His eyes were fixed on me, and for the first time I noticed the red in them, and a peculiar twitch in the lids.

"Did you find the Blue Bird," I asked quietly.

"Find it?" He laughed—and it was not a pleasant laugh. "I used to think it lay in books, in art, in music." Again he gave way to a fit of devilish mirth. "What damned fools we are, old man, what damned fools. But you mustn't tell her." He leaned over the table and spoke confidentially. "She'd never understand; that's why I got rid of her." He lifted his glass to the light, looking at it as a connoisseur looks at a rare vintage, while all the time a strange smile—a cruel smile—hovered round his lips. "Music—art," his voice was full of scorn. "Only we know better. Did I ever tell you about that grip I learned in Sumatra—the Death Grip?"

He suddenly fired the question at me, and for a moment I did not answer. All my fears were rushing back into my mind with renewed strength; it was not so much the question as the tone—and the eyes of the speaker.

"No, never." I lit a cigarette with elaborate care.

"Ah! Someday I must show you. You take a man's throat in your right hand, and you put your left behind his neck—like that." His hands were curved in front of him—curved as if a man's throat was in them. "Then you press and press with the two thumbs—like that; with the right thumb on a certain muscle in the neck, and the left on an artery under the ear; and you go on pressing, until—until there's no need to press any longer. It's wonderful." I can't hope to give any idea of the dreadful gloating tone in his voice.

"I got a Prussian officer like that, that day," he went on after a moment. "I saw his dirty grey face close to mine, and I got my hands on his throat. I'd forgotten the exact position for the grip, and then suddenly I remembered it. I squeezed and squeezed—and, Ginger, the grip was right. I squeezed his life out in ten seconds." His voice rose to a shout.

"Steady, Hugh," I cried. "You'll be frightening Elsie."

"Quite right," he answered; "that would never do. I haven't told her that little incident—she wouldn't understand. But I'm going to show her the grip one of these days. As a soldier's wife, I think it's a thing she ought to know."

He relapsed into silence, apparently quite calm, though his eyelids still twitched, while I watched him covertly from time to time. In my mind now there was no shadow of doubt that the doctor's fears were justified; I knew that Hugh Latimer was insane. That his loss of mental balance was periodical and not permanent was not the point; layman though I was, I could realize the danger to everyone in the house. At the moment the tragedy of the case hardly struck me; I could only think of the look on his face, the gloating, watching look—and Elsie and the boy...

At half-past nine he went to bed, and I had a few words with his wife.

"Lock your door to-night," I said insistently, "as you value everything, lock your door. I am going to see Cremer to-morrow."

"What's he been saying?" she asked, and her lips were white. "I heard him shouting once."

"Enough to make me tell you to lock your door," I said as lightly as I could. "Elsie, you've got to be brave; something has gone wrong with poor old Hugh for the time, and until he's put right again, there are moments when he's not responsible for his actions. Don't be uneasy; I shall be on hand to-night."

"I shan't be uneasy," she answered, and then she turned away, and I saw her shoulders shaking. "My Hugh—my poor old man." I caught the whispered words, and she was gone.

I suppose it was about two that I woke with a start, I had meant to keep awake the whole night, and with that idea I had not undressed, but, sitting in a chair before the fire, had tried to keep myself awake with a book. But the journey from France had made me sleepy, and the book had slipped to the floor, as has been known to happen before. The light was still on, though the fire had burned low; and I was cramped and stiff. For a moment I sat listening intently—every faculty awake; and then I heard a door gently close, and a step in the passage. I switched off the light and listened.

Instinctively, I knew the crisis had come, and with the need for action I became perfectly cool. Soft footsteps, like a man walking in his socks, came distinctly through the door which I had left ajar—once a board creaked. And after that sharp ominous crack there was silence for a space; the nocturnal walker was cautious, cautious with the devilish cunning of the madman.

It seemed to me an eternity as I listened—straining to hear in the silent house—then once again there came the soft pad-pad of stockinged feet; nearer and nearer till they halted outside my door. I could hear the heavy breathing of someone outside, and then stealthily my door was pushed open. In the dim light which filtered in from the passage Hugh's figure was framed in the doorway. With many pauses and very cautious steps he moved to the bed, while I pressed against the wall watching him.

His hands wandered over the pillows, and then he muttered to himself. "Old Ginger—I suppose he hasn't come to bed yet. And I wanted to show him that little grip—that little death-grip." He chuckled horribly. "Never mind—Elsie, dear little Elsie; I will show her first. Though she won't understand so well—only Ginger would really understand."

He moved to the door, and once again the slow padding of his feet sounded in the passage; while he still muttered, though I could not hear what he said. Then he came to his wife's door and cautiously turned the handle...

What happened then happened quickly. He realized quickly that it was locked, and this seemed to infuriate him. He gave an inarticulate shout, and rattled the door violently; then he drew back to the other side of the passage and prepared to charge it. And at that moment we closed.

I had followed him out of my room, and, knowing myself to be far stronger than him, I threw myself on him without a thought. I hadn't reckoned on the strength of a madman, and for two minutes he threw me about as if I were a child. We struggled and fought, while frightened maids wrung their hands—and a white-faced woman watched with tearless eyes. And at last I won; when his temporary strength gave out, he was as weak as a child. Poor old Hugh! Poor old chap!...

Sir William Cremer came down the next day, and to him I told everything. He made all the necessary wretched arrangements, and the dear fellow was taken away—seemingly quite sane—and telling Elsie he'd be back soon.

"They say I need a change, old dear, and this old tyrant says I've been restless at night." He had his hand on Sir William's shoulder as he spoke, while the car was waiting at the door.

"Jove! little girl—you do look a bit washed out. Have I been worrying you?"

"Of course not, old man." Her voice was perfectly steady.

"There you are, Sir William." He turned triumphantly to the doctor. "Still perhaps you're right. Where's the young rascal? Give me a kiss, you scamp—and look after your mother while I'm away. I'll be back soon." He went down the steps and into the car.

"And very likely he will, Mrs. Latimer. Keep your spirits up and never despair." Sir William patted her shoulder paternally, but over her bent head I saw his eyes.

"God knows," he said reverently to me as he followed Hugh. "The brain is such a wonderful thing; just a tiny speck and a genius becomes a madman. God knows."

★

Later on I too went away, carrying in my mind the picture of a girl—she was no more—holding a little bronze cross in front of a laughing baby—the cross on which is written, "For Valour." And once again my mind went back to that little plot in Flanders covered with wooden crosses.

THE MAGIC OF MUHAMMED DIN

Frederick Britten Austin

published in the *Strand Magazine*, vol. 54 (August 1917)

British war stories not only depict Britons engaged in global warfare abroad, but also scrutinize non-British, non-white agents. Adventure tales such as 'The Magic of Muhammed Din' acknowledge the fact that the war was fought, if not directly then indirectly, everywhere in the British Empire. Britten Austin's jingoistic tale introduces its readers to a German agent provocateur who travels to India and tries to stir up insurrection among the Muslim population. The German agitator's plans are thwarted by the loyal fakir and hypnotist Muhammed Din, who exposes the spy as a fraud and delivers him to the British authorities. While Britten Austin (1885–1941) chooses an Indian protagonist as the hero of his tale, he nevertheless does not spare us a hefty dose of patronizing racism in his depiction of the easily duped but ultimately childishly loyal Indian population. The engagement of short fiction with the global nature of war is not always unproblematic from a modern viewpoint, and often reveals the deeply ingrained xenophobia and racist prejudice of its time.

THE INTENSE HEAT OF THE DAY WAS ALREADY A MEMORY OF uneasy sleep, and the distant hills seen across the plain of grey, sun-baked mud were soft in a soft sky. Right across the horizon, as seen from the Political Officer's bungalow, stretched the mountain range, rising from deep blue at the base through a gradation of fairy amethyst and turquoise to a delicate pink suffusing the summits. The Political Officer, his left elbow resting on his writing-table, his fingers caressing the bowl of the old briar whose stem was gripped between white teeth, tobacco-smoke wreathing away from him, contemplated it with bent brows and narrowed eyes. The gaze of that lean face, sallow with many Indian summers, roved not over the distant prospect, tempting though were the transitions and flaws of changing colour on crag and peak to left and right of the point on which his vision was fixed. His expression was stern, the thrust-forward of his clean-cut jaw predominant. Æsthetic enjoyment of the aspect of the frontier hills thus perfidiously beautiful in the evening light had no part in his meditations.

The curtain of the door was plucked aside. A long-robed native, white-bearded, entered noiselessly, bowed, with arms outstretched from his sides, stood erect and waited for orders.

The Political Officer responded with a nod to the *"Salaam, Sahib."* His gaze detached itself from the distant view, ranged keenly over the tall figure in front of him. Under the swathes of the green *pagari* that narrowed the brown forehead a pair of dark eyes of strange intensity met his own. The disturbing effect of their direct gaze was heightened by the bushy white brows under which they glowed. The big, beaked nose, thin-bridged, emphasized their power. The long, white beard spreading over the breast solemnified them with a hint of ancient wisdom. The eyes of the white sahib and the ascetic *Haj* (as his green turban proclaimed him) met unflinchingly.

"The *Sahib* asked for the fakir Muhammed Din—is it well, *Sahib?*"

"It is well, *Haj,*" replied the Political Officer, a twinkle in his eye and a subtle emphasis on the title.

"Did not the Prophet throw his green mantle over Ali that he might himself escape from his enemies, O Protector of the Religion?" replied the fakir, a little piqued.

"*Maloom*" ("it is known"), said the Political Officer, curtly but with a tone of friendliness. "I called you not to discuss the religion, but to protect it. I have work for you, Muhammed Din—dangerous work."

"It is well, *Sahib.*"

"An emissary of our foes is among the tribes, Muhammed Din, and is preaching a false gospel to them. War and the woes of war will surely follow if we do not still his tongue. Listen! You have heard that the infidel Caliph Willem of the West has falsely proclaimed himself a follower of the Prophet that he may use the power of true believers to further his own wicked ends?"

"It is known, *Sahib.*"

"He has sent one of his tribe, dressed as a fakir, into the hills to preach a new Jehad. Already the *mullahs* (priests) are gathering about him. This fakir calls himself Abd-ul-Islam, but he is a Feringhi, no true believer, and no true friend to the religion. Yet he is leading many astray, for he deludes them with a false magic. You will see for yourself. You remember the magic pictures you saw at Karachi?"

"I remember, *Sahib.*"

"It is such magic as that. There is none but Muhammed Din I might safely trust to close the mouth of such a rogue; therefore, Muhammed Din"—the eyes of white *sahib* and Moslem fakir again looked into each other—"I am sending you on the mission. I asked you to come as a fakir because I judged that to be your best disguise. You have come as a *Haj,* which is even better. I do not want this impostor killed, if it can be helped. I want him exposed, discredited. I send you, Muhammed Din." He looked at him with significance as he added: "You may find an old acquaintance."

The fakir stroked his long beard.

"He shall be brought to you riding backwards upon an ass, and the women shall mock at him, *Sahib.* I swear it."

The Political Officer smiled.

"None can if you cannot, Muhammed Din. Now I will explain these things to you more fully."

The Political Officer spread a map across the table and pointed out the route of the German agent across the Persian frontier and among the hills. His present abiding-place was fairly accurately known. The pseudo-fakir attentively considered the ways to it. Then he drew himself erect.

"It is well, *Sahib.* I will now go."

"You have a plan, Muhammed?"

The fakir smiled grimly:

"This dog has his false magic, *Sahib,* but Muhammed Din knows many magics that are not false. I have sworn."

"Go, then. Allah be with you!"

"And with you, *Sahib!*"

Muhammed Din salaamed once more, lifted the curtain, and passed out. The Political Officer watched him go across the compound, and then bent down to his work again with a little outbreathing of satisfaction. The Secret Service had no more reliable man than Muhammed Din.

The squalid little village high up in a cleft of the brown and barren hills, that gleamed golden aloft where they cut sharply across the intense blue of the sky, was filled with an uncommon concourse of tribesmen. And yet more were arriving. Down the stony paths which led to the village from the heights, up the boulder-strewn, dried-up stream-bed which afforded the easiest passage from below, the hillmen hurried in little groups—a bearded *khan,* a modern rifle on his shoulder, his cummerbund stuck full of knives, followed by a ragged rabble of retainers, variously armed. Their weapons were mementoes of generations of rifle-stealing and gun-running. Lee-Enfields, Lee-Metfords, Martinis, Sniders—all were represented. Not a few carried the old-fashioned *jezail,* the long-barrelled gun with inlaid, curved stock. All had knives.

They swarmed on the rough roadway between the squat stone, windowless houses whose loopholes were eloquent of their owners' outlook on life. They clustered round the stone-parapeted well in the centre of the village, so that the women with the water-pots were richly provided with an excuse for loitering. The clamour of excited voices resounding from the walls was re-echoed at a fiercer shout from the steep, towering hillsides, stone-terraced near the village into plots of cultivated land.

This was no ordinary assemblage. From far and near the tribesmen swarmed in, and men met face to face whose habitual encounter would have sent both dodging to cover, rifle to the shoulder. The blood-feuds were laid aside. Families that for months had lived in terror of their neighbours across the village street, quitting their domiciles stealthily by the back way when they had occasion to go out, while the sudden rifle-shot of the concealed marksman added steadily to the tale of vendetta victims on both sides, mingled now with the throng, albeit cautiously. Men whose dwellings were a doorless tower which they entered and left by a basket on a rope, who tilled their fields with ever a rifle in their hand, strode now down the street, their dark eyes roving from side to side, and passed their adversaries with scarce a scowl. Mullahs, Koran in hand, their young disciples at their skirts, threaded their way through the crowd, giving and receiving pious salutation, exhorting, preaching, inflaming the fanaticism of passions naturally fierce. The blood-feuds between man and man, village and village, were forgotten in the reawakened, never-extinguished feud between Islam and the infidel. Behind the priests marched men armed to the teeth, their faces working in a frenzy, their eyes inflamed. They were *ghazi*—wrought up to the pitch of fervour where their own life is a predetermined sacrifice, so that they may first slay an unbeliever, sure of immediate Paradise as their reward.

Above the murmur of voices came the continual drone:—

"*La Allah il Allah!* There is no God but God, and Mohammed is His Prophet!"

It re-echoed down the valley in sudden shouts.

Into this excited throng strode the green turban, the venerable figure of Muhammed Din, piously telling his beads. Men jostled one another out of his way, for this fakir was quite obviously an especially holy man, one who had made the pilgrimage. Giving and receiving the Moslem greeting, "May the peace of Allah be with you!" he inquired the house of the village mullah, and made his way towards it.

He met the priest just on the point of quitting his dwelling. The mullah had a busy and important look. It was a great day for him.

"The peace of Allah be with you!" said Muhammed Din.

"And with you, O holy man!" replied the mullah. He scented an application for hospitality. "Blessed is the day that you come to us, for Allah worketh wonders in my village. Many have come to witness them. Alas! that you did not come before, O holy one, or my house that I have already given up to others would be yours!"

"A corner and a crust of bread, O Mullah!"

"Alas! Allah be my witness! Neither remains to me, O holy one—but I will lodge you with a pious man when the saint whom Allah has sent to us has finished the wonders he is about to show. I must hurry, O holy one! for the moment is at hand. The peace of Allah be with you!"

"Allah has guided my footsteps to you, O Mullah, for I have come from a far land to see these wonders. I will accompany you, for it is His will."

"Hurry, then!" said the priest, irritably, "or Shere Khan's house will be full. Allah knoweth that I praise Him for thy coming!" he added by way of afterthought.

The house of Shere Khan, the headman of the village, was besieged by a turbulent crowd of tribesmen, who jostled one another for entrance. In view of the limited space within, only those known to be most influential were admitted. They deposited their weapons as they entered.

Muhammed Din followed the mullah, who bustled in with an air of great importance. The largest room of Shere Khan's house, a gloomy, stone-walled apartment, almost completely dark since the loopholes high up were stuffed with rags, was set aside for the occasion. More than two-thirds of it was already filled with tribesmen, who squatted on the floor. The remaining portion was rigidly kept clear by one or two of Shere Khan's armed retainers. "Sit farther back, O Yakub Khan! More space, O Protector of the Poor! Farther back, O Yusuf, lest the miracles about to be performed by the will of Allah scorch thee! Back, back, O children of the Prophet! I entreat ye!" The entreaty was emphasized by sundry kicks which the sentries grinningly delivered with a sense of the privileges proper to such an occasion.

The wall at the end of the clear space was whitened. High up on the other wall, behind the tribesmen, was a newly-erected box of wood, large enough to hold a man, supported on pillars of light timber, and only to be reached by a ladder, of which there was at the moment no sign. The tribesmen turned their heads curiously towards this unusual contrivance and nudged and whispered to one another.

"Behold the cage in which the saint keeps the devils over which Allah and the Prophet have given him power!"

Those who were nearest it stirred uneasily.

"What if it should be the will of Allah that they break out of the cage!"

"We are God's and unto God shall we return!" replied his neighbour, nervously, quoting the verse of the Koran which gives protection in time of danger. "May Allah protect us!"

Muhammed Din sat modestly among the throng, telling his beads with bent head.

"What thinkest thou of these wonders, O holy one from a far land?" asked the man next him.

"The wisdom of Allah is inscrutable and much that is hidden shall be yet revealed," replied Muhammed Din, solemnly.

There was a stir of expectation throughout the gloomy apartment. The mullah entered by a door at the farther end, near the whitened wall, uttered a sonorous benediction, and sat down, with grave self-satisfaction, in the front row.

One minute more of tense waiting—and then, amid a low murmur from the assembly, the curtain at the far door was again lifted. The "Saint" appeared. For a moment he stood in a dramatic pose, illumined by a ray of light from without as he held back the curtain. Then, dropping it, he strode solemnly forward into the cleared space. Every eye gazed at him with an avid curiosity. The light in the doorway had revealed him as a youngish man, despite the full beard which lent him dignity. His stately carriage of the long Moslem robes, dimly perceived in the gloom, was worthy of his *rôle*.

He stretched out his hands.

"The peace of Allah be with you!" he said in a deep tone that had only the faintest tinge of a European accent.

In a low deep chant of awed voices the assembly returned the salutation.

"O children of the Prophet! Men of the hills! Greeting! Greeting not from me but from the greatest Sultan of the world!" He spoke in their own dialect, but with a strong admixture of Persian words. "Listen! Ye know already—for his fame has passed the confines of the earth—that the great Sultan Willem of the Franks was visited by a vision from God, and that having had truth revealed unto him he turned aside from the error of his ways and embraced the true faith. Written in great letters of gold over the Sultan's palace shall ye find the sacred words: "There is no God but God and Mohammed is His Prophet!"

He stopped to allow his words their full effect. A murmur of wonderment came from his audience. "A-ah! God is great! Unto Him be the praise!"

He resumed.

"And with him turned all his vizirs and mullahs and khans from the false belief and called on Allah and Mohammed. I—even I, Abd-ul-Islam, who stand before you—am one of them. The Sultan Willem issued a decree to all his people that they should believe in the true faith—and lo! Allah wrought a miracle and they all believed, destroying their false mosques and building new ones to the glory of the Prophet. Great is Allah and Mohammed His Prophet that these things should have come to pass, O children of the Faith! They are hard of belief, for the Franks ye well know are a stiff-necked race. Yet such it is, and my Lord the Sultan hath sent me on an embassy to you that I may tell you these marvellous things. And that ye may more readily believe, Allah in His great mercy has given me power to show you these wonders with your own eyes." His tone took on a deeper, more sonorous solemnity. "O Allah! Allah! In the name of the Prophet, vouchsafe that these thy children may see the great Sultan Willem as he is at this moment!"

He clapped his hands sharply together.

Instantly a beam of intensely white light shot across the dark apartment from the "cage" and fell upon the white wall at the other end. The "Saint" stepped quickly out of the radiance. On the white surface there suddenly appeared a life-size portrait of His Imperial Majesty Kaiser Wilhelm II.—*gowned in long robes and coiffed with a turban*. A gasp of astonishment broke from the peering spectators in the dark room. Once more the "Saint" clapped his hands. The Imperial figure walked in stately fashion straight towards the audience—seeming that in another moment it would be walking out in the air over its heads—stopped, stretched out its right hand, smiled. The muscles of its face moved, the mouth opened—in a speech that none heard. *"Aie! Aie!"* broke from the spellbound tribesmen.

"Alas! that he is so far away that ye cannot hear his words!" lamented the "Saint." "But I can hear them. He tells you to believe in me, who am his messenger, by the grace of Allah and the Prophet. O Allah, vouchsafe that these Thy followers may witness with their own eyes the conversion of the vizirs to the true faith!" Again a clap of the hands, and the picture on the wall changed.

The tribesmen gazed at what to a Western eye would have been an obviously cardboard imitation of an Oriental room with a dais on one side of it. On that dais stood the figure in Moslem robes. Filling the remainder of the room was a throng of men in German uniforms, *pickelhäube* on their heads. They advanced one by one to the figure on the dais, knelt, offered up their spiked helmets, and received in exchange a turban from their graciously-smiling lord.

"See, O people, and believe!" cried the "Saint."

"Aie! Aie!" came the response. "We see and we believe! God is great! There is none great but God, and unto Him be all the praise!"

"Listen! O true believers! The Holy Prophet laid a command on the great Sultan Willem that he should immediately convert all the Frankish nations to the true faith. And the Sultan Willem gave glory to Allah that this command was laid upon him. He sent forth his armies in the great Jehad. The Sultan's armies are the most numerous and bravest in the whole world—not Timur nor Rustum might have stood against them—and none may count the number of their victories in the great war against the infidel Franks. Their triumphs are as the rocks on the hill-sides, beyond reckoning and eternal. All the nations of the Franks fled before them, and were slain like dogs as they ran. And most of all fled before them and were slain the insolent English dogs that, thinking themselves far away from the power of the Sultan Willem, are puffed up with a vain pride and tread upon the neck of the true believer in the land beyond the Indus—nay, who invade your hills and lay waste your crops, seeking to destroy the one true faith. Is it not so?"

"Allah knoweth! He speaketh through thy lips, O holy One!" was the chorused reply from the darkened room. There could be no denial of any statement from a source of such sanctity.

"Look then upon the battle and the destruction of the English dogs!" cried Abd-ul-Islam, giving the signal once more.

Immediately another picture appeared upon the wall—a picture of pseudo-British troops, uniformed so as to be familiar to the tribesmen, taking up a position for battle.

"Watch! O children of the Prophet!" cried the wonder-worker. "Behold the djinns which the Sultan Willem has under his command—for to him has the Prophet given the power of Solomon—behold the djinns that go before the Sultan's army destroying the English infidels!"

Great founts of black smoke leaped up among the soldiers on the wall—debris was flung high into the air—bodies lay upon the ground, visible where the smoke cleared. The soldiers fired quickly from behind cover, dodged, flung up their arms, and fell smitten by an invisible foe. The picture, though a "fake," was cleverly done and would have deceived more sophisticated spectators. The tribesmen did not suppress their exclamations of awe and wonder.

"Behold!" cried the showman. "The soldiers of the Sultan advance!" A serried line of German infantry swept across the picture, bayonets levelled, and the survivors of the defending troops fled before them. The line changed direction and marched straight towards the spectators, an irresistibly advancing menace, swelling larger and larger, uncannily silent.

Shrill cries of alarm broke out from the darkened room. *"Aie! Aie!* Allah protect us! We are God's and unto God shall we return!"

The line of infantry swelled to a superhuman immensity, seemed on the point of reaching the spectators—and then there was darkness.

From the gloom came the voice of the German emissary.

"You have beheld, O children of the true Faith, the infidel English ran like dogs!"

"Like dogs they ran! With our own eyes we have seen it, praise be to Allah! Death to the infidel!"

"Now see the soldiers of the Prophet, the victorious army of the Sultan, destroying the Christian mosques in the conquered country!" announced the showman, in a voice of triumph.

On the wall was thrown the picture of a Belgian village church. German soldiers were busy about it. Then volumes of smoke began to issue from the windows, tongues of flame. The roof fell in. The church was reduced to a ruin.

"Behold! Ye see with your own eyes!"

"We see, we see! God is great! Unto Him be the praise!" came the reply from the spectators.

"Now see others!" cried the German. "This is the work of the Sultan's armies—will ye now doubt that he has set his face against the Christian infidels?"

Picture after picture of ruined and desolated churches followed upon the wall. The German authorities had evidently prepared a special film of them. Cries of wild approbation broke from the fanatical tribesmen, the mullahs loudest.

"Once more, O people, look upon the English prisoners, whose lives have been spared because they have embraced the true faith, being led through the Sultan's capital!"

A film of a few British prisoners from Gallipoli being marched through the streets of Constantinople was then shown, amid shouts of applause.

The picture was taken off, but the beam of light still blazed across the room. The German placed himself full in it.

"Ye have seen with your own eyes, O warriors of the hills! Praise be to Allah for His mercies! Ye will no longer doubt. In the name of the Prophet, the Sultan Willem, the protector of Islam, commands that ye rise up and sweep beyond the Indus. Everywhere the power of the English is broken. With your own eyes ye have seen it. Only on your borders do they still keep up a vain show. Rise up, O children of the Prophet, and sweep these dogs of infidels into the sea! The rich lands of India and much loot will be the reward of your valour. Paradise awaits those who fall in the sacred fight! The green banner of Islam shall wave over the entire earth, for there is no God but God, Mohammed is His Prophet, and the Sultan Willem is His chosen instrument!"

Karl Schultz felt an inward glow of triumph at his own histrionic power as, his words ringing sonorously through the stone apartment, he stood in the full blaze of light and raised his arm. It evoked loud shouts of fanatic frenzy from the excited assembly. They clamoured to be led against the infidel there and now. He kept his arm outstretched as though to still the tumult, as though his discourse were yet unfinished.

But the cries would not cease. "Great is Allah! Death to the infidel! Death! Allah! Allah! There is no God but God! Allah! Allah! Allah! Death to the infidel—death!"

Suddenly there was a new element in the vociferation, a movement among the assembly far back in the dark room. "Make way for the holy man with great tidings from India! Make way for the *Haj!* In the name of the Prophet—make way, dogs that ye are!"

Schultz looked towards the venerable figure of Muhammed Din pressing through the throng. A sudden doubt leaped up in him, was extinguished in self-confidence. The strange fakir approached. The wild clamour of the tribesmen was stilled in curiosity. They fell back in a sudden awe.

Schultz watched the venerable stranger advance solemnly, silently, into the blaze of light in which he himself stood. Again he was conscious of an instinctive tremor. "The peace of Allah be with thee, O *Haj!*" he said, and he found that he had deliberately to control his own voice. There was something uncannily impressive in the advance of this silent, dignified old man.

"And with all the faithful!" came the sonorous reply, enigmatic to the German's ears.

He found himself looking into a pair of strangely disturbing eyes; heard, with a wild reeling shock of the spirit, his own tongue spoken in a low, level Oriental voice.

"Move not a finger and make not a sound, Schultz Sahib, or you are a dead man!" Schultz Sahib's eyes glimpsed the muzzle of a pistol not six inches from his chest. "*Smile, Sahib!* or your friends may interrupt us."

Having once ceded to the menace of the pistol, the German's brain could not resist the command of the imperative eyes that seemed to be boring deep into him. He *smiled*—a deathly smile.

"You have forgotten me, Schultz Sahib? It is not so long since we worked together on the railway. One of us at least learned a great deal about the other in those days, *Sahib. Smile!*—keep smiling!"

A wild revolt surged up in the German, subsided, without exterior evidence, under the glare of the dominating eyes which held his fascinated. He tried to turn away his gaze, was checked by the level, purposeful voice of the fakir.

"Keep your eyes on mine, *Sahib!* Look elsewhere and you are dead before you have looked!"

He heard the words reverberating through him, endlessly re-echoing in chambers of his soul magically open to them. He felt himself fixed, immobile, in a strange paralysis of the faculties. The terrible eyes looked into his that he could not close—he felt, as it were, waves of immeasurable strange force flowing from them, rolling over him, submerging him. And yet still he looked into the eyes of the fakir, his own eyes an open port to their influence.

A subtle, pervading odour ascended his nostrils, filled his lungs, mounted to his head. His brain grew dizzy with it. And still the compelling eyes held him, prevented him from turning his own eyes to the source of the odour. He lost the sense of his environment, was oblivious to the awed tribesmen staring silently at the pair in the blaze of light. He saw nothing but the eyes—lost consciousness of his own body. He stared—and lost consciousness even of the eyes at which he stared.

There was vacuity, oblivion, an annihilation of time—and then out of that vacuity a voice commenced to speak. He heard it with a shock of the nerves—it crashed through darkness with a mighty power. He seemed suspended like a lost spirit in everlasting night, fumbling around the vague yet massive foundations of the world—indefinitely remote from all that he had ever known. He could not detach himself from those foundations. They quivered under the booming voice, communicated an unpleasant thrill to the core of him. An awful unimaginable disaster seemed to envelop him. The tiny germ of consciousness that was still his fought for extension, strove to see. All was blackness—blackness. And still the voice went on relentlessly, driving through darkness, like a ploughshare thrust forward by the firm grip of a mighty and inexorable hand. Immeasurable results seemed dependent on its progress. He listened to it—and as he focused himself on the listening, a dim perception of his environment came to him. He was vaguely conscious of a sea of faces, upturned, listening—as he himself listened. Those faces—they were in some relation to him, there was a link between them and him—he could not determine it. He listened. The words rang like sounding brass, the vowels roaringly sonorous, the consonants clashing. He concentrated himself on their meaning—penetrated to it suddenly as through veils smitten asunder.

"*Lies and again lies, O children of the Prophet! A mockery of lies! The Sultan Willem is a servant of Shaitan who feigneth religion that he may lure true believers to their damnation while they unwittingly serve the Evil One!*" His perception leaped up, clawing at danger, and then was dragged down again, engulfed. He felt himself like a man drowning in black waters at night—down—down—and then, fighting obscurely, he shot up again, heard the inexorable voice continuing: "*This magic you have looked upon is a false magic—the magic of unbelievers in league with Eblis!*" He heard the re-echoing denunciation in a spasm of full consciousness—was suddenly cognizant of the sea of faces, of fierce passions exhaling from it—was completely aware of the menace of utter ruin. A great revulsion surged in him. This must be stopped—stopped! The necessity for instant protest was an anguish in him. All of himself that he could summon from the darkness as his own shrieked the negative, and yet he did not utter a sound—knew that he did not.

"Climb up into that box some of you, and ye shall find no magic but a Frank there!" He strained with all his soul towards the faculty of speech—felt his powers vanquishing the spell of dumbness—on the verge of utterance shaped his words of denial. *"Lo! have I not spoken the truth? Yea, I cannot speak other than the truth, for I am the runaway servant of Muhammed Din, and his sanctity hath broken the compact between me and the Evil One!"* In staggering horror he realized—*the voice was his own!*

He stood fixed, incapable of movement, and saw—like a man that has dreamed and cannot yet distinguish dream from reality—the mob of tribesmen surging obscurely in the long stone room, saw the blinding white eye of the lantern still shining steadfastly upon him—saw it waver, swing from side to side, and then, with one last blinding flash, disappear. In the utter darkness he heard shouts and shrieks and fierce derisive laughter. He heard crash upon crash as heavy objects were flung from a height at the other end of the room. He heard a piercing yell, an agonized, appealing utterance of his own name. For a brief second it shocked him into complete consciousness—*his operator!* Then, ere he could break his invisible bonds, he felt a pair of cool hands pressed tightly against his brow, over his eyes, and he relapsed totally—with a last little gasp—into nothingness.

He awoke again to see the tribesmen surging round him, fiercely shouting. The room re-echoed with reiterated cries of *"Sharm! Sharm!"** and a howl that was so unmistakably for blood that it chilled him to the heart. The room was lighter now—the rags had been pulled down from the high loopholes in the wall. He saw Muhammed Din standing before him, fending off his adversaries.

---

*   Sharm, a stain of dishonor that can only be obliterated in blood. The conception that underlies the blood-feud.

He was still incapable of voluntary movement. A great faintness swept over him. He reeled back; found himself supported by the angle of the wall. He had been thrust back there all unconscious of the movement.

Dazed and sick, he heard Muhammed Din speaking.

"O children of the Hills, Allah and His holy Prophet sent me to you to rescue you from the snare of the Evil One. On me is laid the charge of vengeance upon this wretch, who was my slave ere he became the possessed of Shaitan. But this much of vengeance will I grant ye, for this much is just. He made a mock of you. Make ye a mock of him. Let him be driven out of the village, face tailwards upon an ass. The women and children shall cry derision upon the runaway servant who came to deceive you as a saint with the false magic of Shaitan!"

Staring speechlessly before him, the exposed charlatan heard the howls of approval of the mob. His faintly-working intellect wondered how the mullah was taking this deception—perhaps even yet— He saw Muhammed Din hold up a large bag of money. He recognized it with a last hopelessness.

"This gold"—Muhammed Din emptied some of it upon his hand—"this gold hath my servant surely received from Shaitan. It is accursed unless some holy man receive it. Therefore to you, O Mullah, do I give it."

The mullah snatched at it.

"Great is Allah and for the meanest of His creatures doth He provide!" he said. "Thou speakest truth, O holy fakir: Praise be to Allah that I am here to protect the faithful from the accursed magic of this gold. As to this wretch, accursed of Allah, let him be driven quickly forth as thou sayest, O holy one! It is meet that thy vengeance should not have to linger."

There was a rush at the fallen magician. He swooned into their arms.

Some little time later, when the last stone had been flung and the last epithet of mocking insult had ceased to echo from the hills, Schultz Sahib, his hands bound behind his back, his feet tied under the belly of his mount, raised his eyes from the ass's tail that he had been contemplating.

"Thou hast won, O Muhammed Din—but even yet I do not understand. What happened?"

The fakir smiled.

"Thou hast thy magics, Schultz Sahib—what thinkest thou of the magic of Muhammed Din? Hurry, O Willem, hurry!" he cried, as his stick descended with a resounding thwack upon the hindquarters of the ass. "Thou art laggard in thy invasion of the territories of the English!"

The Political Officer listened to the story, and, embracing hypnotism in the studies of his exile, made a note of it.

THE NAVY-UNDER-THE-SEA

"Bartimeus" (Lewis Anselmo da Costa Ricci)

collected in *The Navy Eternal* (London: Hodder & Stoughton, 1918)

Ricci (1886–1967; he later anglicized his surname to Ritchie) was a naval officer and popular writer of naval stories about whom we know relatively little. Sheffield Hallam University's *Reading 1900–1950* project points out that Ricci probably adopted his pen name because he was blind in one eye following an attack of "Malta Fever" (brucellosis)—Bartimeus is the blind beggar in the New Testament who is healed by Jesus Christ. Ricci's stories appeared in a range of magazines and were collected in a number of volumes, including the 1935 *"Bartimeus" Omnibus* of sixty-five stories. Ricci's wartime collection, *The Navy Eternal*, was clearly a publicity exercise for the navy. It introduced readers to all the various branches of the modern navy, including the Royal Naval Air Service (later merged with the Royal Flying Corps to form the Royal Air Force) and the submarine crews of the Royal Navy. Although submarine warfare during the First World War is now mostly associated with German U-boats and atrocities such as the sinking of the passenger liner RMS *Lusitania* in 1915, Britain had in fact had submarines in operation since 1901. Ricci's story is one small attempt to draw attention to the risky and uncomfortable lives of British submarine crews, and he was at pains to emphasize the difference between German submarine warfare and its English equivalent.

T HE YEAR OR SO BEFORE THE WAR FOUND THE SUBMARINE Service still in its infancy, untried, unsung, a jest among the big-ship folk of the Navy-that-Floats, who pointed with inelegant gestures from these hundred-feet cigar-shaped egg-shells to their own towering steel-shod rams and the nineteen-thousand-odd tons behind each of them.

The Submarine Service had no leisure for jests at that time, even if they had seen anything particularly humorous about the comparison. In an intensely grim and practical way they were dreamers, "greatly dreaming": and they knew that the day was not far off when these little wet ships of theirs would come into their own and hold, in the bow and stern of each fragile hull, the keys of death and of hell.

The Navy-that-Floats—the Navy of aiguillettes and "boiled shirts," of bathrooms and Sunday-morning divisions—dubbed them pirates. Pirates, because they went about His Majesty's business in football sweaters and grey flannel trousers tucked into their huge sea-boots, returning to harbour with a week's growth of beard and memories of their last bath grown dim.

The Submarine Service was more interested in white mice* than pirates in those days, because it was growing up; but the allusion stuck in the memory of one who, at the outbreak of war, drew first blood for the submarines. He returned to harbour flying a

* White mice were carried in the early types of submarines to give warning, by their antics, of an escape of gas.

tiny silk Skull-and-Crossbones at his masthead, to find himself the object of the Navy's vociferous admiration, and later (because such quips exchanged between branches of the Naval Service are apt to get misconstrued in less-enlightened circles) of their Lordships' displeasure.

The time had come, in short, when it was the turn of the Submarine Service to develop a sense of humour: humour of a sort that was apt to be a trifle dour, but it was acquired in a dour school. They may be said to have learned it tickling Death in the ribs: and at that game he who laughs last laughs decidedly loudest.

The materials for mirth in submarine circles are commonly such as can be easily come by: bursting bombs, mines, angry trawlers, and the like. Things not in themselves funny, perhaps, but taken in conjunction— However...

A sower went forth sowing; she moved circumspectly at night on the surface and during the day descended to the bottom, where her crew slept, ate sausages and fried eggs and had concerts; there were fourteen items on the programme because the days were long, and five instruments in the orchestra. For two nights she groped her way through shoals and sand-banks, negotiating nineteen known minefields, and only the little fishes can tell how many unknown ones. Early in the third night she fixed her position, completed her grim sowing (thereby adding a twentieth to the number of known minefields within a few square miles off the German coast) and proceeded to return home. At dawn she was sighted by two German seaplanes on patrol; she dived immediately, but the winged enemy, travelling at a hundred miles an hour, were on top of her before the swirl of her dive had left the water.

Now it must be explained that a certain electrically controlled mechanism in the interior of a submarine is so constructed that if any shock throws it out of adjustment, a bell rings loudly to advertise the fact. As the submarine dived, two bombs dropped from the clouds burst in rapid succession dangerously adjacent to the hull.

The boat was still trembling from the concussion when sharp and clear above the hum of the motors rang out the electric bell referred to.

"Maria," said a voice out of the shimmering perspective of machinery and motionless figures awaiting Death, "Give the gentleman a bag of nuts!"

In spite of nearly three years of war, the memory of the days when the big Navy laughed at its uncouth fledgling has not altogether died away from the minds of the Submarine Service. Opportunities for repartee come none too often, but they are rarely missed.

Now the branch of the parent Navy with which the Submarine Service has remained most in touch is the department concerned with mines and torpedoes. The headquarters of such craftmanship is properly a shore establishment: but following the custom of the Navy it retains the name of the hulk from which it evolved, and is known in Service circles as H.M.S. *Vernon*.

A certain submarine was returning from what (to borrow a phrase from German naval *communiqués*) may be described as an enterprise. It was one which involved a number of hazardous feats, not least of which was navigating submerged in an area from which the enemy had removed all buoys and lights, and was patrolling with destroyers and Teutonic thoroughness.

The submarine was proceeding thus at slow speed with her crew at their stations. Their countenances wore expressions similar to those on the faces of the occupants of a railway carriage travelling through a tunnel. One, a red-pated man, tattooed like a Patagonian chieftain, sat with his lips pursed up in a soundless whistle, watching a needle flicker on a dial, while he marked time to an imaginary tune with his foot.

A sharp metallic concussion jarred the outer shell of the fore compartment. It was followed a second later by another, farther aft, and then another. Six times that terrible sound jolted the length of the boat, and then all was silence. The noise made by a mine striking a submarine under water is one few have lived to describe, yet every man there interpreted it on the instant.

They waited in the uncomfortable knowledge that mines are sometimes fitted with delay-action primers which explode them some seconds after impact. Then suddenly the tension broke. For the first time the red-headed man took his eyes from the dial, and his foot stopped its noiseless tattoo.

"Good old *Vernon!*" he said sourly. "Another blasted 'dud'!"

Once clear of their own bases and the sight of war signal stations, the submarine is an outlaw on the high seas, fending for itself in the teeth of friend or foe. True there is an elaborate system of recognition signals in force, but the bluff seamen in command of the armed auxiliaries that guard the seaways round the coast have a way of acting first and talking afterwards. It is the way of the sea.

A homing submarine on the surface encountered one of these gale-battered craft, and in spite of vehement signals found herself under a rain of projectiles from the trawler's gun. Realizing that the customary signals were of no avail, the commanding officer of the submarine bethought him of a still more easily interpreted code. The second-in-command dived down the conning-tower, snatched the tablecloth off the breakfast table, and together they waved it in token of abject surrender.

The trawler ceased fire and the submarine approached near enough to establish her identity with hand-flags. The white-bearded skipper of the trawler was moved to the depths of his Methody soul.

"Thank God!" he signalled back, "thank God I didn't hit you!"

"Amen!" replied the hand-flags, and then after a pause: "What did *you* do in the Great War, daddy?"

Those who go down to the bottom of the sea in submarines are wont to say (in public at all events) that since they gave up groping among the moorings of the Turkish minefields in the Narrows, very little happens to them nowadays that is really exciting.

This of course is largely a question of the standard by which you are accustomed to measure excitement. Half an hour's perusal of the official reports made by the captains of these little wet ships on return to harbour almost leads to the supposition that each writer stifled his yawns of boredom with one hand while he wrote with the other.

Yet to the initiated Death peeps out half a dozen times in the length of a page, between the written lines in which he is so studiously ignored. The culmination of years of training, ten seconds of calculated judgment and a curt order, which cost the German Navy a battleship, is rendered thus into prose: "5 a.m. Fired both bow torpedoes at 1,200 yards range at last ship in line. Hit. Dived."

But let us begin at the beginning...

At three o'clock one summer morning a British submarine was sitting on the surface admiring the face of the waters. There was a waning moon, and by its light she presently observed a line of German light cruisers stealing across her bow. She waited, because they were steering west, and it is not the custom of such craft to go west alone; two minutes later she sighted the smoke of five battle cruisers also going west. She allowed the leading ship to come within 800 yards and fired a torpedo at her; missed, and found herself in the middle of a broadside of shell of varying calibres, all pitching unpleasantly close. She dived like a coot, and with such good-will that she struck the bottom and stopped there for a quarter of an hour putting things straight again.

At 4 a.m. the submarine climbed to the surface and found two squadrons of battleships blackening the sky with smoke, screened by destroyers on all sides and brooded over by Zeppelins. She fired at two miles range and missed the flagship, halved the range and fired again—this time at the last ship in the line—and blew a hole in her side through which you could drive a motor omnibus. She then dived to a considerable depth and sat and listened to the "chug" of the destroyers' propellers circling overhead and the detonations of their explosive charges. These gradually grew fainter as the hunt moved away on a false trail.

The submarine then came up and investigated; the remainder of the German Fleet had vanished, leaving their crippled sister to the ministrations of the destroyers, who were visible casting about in all directions, "apparently," says the report dryly, "searching for me." The stricken battleship, with a heavy list, was wallowing in the direction of the German coast, sagging through a right-angle as she went. The menace that stalked her fetched a wide circle, reloading on the way, and took up a position ahead favourable for the *coup de grâce*. She administered it at 1,500 yards range and dived, praising Allah.

Later, having breakfasted to the accompaniment of distant explosions of varying force, she rose to the surface again. It was a clear sunny morning with perfect visibility; the battleship had vanished and on the horizon the smoke of the retreating destroyers made faint spirals against the blue.

Since British submarines specialize in attacking enemy men-of-war only, their operations are chiefly confined to waters where such craft are most likely to be found. Those who read the lesson of Jutland aright will therefore be able to locate roughly the area of British submarine activity.

In the teeth of every defensive device known to Kultur, despite moored mines, explosive nets, and decoys of fiendish ingenuity, this ceaseless patrol is maintained. Winter and summer, from sunset to dawn and dawn to sunrise, there the little wet ships watch and wait. Where the long yellow seas break in clouds of surf across sandbanks and no man dares to follow, they lie and draw their breath. Their inquisitive periscopes rise and dip in the churning wake of the German minesweepers themselves. They rise out of the ambush of depths where the groundswell of a forgotten gale stirs the sand into a fog; and an unsuspecting Zeppelin, flying low, lumbers, buzzing angrily, out of range of their high-angle gun.

Here too come other submarines, returning from a cruise with the murder of unarmed merchantmen to their unforgettable discredit. They come warily, even in their own home waters, and more often than not submerged; but they meet the little wet ships from time to time, and the record of their doubtful achievements remains thenceforward a song unsung.

A British submarine on patrol sighted through her periscope the periscope of another submarine. So close were the two boats that to discharge a torpedo would have been as dangerous to one as the other, and the commanding officer of the British boat accordingly rammed his opponent. Neither boat was travelling fast, and he had fully three seconds in which to make his decision and act on it.

Locked together thus, they dropped down through the depths; the German blowing all his tanks in furious efforts to rise; the other flooding every available inch of space in a determined effort to force his adversary down and drown him.

Now the hull of a submarine is tested to resist the pressure of the water up to a certain depth; after that the joints leak, plates buckle, and finally the whole structure collapses like a crumpled egg-shell. With one eye on the depth-gauge the British lieutenant forced the German down to the safety limit and, foot by foot, beyond it. Then gradually they heard the enemy begin to bump along their bottom; he had broken away from the death-lock and was rolling helplessly aft beneath their hull. The sounds ceased and the needle on the dial jerked back and began to retrace its course. The British submarine rose, to contemplate a circle of oil slowly widening on the surface in the region of the encounter.

Few of these grim games of Peep-bo! are without a moral of some sort. A gentleman adventurer within the mouth of a certain river was aware of a considerable to-do on board flag-draped tugs and river-craft; he himself shared in the universal elation on sighting through his periscope a large submarine, also gaily decked with flags, evidently proceeding on a trial trip. He waited until she was abreast of him and then torpedoed her, blowing her sky-high. Remained then the business of getting home.

Dashing blindly down towards the open sea with periscope beneath the surface, he stuck on a sandbank and there lay, barely submerged. A Zeppelin at once located him: but in view of his position and the almost certain prospect of his capture, forbore to drop bombs; instead she indicated his position to a flotilla of destroyers and stood by to watch the fun. The commander of the submarine raised his periscope for a final look round and found a destroyer abreast his stern torpedo tube. He admits that things looked blackish, but there was the torpedo in the tube and there was the destroyer.

He fired and hit her; the next instant, released from the embrace of the mud by the shock of the discharge, the submarine quietly slid into deep water and returned home.

In big brass letters on an ebonite panel in the interior of the submarine is her motto—one word: RESURGAM.

There are both heights and depths attainable by the Spirit of Man, concerning which the adventurer who has been there is for ever silent. His mother or his wife may eventually wring something out of him, but not another man. Readers of the following narrative must therefore content themselves with the bald facts and the consolation that they are true. What the man thought about during his two hours' fight for life: how he felt when Death, acknowledging defeat, opened his bony fingers and let him go, is his own affair—and possibly one other's.

Disaster overtook a certain British submarine one day and she filled and sank. Before the engulfing water could reach the after-compartment, however, the solitary occupant, a stoker petty officer, succeeded in closing the watertight door. This compartment was the engine-room of the boat, and, save for the glimmer of one lamp which continued to burn dimly through an "earth," was in darkness.

Now it happened that this solitary living entity, in the unutterable loneliness of the darkness, imprisoned fathoms deep below the wind and sunlight of his world, had a plan. It was one he had been wont to discuss with the remainder of the crew in leisure moments (without, it may be added, undue encouragement) by which a man might save his life in just such an emergency as had now arisen.

Briefly, it amounted to this: water admitted into the hull of a sub-marine will rise until the pressure of the air inside equalizes the pressure of the water outside: this providing the air cannot escape. A sudden opening in the upper part of the shell would release the pent-up air in the form of a gigantic bubble; this, rushing surface-wards, would carry with it an object lighter than an equal volume of water—such, for instance, as a live man. It was his idea, then, to admit the water as high as it would rise, open the iron hatchway through which torpedoes were lowered into the submarine, and thus escape in the consequent evulsion of imprisoned air. It was a desperate plan, but granted ideal conditions and unfailing luck, there was no reason why it should not succeed. In this case the conditions for putting it into execution were, unfortunately, the reverse of ideal.

The water spurted through the strained joints in the plating and through the voice-pipes that connected the flooded forepart with the engine-room. With it came an additional menace in the form of chlorine gas, generated by the contact of salt water with the batteries; the effect of this gas on human beings was fully appreci-ated by the Germans when they adopted it in the manufacture of asphyxiating shells…

To ensure a rapid exit the heavy torpedo-hatch had to be dis-connected from its hinges and securing bars, and it could only be reached from the top of the engines. The water was rising steadily, and the heat given off by the slowly cooling engines can be better imagined than described. Grasping a heavy spanner in his hand, the prisoner climbed up into this inferno and began his fight for life.

His first attempt to remove the securings of the hatch was frustrated by the weight of the water on the upper surface of the submarine; this would be ultimately overcome by the air pressure inside, but not till the water had risen considerably. Every moment's delay increased the gas and some faster means of flooding the compartment had to be devised. The man climbed down and tried various methods, groping about in the choking darkness, diving below the scummy surface of the slowly rising tide to feel for half-forgotten valves. In the course of this he came in contact with the switchboard of the dynamo and narrowly escaped electrocution.

Shaken by the shock, and half suffocated by the gas, he eventually succeeded in admitting a quicker flow of water; the internal pressure lifted the hatch off its seating sufficiently to enable him to knock off the securings. The water still rose, but thinking that he now had sufficient pressure accumulated, he made his first bid for freedom. Three times he succeeded in raising the hatch, but not sufficiently to allow him to pass: each time the air escaped and each time the hatch fell again before he could get through.

More pressure was needed, which meant that more water would have to be admitted from the fore-compartment, and with it unfortunately more gas. First of all, however, the hatch had to be secured again. The man dived to the bottom of the boat and found the securing clips, swam up with them and secured the hatch once more. Then he opened the deadlight between the two compartments a little way, increased the inrush of water, and climbing back on to the top of the engines knocked the bolts away.

As he expected the hatch flew open, but the pressure was not now sufficient to blow him out. He started to climb out, when down came the hatch again, and fastened on his hand, crushing it beneath its weight. By dint of wedging his shoulder beneath the hatch he succeeded in finally releasing his hand and allowed the hatch to drop back into its place.

Loss of consciousness, nerve, or hope would have sealed his doom any moment during the past two hours, but even in this bitter extremity his indomitable courage refused to be beaten. Gassed, electrocuted, maimed, cornered like a rat in a hole, he rallied all his faculties for a final desperate effort. Crawling down again, he swam to the deadlight and knocked off the nuts to admit the full rush of water. The compartment would now flood completely, but it was his last chance. He climbed back under the hatch and waited.

The water rose until it reached the coaming of the hatch; with his final remnant of strength he forced up the hatch for the last time. The air leaped surface-wards, driven out by the water which impatiently invaded the last few feet it had striven for so long. With it, back through a depth of sixty feet, back to God's sunlight and men's voices and life, passed a Man.

The Navy-that-Floats and the Navy-that-Flies usually go about their work sustained by the companionship of others of their kin. From first to last their ways are plain for all men to behold. They fight, and if need be, die, heartened by the reek of cordite-smoke and cheering, or full-flight between the sun and the gaze of breathless armies. It is otherwise with the Navy-under-the-Sea.

Submarines may leave harbour in pairs, their conning-towers awash, and the busy hand-flags exchanging dry witticisms and personalities between the respective captains. But as the land fades astern, of necessity their ways part; it is a rule of the game in the Submarine Service that you do your work alone; oft-times in darkness, and more often still in the shadow of death.

There is appointed an hour and a day when each boat should return. After that there is a margin, during which a boat might return; it is calculated to cover every conceivable contingency;

and as the days pass, and the slow hours drag their way round the wardroom clock on board the Submarine Depot Ship, the silences round the fireplace grow longer and there is a tendency in men's minds to remember little things. Thus he looked or lit a pipe: scooped the pool at poker: held his dog's head between his hands and laughed... After that a typewritten list of names is pinned on the wall of the little chapel ashore, and here and there among the rows of quiet houses on the hill some white-faced woman folds up empty garments and slowly begins to pack... That is all. From first to last, utter silence and the Unknown.

In this way has been begotten a tradition peculiar to the Navy-under-the-Sea. In the parent Navy it is not meet to talk "shop" out of working hours; in the Navy-under-the-Sea every aspect of life is a jest; but neither in seriousness nor in jest does one refer to Death.

A certain lieutenant in command of a British submarine was returning from patrol in waters frequented by German men-of-war, when he rescued the crew of a Danish steamer torpedoed and sunk by a German submarine. It was blowing a gale and his timely intervention saved the lives of the castaways.

The Depot Wardroom listened to the tale and approved. It even warned the hero that he might find himself the possessor of a pair of presentation binoculars if he weren't careful. The hero expressed his views on that aspect of the affair (they need not be repeated here) and straightway forgot the incident.

He was on his way back from his next spell of patrol work a few weeks later when he again encountered in an open boat the crew of another torpedoed ship. They were Dutch this time, and they had been pulling for nineteen hours in a winter gale, so that their hands were flayed to the bone. These he also rescued and brought back with him to the base; thence they were sent in comfort to their native land to reflect at leisure on Germany's methods of conducting submarine warfare, as compared with those of Great Britain.

A few days later a deputation of his brother submarine captains summoned the hero to the wardroom (what time the sun had risen over the fore-yard), and there, to the accompaniment of cocktails and an illuminated address, solemnly presented him with a pair of binoculars subtly fashioned out of beer-bottles: in the wording of the gunner's supply note that accompanied them "complete in case, tin, black-japanned." That all things might be done decently and in order, the recipient was bidden to sign an official receipt-note for the same.

Now the moral of this may appear a trifle obscure; but it serves to illustrate the attitude towards life of the Navy-under-the-Sea. The lives of these defenceless victims of Hunnish brutality had been saved—therefore the occasion demanded not heroics, but high mirth. The hero of the affair admits to having partly missed the joke. But this may be accounted for by the fact that the binoculars were empty, and that later on, when presented with his monthly mess-bill, he discovered that the official receipt which bore his signature included the cocktails ordered by the deputation during the presentation ceremony. So much for the Jest of Life.

There is a private magazine which appears monthly in a certain east-coast port; it is edited by a submarine officer, written by submarine officers, and its circulation is confined chiefly to the Navy-under-the-Sea: but it affords the truest and clearest insight that can be obtained of the psychology of the Submarine Service.

The success of a publication of this nature depends upon raw personalities—indeed there is very little other "copy" obtainable;

the readers demand it voraciously, and the victims chuckle and tear off the editor's trousers in the smoking-room. Month by month, as you turn the witty pages, familiar names reappear, derided, scandalously libelled, mercilessly chaffed to make the mirth of the Mess. Then abruptly a name appears no more.

> "Art called away to the north,
>   Old sea-dog? Yet, ere you depart,
> Clasp once more this hand held forth...
>   Good-bye! God bless your dear old heart!"

The above lines are quoted from the magazine in question, with the editor's permission, and in reverent memory of a very gallant officer, to sum up, as no prose could, the attitude towards Death of these "gentlemen unafraid."

It happened that another of Britain's little wet ships went into the northern mists and returned no more. As was the custom, a brother officer of the Submarine Service went ashore to tell the tale to the wife of her commanding officer, returning from the task white and silent.

A few months later the officers of the flotilla to which the boat had belonged were asked to elect a sponsor for the little son of their dead comrade. Now since the life of any one of them was no very certain pledge, they chose three: of whom one was the best boxer, another the best footballer, and the third owned the lowest golf handicap in their community. In due course the boy was destined to become a submarine officer also, and it behoved the Submarine Service to see that he was brought up in such a way as to be best fitted for that service, sure of hand and heart and eye.

Thus in life and death the spirit of the Navy-under-the-Sea endures triumphant. Prating they leave to others, content to follow their unseen ways in silence and honour. Whoever goes among them for a while learns many lessons; but chiefly perhaps they make it clear that the best of Life is its humour, and of Death the worst is but a brief forgetting...

MADEMOISELLE FROM ARMENTEERS

Stephen Morehouse Avery

collected in *C'est la Guerre! The Best Stories of the World War*,
edited by J. G. Dunton (Boston, MA: Stratford, 1927)

Avery (1893–1948) was a professional writer best known for his Hollywood screenplays, but before turning to cinema, he wrote fiction for a range of big American magazines. The title of his short story, 'Mademoiselle from Armenteers', affectionately references the wartime song, which was popular among British and American soldiers. The song's lyrics are quoted repeatedly throughout the story, but while the lyrics are fundamentally comic and (at least in the most explicit versions) rather lewd, this story poignantly re-writes the tale of the 'Mademoiselle from Armentières' as a tragedy.

O F COURSE, YOU'VE HEARD THAT SONG ABOUT "HINKY, DINKY, Parlez-vous?" Well, every one of its maudlin verses is a slander of a sweet youngster who gave away too much happiness—in hope, perhaps, that a few crumbs of it would find its way back to her. And a crumb did, thank God.

That is not to advocate any new standard of conduct, either, or to deny a moral prejudice as complete as any one's, probably. But with a little understanding of human nature, French mud, and the fatalism astride a howling shell, too much broadmindedness is not required to win a hearing for Mademoiselle from Armentières. If you can know her, as I did, perhaps you will judge her—as I did.

In May of '17, my nerve-strained and weary battery hooked in, pulled out from the damnable Ypres salient, and trekked for the comparative peace of Armentières. It was a quiet sector, so they said; a lull in the long, harrow-ridden line; a sort of peace by mutual consent except for an occasional five-nine which whined among the smokestacks of the town to crash against the nerves of the war-blasé inhabitants and remind them that "all this is very nice, but we're only a few miles away," or however one says that in German. Then one of our otherwise content battery commanders would be ordered to send over a retaliation salvo and the day's war was done. It looked mighty good after Ypres.

Actually, we didn't stop in Armentières, but dragged twelve kilometres beyond it along the Rue de Lille to a position near Bethune, a tiny village which, with a fountain in the centre of the square and a pub at each corner, had started out to be a town and, in the first eight hundred years, hadn't quite made it. A mere fringe of little grey houses surrounded the square, deserted now but for a few old men, a few wounded, and three women: two laundresses and Madame Peritot who ran the Cheval Blanc. Two thousand yards east was the British front line, and five hundred more, a desolate, brown, shell-chewed strip, reached the Germans. Behind us, the chimneys of Armentières broke the sharp black line of the sunset horizon and in the north were purple blurs—Aubers, Messines Ridge.

So we shoved our eighteen-pounders into pits behind a tall hedge and picked up officers' mess and quarters in a small, but tidy, farmhouse under a knoll about a kilometre from the village. The men, under the eagle eye and gifted profanity of Sergeant Nye, spread out down the slope.

The garden of our farmhouse was full of lilacs and roses just then, and we had our mess table set out there. Soft nights—they seemed to soften whatever Tommy's beloved camp ditty—reached us over the vine-grown wall: "Carry Me Back to Dear Old Blighty," or that Hinky-Dinky thing which I have learned to hate.

I recall the particular evening, almost a month later. Colonel Balton had come down from Brigade H.Q. to look us over and, I suspect, to try some of the 1893 Vouvray which our fellows had unearthed. We had a jolly crowd that spring, anyway. What was a colonel's mess compared to our charming *al fresco* dinners in a lilac-scented garden, a bare trench-mortar distance from the enemy? I can see them, from the subaltern twins, distinguished only by the different cocky angles of their caps, past the very Oxford and ludicrously proper Senior Lieutenant, up to my battery assistant and best pal, Captain Rodney Bonnivale, nicknamed Bonny. And that he was, a blue-eyed, crisp-haired lad, as gay as he was stout-hearted in spite of the fact that he'd been clipped and battered in every rotten show from the Dardanelles to the Somme. I always had an idea that Bonny's blitheness masked a nervous system about to crack: some trouble in England rather than the war. He hadn't been back since the first hundred thousand took him to Flanders.

It was not the sort of thing one talks about, but I was tempted to say something as we were returning together after pushing the colonel's car off on a back road toward headquarters. "You need a leave, Bonny," I told him, "just about as bad as any one in the B.E.F. When do you want to go?"

He eyed me suspiciously, but the darkness gave me a mask. "What's the matter, Major?" he said. "My calculations going wrong?"

Heaven knows, it wasn't that. Bonny knew more about calibration, charge and meteor corrections, ballistics, and all of it than any fellow I had. His experience was all practical and invaluable.

"Nothing of the sort," I said. "You're under par. You're not sleeping. That pip-squeak hitting in the road yesterday had you trembling for an hour. You ought to go."

He laughed. "All right, Major Bob, since you want to get rid of me. But go where?" He hummed the tune. "But Blighty is no place for me."

We went on in silence. I was thinking. As we neared the farmhouse a rifle shot rang out down the road, and our sentry stuttered challenges. A raid? I began jog-trotting toward the sentry post, Bonny at my heels. I noticed, looking back, that he was half staggering. Was it too much Vouvray? Oh, no; it was too much of the glory of war; too many lumps with upturned blackened faces, lying unnaturally flat on the ground. The quiet sector was giving him time to remember.

We'd only made half the distance when a blink of my flashlight showed the corporal of the guard and a relief putting rough hands upon a struggling and dishevelled little French poilu. They dragged him toward the farmhouse. His faded blue breeches bagged almost to his ankles.

Bonny strolled up to the house with me to consider the case officially. Both of us had enough early schooling in France to speak the language. It might be sport. I sat at my table in the tiny sitting-room and Bonny stood over by the door.

The corporal jerked the prisoner in, still struggling. "This 'ere frog sneaks up the road, Major," he spluttered, "and takes a pop at Private Digges 'ere, sir."

Private Digges, scarce able to contain his rage, stood in the doorway holding the offending weapon, a heavy French army rifle, murderous bayonet fixed. It seemed almost too big for the diminutive prisoner to carry. "'Is bullit clips right by me ear, Major."

The faded little Frenchman turned his glare from Private Digges to me, and I saw at once that he was no more than a boy, a smooth and white-faced lad of sixteen, perhaps, with grey eyes too large for his face and a short tilted, un-French nose. *"Vous êtes Anglais,"* he said. "Ingleesh," he repeated, pointing to Digges. "I think it was *une* Boche. I mus' keel a Boche tonight." He was trembling.

I dismissed the corporal and Private Digges. Bonny stood by, half amused, half interested, and the prisoner kept glancing at him quickly and then turning back to me. "Why must you kill a Boche tonight?" I questioned. "Why won't to-morrow night do? How old are you? Fifteen?"

His voice was very low and his effort with English so quaint that I avoided French. *"Moi? Mais non,* I am twenty. I was youngest all but one. I have two brothers and a younger brother and each is killed. Thees"—he pulled at the blue bag of a trouser leg—"thees is Henri. Thees shoe are Raoul." The heavy hobnailed boot was loose upon his foot. "To-day I hear how my youngest brother, *mon petit* Paul, is kill, too. I have take very good care of Paul since he was little with me." The grey eyes began to swim and his chin quivered like a girl's. *"Alor, vous savez, mon Général Anglais,* I mus' shoot one Boche tonight."

Bonny pulled a chair away from the adjutant's desk. He touched the prisoner on the shoulder. "You are very tired," he said. "Won't you sit down, Mademoiselle?"

Our prisoner flushed, backed away from him and then sat down. Very small hands came up over those big grey eyes and some curls of dark, close-bobbed hair escaped the blue cap. Who can laugh, or weep, as the French? Mademoiselle—and I such a complete blithering ass!

Well, what to do? Bonny stood there patting her shoulder and laughing at me. "I think you need a leave, Major Bob. Your eyes are going bad. Now tell us where you come from, Mademoiselle."

She pointed blindly without looking up. "Armentières," she said and went on sobbing.

Bonny lighted a cigarette. "I fancy I'd better take her down to Madame Peritot, Major. We can kill the Boche for her to-morrow."

"You needn't go," I said. I wanted to see Madame Peritot about something, anyway. "I'll take her down."

She looked up quickly enough at that, startled. *"Non-non-non!"* She shook her head vehemently and pointed to Bonny. "You!" she said.

That settled that.

My business with madame, a matter of provisions to vary the men's mess, had to wait ten days. I'd been summoned to

Brigade H.Q. to study a new target series and to exchange map corrections, and by the time I really struck down the back path to the village, I'd forgotten all about the mademoiselle from Armentières.

Corliss, one of the subaltern twins, was with me. He called my attention to the unusual number of our fellows on the path. "Sergeant's been loosening up on passes," he said. "God knows what they can find to amuse themselves with in this place."

They found something, though. I noticed that the lads returning were in high mood and nearly every one of them wore, tucked in cap or tunic, a rose which he tried to conceal when he saw me coming. But I knew them for the same Tommies who had stood in the mud and blood of Ypres and maintained battery fire three secs until the gas burned their eyes and they couldn't lift a shell—and I refused to see these non-regulation roses.

"*Ah! Bon soir, mon Commandant!*" Madame met me at the door of the Cheval Blanc with a machine-gun burst of staccato French. "So you are here. *Eh, bien!* You have come back."

We were fast friends, Madame Peritot and I, or "Madame Petticoat," as the men called her. She took us inside to a marble-topped table in a corner of the long, mirror-lined room, with the same red-plush wall bench, the same gaudy prints, and at the far end the same carved bar with another mirror and a hundred many-coloured bottles behind it—the same because there must be fifty thousand of them in France. Fifteen or twenty of our men crowded to the bar, laughing and talking the mixed dialects of the four corners of England and a little pidgin-French.

Madame, with great ceremony, poured out three tiny glasses of cherry brandy, molten rubies. "Andrée would not give you this," she said to Corliss, shaking her finger. "*Mais non,* she gives only the colour to drink which matches the complexion. If you are dark, *comme mon commandant ici,* a red drink, yes. Or if you have grey eyes like hers, or green, a *crème de menthe. La!* But blond like you, Lieutenant, ah, poor Andrée has no blue—but she gives you cognac which is yellow enough."

Corliss did not understand very well. I was puzzled. "Andrée?"

Madame seized my hand. *"Ah, mille fois, Commandant, je vous remercie.* I thank you every hour of my saddened life for sending to me that pretty babe. She makes everybody laugh. She makes me sing. Hear the 'It's a Long Way to Tipperary.'" Madame beat time, tapping her glass on the table. "Listen to her laugh now. And she will give only four drinks each—which is bad for my business. But Bethune is alive with her."

The men had not noticed my presence and their gaiety was unrestrained. The group divided and through it to a battered piano against the wall came a young French girl, an apron over the simple and yet charming frock: grey, trimmed and belted with apple green, which Madame Petticoat had found for her. Somehow, with her dark, short curls flying, her eyes did not seem so much too big for her face, and there was a piquant unexpectedness about her which made her pretty. Great Lord! After the hell and dirt we'd seen she was pretty and bright as spring's first daffodil. I dare say I'm old. I wanted to weep.

When she'd done singing a French ballad with its inevitable plaintive note, and the keys of the old piano, a dozen of them ivoryless, had called forth the concluding jangle, she turned and saw us. Why should she flush?

"Andrée! *Voici ton ami, le commandant."* Madame called to her.

Several of the men went close to her to murmur *au revoir* as they departed. Some had mentioned mess call.

I spoke to her in French when she came over. "You have postponed shooting your Boche, Mademoiselle? It is better to make us all gay. Perhaps you are happier, too."

"*Non.*" She made a vague little gesture. Then brightening, she said, "You know, I speak a very nice Ingleesh because I visited to Breestol. *Mais, non, mon général,* I cannot be very happy again, but nobody is, is they?"

I had to smile. "Not too happy," I said.

"So you see?" Her earnestness was a delight. "One might as well laugh and sing. *Non?*"

I could not help observing her sidelong glances at the open door and a little questioning in her eyes. A moment later she went behind the bar and put on a perky hat, apple green again, adjusting it for minutes in front of the mirror.

"Ah!" exclaimed Madame, "*La jolie bébé.*" The pretty babe!

When she came back I asked if she were going out. "Doesn't Madame watch out for you better than that?"

Andrée smiled. "She watches out very much." Why she was preoccupied I couldn't guess.

And then it was too late for guessing. A whispered exclamation escaped Andrée. Without so much as a bow she fluttered away from us, through the open door. Out there, slid up silently against the broken kerb, was the colonel's staff motor and stepping grandly out of it was my very best battery assistant and choicest friend, Captain Rodney Bonnivale.

I admit staring. Madame sat with her hands clasped, rapt. I saw Bonny smile down at Andrée, not even seeing us, and when he touched her arm to put her in the car she looked up at him with eyes in which there was a lot more than any man could earn in fifty years, much less ten days.

Bonny waved to the chauffeur to proceed, and they whisked along the winding road which goes to—well, wherever such roads go.

Bonny followed me into my farmhouse office. We'd had a shoot that morning. The front was waking up and the enemy was feeling along the road for our battery, uncomfortable, but evidence at least of our effectiveness. Three of their shells ploughed into the village square and I heard murmurs among the gun crew: "The Cheval Blanc!—Andrée?"

But it was all right. As soon as Cary came up to relieve him, Bonny had trotted off down the path, and now here he was back again, smiling, sunk in my only comfortable chair, smoking my next-to-last cigarette. He was a different man, bright-eyed, real colour, and the infectious good humour as of old.

"You know, Major Bob," he began, suddenly putting on a long face, "I suppose you were right about that leave. I feel sort of knocked about. You see I don't sleep. A week would about fix me up, don't you think?"

I was writing a report and didn't look up. "Since our conversation on the subject, Captain Bonnivale," I said, "you seem to have recuperated wonderfully without a leave." I could imagine the expression on Bonny's face, so I went further. "You know something is stirring out there, Captain. I've cancelled leaves for the entire battery."

He was silent for a minute, trying to fathom the depth of my seriousness. Finally he stood up. "You may go to blazes, Major." He stamped toward the door.

"Wait a minute, Bonny," I said. "Are you going to England?"

"You old devil," he said laughing. He sat down again and took my last cigarette…

I know all sides of this story—every detail. Bonny told me, and Andrée, and Madame, and a soldier's diary, everything I didn't see. I know that he carried her half-way down the path that first night and that when he turned her over to Madame and told her good night, he was the nearest thing of flesh and blood she had, and she asked him not to leave her. But he did.

He was back the next afternoon, though, and found her in one of Madame's best dresses, much tucked. But there was a comb in her short curls, studded with little beads of red glass, gorgeous. "Isn't it a beauty?" said Andrée, and he replied that it was. Only his "it" meant something more inclusive than hers.

Then they were walking across the fields and once, when they met a little boy under a tree, Andrée wept. And once, when they saw a furious old peasant who couldn't curse his donkey into another step, Andrée fairly died with glee. Bonny laughed, too. And soon the peasant laughed, too.

"*C'est la guerre,*" he said.

"He should have a new name for his donkey," said Andrée. "He should use name Verdun."

They found a tinier village than Bethune where Bonny bought an omelet confiture and a bottle of wine. Andrée ate most of the omelet while he drank most of the wine. "*Non, non, non,*" she said, when the madame offered to show them her very best rooms.

They had many such adventures during my ten days' absence, before Bonny's clever wrangling had lifted him to the dignity of the colonel's staff car. The last time, returning through evening purple, Andrée stopped beside a low wall on the outskirts of the village and lifted up her smooth, young arms to Bonny. "Oh," that was all she said.

But Bonny, on the way back to camp, overhearing a couple of the men humming, "Mademoiselle from Armentières, parlez-vous," gave them two days' fatigue duty for dirty equipment and being unshaved.

"Are you going to England, Bonny?" I repeated the question.

He went to the window and stood looking out without answering. A five-nine drove into the hilltop above us, a pillar of sudden smoke, a shower of falling earth. Bonny dodged.

Strange, that. I'd seen him under terrific bombardment, gas, H.E. shrapnel like hail, and he'd never blinked an eye. These isolated bursts seemed to get him. "No, not England," he said, turning back into the room. "There's a mess back there. But I'd like a week."

"Take two, Bonny. I'll arrange it."

He grinned. "I'll tell you, Major Bob. We both know there is going to be a show on the line. The signs are plain. No, I'll not be so far away I can't get back when she breaks."

"Nonsense!" I said. "I don't want you around." There was a risk in these war friendships. Their very intensity courted heartbreak. I didn't want him around.

Well, I was wrong. I thought I had everything figured out, but I hadn't. Bonny disappeared, but Andrée was at the Cheval Blanc, gay as a lark, every one of the following four afternoons. It was too deep for me.

The fifth night the enemy put on their show. As soon as it was dark our fellows up front began to put up their signal lights—red, blue, yellow, green, like a fireworks display. Beyond, under the moon, was a black murk. At exactly nine-ten with a frightful detonation, our whole line seemed to blow up. The ground trembled and up there a pall of black smoke hung like a fallen thundercloud. What good is courage?

I knew our turn was next; the S.O.S. from the infantry and the German bombardment came at the same moment. Everything came over: miniés, pineapples, a rain of five-nines, and each of them a volcano. Everywhere the ground burst open. A shell hit in the farmhouse garden and knocked me against the wall. The whole top of the knoll above us was torn off. The road was a pit. And in the midst of it I manned my eighteen-pounders with the gamest crew in the R.F.A.

I had the order to drop down to two thousand yards. I felt better when we got going, slowly at first, then faster and faster until those six guns were slugging like some gorgeous battering-ram machine— like the fists of Britain. A shell got a direct hit on our number six gun and—ah, well! one of them was Cary.

Infantrymen were drifting by us. Some young kid of a subaltern reformed a line of them on our hillside. I kept a relief-gun crew and sent the rest of our lads under the senior lieutenant to join them. They went back into it with a shout—into that. There is no real limit to men.

All down the lines for miles our unsilenced batteries were blazing away. "Drop to a thousand," came over the 'phones. So the enemy was in our line.

Something happened. I don't know what. I wasn't hit, but I just sat down and couldn't talk. And there was Bonny bending over me. "All right, old top? Give me the 106 fuze, eh? I'll take 'em, Major."

I was assisted back to the wreck of our farmhouse. I heard our guns going as I'd never heard guns going before. Open sights, direct fire, I knew. Bonny should have been a colonel. There was a faint cheer up front. Some one ran by the farmhouse shouting. "Lift! Lift!" So the Germans were going back, then.

It was a fine show. Only about fifteen hundred men paid the great price to see it—just a little side show compared to others.

The next morning was bright and blue. We were in the peace sector again. Except for ugly pits everywhere and considerable wreckage, nothing was changed. The village had been spared to a large extent, though its small clock-tower had been tumbled into the square and its window glass was smashed.

But where was Bonny? He'd vanished as surprisingly as he'd appeared. I thought he might at least have waited until morning. How did he know I was going to be all right? Andrée sent me a cordial and a cake.

A week slipped by, blue sky for days and nights under a horned moon. But I was tired of the war. If it only could have been a cricket war and ended after six months! But I was a different man now, seven hundred years old. Bonny seemed to stay young, though. Somehow I used to smile whenever I thought of Bonny.

That night I walked down to the village. I'd seen Andrée in the afternoon but I had to walk somewhere. I was worried. Where in the devil had Bonny gone? A counter demonstration to the German affair was brewing. I'd heard the talk.

The Cheval Blanc was empty, except for Madame who was arranging shining glasses in a row on the bar shelf. "Andrée?" she replied to my question. *"En haut,"* and she pointed upstairs.

Madame and I had a drink together and I was about to go, unsatisfied, some way or other. Some one came clattering down the stairway into the dark hall outside. "Madame!" The door pushed open and in boots, breeches and shirt open at the throat like a happy young polo player, Bonny burst in upon us. "Hello, Major Bob," he said without the least hesitation. "About time you paid your duty call. Come on up. I'll show you something pretty."

The old son of a gun! Madame had been terrified until she saw the grin spread across my face. Now she hovered over us and clucked like a hen with a new brood of chicks. I followed Bonny up two flights of dark stairs. "Andrée," he shouted. "Can I bring the major up?"

I've been in a few good homes but never in one so happy as Bonny's. It breathed happiness when the curtains blew in with a night breeze. There were flowers and books on the table. Andrée's execrable crayon sketch of Bonny stood on the mantel. A flower marked their place in a book. And there was Andrée in a long blue thing with a white collar, like—like whatever is prettier than beautiful, like something your eyes can't leave. At least mine couldn't. And Bonny's didn't even try to.

She came and sat in his lap and lighted his cigarette. Then she hopped up to light mine. Then she hopped back to Bonny's lap, and—the lucky devil—I knew that whatever life had done to him— and it had done a lot—he was square with it now.

Bonny and I spoke briefly of the raid and of Cary. He was embarrassed when I mentioned his own work, and because Andrée patted his chin. If my back had been turned, she would have kissed him. I know.

"We go visiting to the sea when his another permission comes," she said. "Will it come soon, *mon Général Anglais?*"

When Bonny went into the other room, looking for matches, she pulled her chair over and put her hand on my sleeve. "Will you make me a promise that nothing happen, *mon général?* Because—if it should happen to him—how do you say—too much—*vous savez?* You see, all this—" she waved to include the room—"all this is given to me like to say, '*Petite Andrée,* much is taken from you, but look what you get in return.' And I say 'good.' I say I will be gay and glad then. And I am. Can you not see for yourself?"

I said something. I don't know what.

"Yes," she went on. She couldn't keep the trill out of her voice. Happy? She'd never been so happy before this. "Yes, like a flower which grows up from rich sadness ground. *Vous comprenez?*—watered with tears. Only ours is a forever flower. No, I will not have him be even *blessé—blessé? Blessé?* How you say?"

I told her. "Wounded."

"Non, non, non. I want him not to be hurt at all. You promise?"

Bonny saved me. "Here!" he called from the doorway. "Are you flirting again, Andrée? I've always told her she liked the British tunic and not me, Major."

"Oh!" She threw up her hands. "That is what your sergeant calls—the bloomin' liar. *Comment?* Not a nice word? Oh, *pardon, général.* But you are verra nice. I am sure you keep your promise. I will set out one little liqueur."

Bonny watched her go. "You know—" he sat down in the chair she had left. "You know, Major, I haven't thought much about getting it. I rather expected it. I haven't cared. I'd bungled things pretty much."

He didn't say anything more. Pretty soon Andrée brought in the tray and we had a gay hour. Finally her poorly concealed yawns gave me a hint.

It was a beautiful night. I felt buoyed and exhilarated all the way back to camp. I was sorry Bonny's leave was up, but I was glad he was coming back. I missed him.

There were orders for me when I reached the farmhouse and the 'phones were buzzing all night long. The enemy had earned a penalty for disturbing the peace sector and a raid was on for late the following night.

Bonny was at my side all during the next day. We got a new gun in to replace our smashed one and a new subaltern filled the gap which Cary left. Bonny was blithe as only he could be.

Toward evening we made a flying visit to the Cheval Blanc, a glimpse of Andrée, a word with Madame. Leaving in the gathering darkness we stood aside to watch that village square fill and empty four times, silently except for the tread of boots or an occasional low command, once with Black Watch, once with Canadians, twice with veteran English lads. How many would see dawn? But we had to make a raid. Hadn't the Germans made one? What were a few more sticks upon this funeral pyre of Europe?

Bonny sat up with me in the farmhouse. I had the 'phones over my ears though we still had an hour or two. Our zero was twelve-forty. I think it was then he told me about the business in England. He'd been married, and badly. During his first visit in Flanders she had caught on with some pompous, profiteering official, immensely rich, and she'd asked Bonny to let her go. "I fixed it so she could bring action," he said. "I didn't care about my reputation particularly, but they were making an ugly business of it all when I heard last." He laughed. "I'm glad of it now. Otherwise there wouldn't have been Andrée. But if a breath of it reached her…"

Something was coming from headquarters. "You have that, Major?… Your best man… Absolutely essential, Major…"

I remembered the stem of that shell during the enemy's raid. I felt like that. I was ordered to send my best man up along the 'phone wires to the front line and to an observation post beyond. He was to stay there if every shell in Germany landed. Yes, he was to stay there—if he could get there. And I had only one best man, only one man who could do the job.

My voice must have sounded strange at H.O. I was shouting. "Yes, all right, Colonel. I'll take care of it. No one here has that work in hand but me. I'll start at eleven-thirty, Colonel, and Captain Bonnivale will remain…"

Oh, no, he wouldn't. Old Bolton must have had a general at his elbow. "You will remain in charge of your guns, Major, and you will send Captain Bonnivale…"

"But Colonel," I shouted back. "He can't possibly…"

"Cut it out, Bob. Do you want to lose your command?" Bonny pulled me away from the 'phone. "Am I going up again? When do I start?"

I wept like a child.

Bonny started laughing. That was his way. "My Lord, Major, give me a chance. I'm not dead yet. I'll get a D.S.O. out of this. I'll just step down to the village a while. Back in an hour. Give me a light, will you, Major?"

Madame told me. An infantry staff occupied her café. Bonny came in and went up the stairs two at a time, singing, which was the only thing he couldn't do. Madame clambered up after him and found them laughing and playing like children. Andrée flushed with the surprise of his visit. They were arranging a picnic for the following afternoon, and Andrée was pleading to be taken to a Y.M.C.A. entertainment which was scheduled in a town twelve miles back. Bonny wasn't so strong for Y.M.C.A. affairs, but he caved in after a minute and agreed.

Madame left them shortly and of course, during the fifteen minutes it took them to tell each other good night, no one can know what they said. But one can know that Bonny didn't say a word about the job ahead of him. When he came downstairs, his features carried an expression of frozen rigidity and his eyes were bright. He hurried directly into the street without a word or a glance.

At eleven-fifteen he came into the farmhouse for his equipment and detailed instructions. I gave them to him, like a sentence while he stood there and laughed at my seriousness. "Why were you so anxious to do the job yourself," he demanded, "if it's as bad as all that? An easy chance for conspicuous service, I call it."

But he knew what the job was, and I knew he did. And he knew why I had wanted it. We didn't go in for melodramatics, but his slap on the shoulder and, "Well I guess I'd better run along," was about all I could take.

I can't remember what I did during the next half-hour. Went crazy, I suppose. I recall wondering if he could get there in a half-hour and yet I know he couldn't. But I went to the gun pits and got on the head 'phones, listening, hoping for the sound of his voice at the other end. There was firing on the line.

Fifteen minutes later I heard him, laughing. My heart was still. "Major?" he said, "that you, Major? Well, here I am with a machine-gun bullet through my foot. How's that for luck?" There was an unfamiliar note in his laughter. "Something's wrong up here, Major. I think the Hun is wise. He is ranging for the line."

Something was wrong. A violent German bombardment concentrated upon our man-choked front-trench system. I don't know whether H.Q. or some opportunist of an infantry colonel deserves the credit. But twenty minutes ahead of zero our fellows went over, leaving empty, smoking trenches for the enemy to pound. It was brilliant!

I was busy with the guns then, laying a creeping barrage ahead of our attack. Bonny's instructions came back with mechanical regularity. It didn't even sound like the Bonny I knew. He was the engine, the wheel now, the soldier.

I was foolish to hope. Like a forest fire, but faster, the red line of enemy fire left those empty trenches and started back to catch our attack. From the road I could see it, a rolling billow of smoke, blacker than night and red at the bottom. "Getting pretty hot out

here," came Bonny's voice. Yes, what could be left of Bonny's observation post when that tidal wave of flame rolled over it? "Major?
Major!" I heard a buzzing on the wire.

I wish I could tell you that Bonny came back and took her to a
white cottage in Brittany. But it didn't happen that way. It almost
never happened that way. Bonny didn't come back.

Well—perhaps one of Andrée's brothers wasn't killed. There
were many mistaken reports. Or perhaps, after these four or five
years, she has met and married a finer man than Bonny. Perhaps
there is one.

The next evening, as soon as I was free, I went down to tell her.
I found Madame, white-faced and brooding at one of the tables at
her deserted café. Andrée had heard—and gone. An hour ago she
had started back along that shell-tortured road which brought her
to us in the first place.

Corliss and I started after her. A fire had started in Armentières
and the smoke-stacks were black against a red sky. Mademoiselle
from Armentières was going back there.

Before very long we made out the little figure plodding along
ahead of us. Corliss started to shout, but I put a hand on his arm.
After all, what could we say? What could we do? I hadn't thought of
that before. We stood there a while in silence, and then we turned
back the way we had come. Hinky, Dinky, Parlez-vous.

PARAPHERNALIA

Mary Borden

published in *The Forbidden Zone* (London: Heinemann, 1929)

Borden (1886–1968) was an American by birth and attended Vassar College, a prestigious American women's college in the state of New York. She travelled extensively before moving to Britain, where she lived for most of her adult life. During the First World War, Borden worked as a nurse in a field hospital near the front, treating injured French soldiers for the French Red Cross. Some of her poems about life as a nurse near the front line were published in *The English Review* while the war was still going on. Borden was already an established novelist by the time Heinemann published her volume *The Forbidden Zone* in 1929. In essence, *The Forbidden Zone* was a war memoir, but it was startlingly experimental for its time as it consisted of Borden's war poetry and an assembly of sketches and stories detailing life in the field hospital and Borden's observations of the ravaged French and Belgian countryside. 'Paraphernalia' is one of the shorter sketches in the volume and deals with one of the recurring dilemmas addressed in Borden's book—the need of the nurse to distance herself from the suffering of her patients, and the impossibility of doing so.

WHAT HAVE ALL THESE QUEER THINGS TO DO WITH THE dying of this man?

Here are cotton things and rubber things and steel things and things made of glass, all manner of things. What have so many things to do with the final adventure of this spirit?

Here are blankets and pillows and tin boxes and needles and bottles and pots and basins and long rubber tubes and many little white squares of gauze. Here are bottles of all sizes filled with coloured liquids and basins of curious shapes and round shining boxes and square boxes marked with blue labels, and here you are busy among your things. You pile the blankets on his exhausted body. You fetch jugs of hot water and boil the long curling rubber tubes in saucepans. You keep corking and uncorking bottles.

Yes, I know that you understand all these things. You finger the glass syringes exquisitely and pick up the fine needles easily with slender pincers and with the glass beads poised neatly on your rosy fingertips you saw them with tiny saws. You flaunt your perfect movements in the face of his mysterious exhaustion. You show off the skilled movements of your hands beside the erratic jerkings of his terrible limbs.

Why do you rub his grey flesh with the stained scrap of cotton and stick the needle deep into his side? Why do you do it?

Death is inexorable and the place of Death is void. You have crowded the room with all manner of things. Why do you crowd all these things up to the edge of the great emptiness?

You seem to have so much to do. Wait. Wait. A miracle is going to happen. Death is coming into the room. There is no time for all this business. There is only one moment between this man and eternity.

You still fuss about busily. You move your feet and rustle your petticoats. You are continually doing things with your hands. You keep on doing things. Why do you keep on doing things? Death is annoyed at you fussing.

The man's spirit is invisible. Why do you light the lamp? You cannot see the God of Death with your splendid eyes. Does it please you to see the sweat on that forehead and the glaze on the eyeballs?

Hush, you are making a noise. Why do you make a noise? No, as you say, he cannot hear you, but cannot you hear? Eternity is soundless, but hush! Let us listen. Let us listen. Maybe we shall hear the stirring of wings or the sighing tremor of his soul passing.

Ah! What are you doing? Why do you move? You are filling the room with sound as you have filled it with objects. You are annoying Death with your ridiculous things and the noise of your foolish business.

What do you say? He is dead? You say he is dead?

And here are all your things, your blankets and your bottles and your basins. The blankets weigh down upon his body. They hang down over the bed. Your syringes and your needles and your uncorked bottles are all about in confusion. You have stained your fingers. There is a spot on your white apron; but you are superb, and here are all your things about you, all your queer things, all the confusion of your precious things.

What have you and all your things to do with the dying of this man? Nothing. Take them away.

Aftermath

ARMISTICE DAY

Stacy Aumonier

collected in *The Love-a-Duck, and Other Stories* (London: Hutchinson, 1921)

As a young man Aumonier (1877–1928) trained as a painter, and he also enjoyed considerable success as a writer and performer of comic sketches before turning to writing fiction. A novelist, essayist and short story writer, he arguably embodies all that was best about the British magazine story scene in the 1910s and 1920s. His stories are sometimes wistful, sometimes hilarious, but always well-crafted, carefully plotted and sensitively written. His output was prolific, but his career as a writer was cut short by tuberculosis, the disease that also claimed his better-known contemporaries Katherine Mansfield and D. H. Lawrence. His story 'Armistice Day' combines many features typical of magazine fiction of its day, including romance and a duel between rivals for the hand of a beautiful woman. In an interesting contrast to the sombre nature of later Armistice Days and Remembrance Sundays, Aumonier depicts his Armistice celebration as a day of euphoria, an occasion on which goodwill and harmony dissolve all class distinctions and on which even resentment towards the German enemy melts away, at least temporarily.

I

ON THE EVENING OF NOVEMBER 10TH, 1918, A FRENCH
officer, in the pale blue uniform of a Captain of Artillery,
was ambling slowly up and down Little Compton Street. There
was about his slow but watchful movements the air of a man who
is being kept waiting. And such indeed proved to be the case. For
after some minutes there came hurrying in his direction a fellow-
countryman, of somewhat similar build to himself, but in mufti.
And the greeting of the latter was:

"Pardon, my dear Anton! I was detained."

They shook hands with cordiality, and repaired to the Monaco.

Over glasses of vermouth they carried on the following conversation in their own language:

"You have heard the news, of course?"

"The Armistice?"

"It is to be signed to-morrow morning."

"Thank God! But that I imagine is not the urgent matter you
wished to discuss with me."

"As you say, Max, that is not the matter. But listen, the war is
to all intents and purposes over. Our cause and our country have
claimed four and a half precious years of our lives. During that time
one had no right to claim any consideration for one's own interests,
if they were in any way likely to affect the great issue. Am I right?"

"Perfectly, my dear Anton."

"But now that it is over one may perhaps indulge a little in
the consideration of one's own personal affairs, eh? Passions that

have—that have slumbered may be assuaged. You remember that little affair of your own at Chambéry many years ago?"

"With that upstart lieutenant in the Dragoons?"

"I had the honour to be of assistance to you. And at the time you said—"

The face of the officer in mufti looked startled.

"My dear Anton, do I understand that you wish to fight a duel?"

The officer addressed as Anton bowed solemnly.

"Can it be that—that English officer, Captain Hignett? I remember you telling me that there had been trouble. Pauline!... Wasn't that the girl's name?"

"She was my fiancée."

"But a duel! My dear old man, the English do not fight duels. Even in our country it is no longer—"

Anton rapped his fist down upon the table.

"There shall be a duel even if it is the last one in the story of the world. A duel, or a thrashing, or a murder."

His eyes rolled, his pale cheeks shook as though with an ague of passion. It was clear from his restless movements that his nerves were all on edge. His neck was scarred by the track of a piece of shrapnel. He was barely thirty-five years of age, but his close-cropped hair was nearly white. His face was lined and twisted, like a man who for a generation has been observing the tortures of the damned.

"I regret this extremely," said his friend.

"You gave me a promise," answered Anton de Thiepval, almost sullenly.

"Which I shall most assuredly keep, old friend. I only repeat—I regret this extremely. The War is over. Let us bury all animosities."

"There are some things which only cowards and poltroons bury."

"Come then. Remind me of the details. It was, I think, two years ago. Things move so rapidly these days. I am myself submerged in the vibrations of tragedy."

"You will remember, my dear Max, I was liaison officer at that time attached to the British 97th Division. I was slightly wounded during the first week of the war and sent to a base hospital at Rouen. It was there I met Pauline. She was the daughter of an advocate at Lamballe, an old Breton family. When I met her she was a ward sister, one of the most beautiful, adorable women who ever lived. I fell desperately in love, and I had every reason to believe she reciprocated my affections. But she was a difficult woman to understand, Max. She made me jealous from the very first. She loved everyone. At first I thought it was the men, and that she was flirting with them. In time I came to understand that it was her way. She had no capacity for flirting at all. She loved everyone, men, women, children, even dogs. She was lavish with her affections. And so absorbed was she in her work that you could safely aver that love with her was pure abstraction. I ceased to be jealous, but I told her plainly that I loved her and wanted to make her my wife. Her answer was always the same. She would smile—oh, ever so kindly and murmur: 'We are all mad, Anton. Wait till this is all over.' I never got anything more satisfactory out of her than that, but it satisfied me. She could not look at me as she did and not mean more. I set my mind, like an alarm clock, against the day when it would all be over. I repeated to myself again and again: 'We are all mad. But one day we shall be sane, and Pauline will be my wife.' When I was discharged from the hospital I was passed as unfit for active service, but owing to my knowledge of English, I was, as I just told you, appointed liaison officer to this British division. It was then that I met Captain Hignett. He was a good-looking man of that lean English kind, reserved but entirely friendly. He too had been wounded while serving in a machine-gun company, and was now a transport officer at Amiens. My work brought me in close touch with him, and we spent many pleasant days and evenings together. I saw nothing of Pauline, although I wrote to her regularly. Her replies were brief and perfunctory, although couched in affectionate terms. I could not complain of this. I knew the poor girl was worked to death, and the world was 'not yet sane.' A whole year passed. And then one day to my delight I heard that she was coming to Amiens. She had been very ill, and her father having some important Government post at Amiens she joined him there for a brief rest. I need not say that I lost no time in paying the family my respects. I found Pauline looking pale and worn, but more adorable than ever. She was surrounded by her family—there were two sisters, a cousin, and an aunt in the household—so I had great difficulty in getting her by herself. But when the chestnuts began to bloom along the side of the canal she would sometimes go there to sit or read, and there I would pour out my heart to her. She appeared to be in a yielding mood, and again and again I imagined she was on the point of succumbing to my entreaties. But it always came back to the same story—*The World was insane*. It was impossible to form judgments, to do things rationally. In such a mood one might act, and then live to repent. Men and women were all behaving in a crazy unbalanced way, eating, drinking, loving, knowing that there might be no to-morrow. I accepted her attitude as a compliance upon the terms of the war being over.

"And then one evening, I made my fatal mistake. I took this Captain Hignett to visit her. I little knew the anguish this was to bring me. He talked in his quiet voice to the father about fishing and shooting.

"You know what these English are. You could not tell from his manner what he was thinking or feeling. He almost seemed to ignore Pauline. He certainly paid her no compliments, and expressed no great anxiety to see her again. Walking home from the house he made no comment about her, or about the family. He talked shop.

"The father, however, had invited him there to dinner the following Sunday. It was on this occasion that I became aware of the preoccupation of Pauline. When I was talking to her I observed her eyes following the stranger... My dear Max, the English are our good Allies. I do not propose to offer any criticism. But I am convinced that they and we will never understand each other. This man embodied in himself the salient characteristics of his race. As the days passed I could not determine whether the man was a fool or a consummate actor. He was almost *gauche* in his attitude towards Pauline, nor could I get him to speak of her. But I saw him glance at her once or twice in a way I did not like. It was the expression of a man either dreaming, mad, or struggling with temptation. I tried to draw him out by enlarging upon my own love for Pauline, and he infuriated me with his attitude of detached patronage. It was as though he could not be bothered with *my* troubles, but he had to work some problem out by himself. A week later I met them walking side by side by the canal, Pauline doing all the talking, and the Englishman frowning and looking very solemn. When they saw me coming Pauline looked distinctly flustered, but Hignett appeared quite unconcerned and he greeted me as though the position were quite normal. I need hardly say that after that there was a coldness between us.

"I was of course prepared to concede that this meeting may have been an accident, but my hopes in this direction were quickly dissipated. They were seen together day after day. My friends brought me reports of clandestine meetings. Pauline, I could see, was profoundly disturbed in my presence. I suspected that she arranged things so that I could never get her alone. She began to adopt towards me that attitude which every lover detests, the attitude of sisterly pity. I consoled myself with the memory of her reflection that the world was not sane. I felt convinced that she would do nothing until the war was over, and then we should all meet on equal ground. Hignett had the advantage of me in that he was stationed at Amiens. My duties called me all over the place, and I was away for days and weeks at a time. But my rage at the perfidy of this Englishman was beginning to reach boiling-point. One day I was under orders to go to the other end of the line, and I knew that I should probably be away for months.

"The night before I left I met Captain Hignett in the street. After a formal greeting I told him I was going and I said sternly: 'Captain Hignett, you have an English expression—*It isn't done!* I would ask you to ponder that carefully in relation to your actions.' He looked surprised, then answered coolly: 'I'm not conscious of doing, or being about to do, anything dishonourable.' I replied: 'Very good! I trust to your honour as an officer and a gentleman,' and I turned on my heel.

"Barely a month passed, Max, barely a month, when the whole world came tumbling about my ears. I was at Bapaume when a friend sent me the soul-destroying news. One of my sources of comfort had been that a few days after my departure Pauline was due to return to Rouen. Now came the news that instead of going to Rouen she had gone to England with Hignett. She had married him at Amiens. I cannot tell you what I suffered. I tried to be sent back to the firing line. I craved for death, extinction. I was only

sustained by the slumbering passions of revenge. My soul raged
with blind anger against this perfidious traitor and the woman who
said that such a thing as marriage was not to be considered 'till the
world was sane.'

"Sane! God in heaven! Was I sane? Was Pauline sane? I couldn't
sleep. My thoughts were poisoned. I had never had a fair chance.
While my back was turned this cool snake had crept in and robbed
the nest that should have been my future home. I developed a
fever, and spent many months lying on my back, raging against
Fate and the universe. When I recovered I promised myself that
when the world was sane again I would shock its smugness with
my insanity. Honestly, old friend, I nurtured the darkest inclina-
tions in my heart. I understood how men have been driven to
the last extremity of the *crime passionelle*. It has only been by
reminding myself constantly that I am an officer, and that this
treacherous friend wears the uniform of an officer of an allied
race, that I am able to force myself to give him the opportunity
of satisfaction."

Max regarded his empty glass thoughtfully.

"You are fully determined, then, to see this thing through?"

"But yes."

"And you demand my assistance?"

"As you say."

"And when is this—this challenge to be delivered?"

"To-night, my friend. We go straight from here."

II

In the library of a square-brick house, with its lawns sloping down
to the river, at Teddington, a tall slim young man was sorting out a

collection of army forms. His clear grey eyes were alight with eagerness. He had just heard the news on the telephone of the probable
Armistice on the morrow, and he hummed gaily to himself at his
work. After some minutes he rang the bell, and an ancient butler
entered. He looked up and said:

"Ah, Mason! I'm expecting a friend to-night to dinner. An
American gentleman, Lieutenant Frazier Brandt. He may be here
at any moment. Show him in."

"Very good, sir."

"What time did my wife say she would be home?"

"Madame said she might be a little late, sir. About eight o'clock.
Shopping, I think, sir."

"Very good. How is my father to-day?"

"The General is pretty well, thank you, sir."

Mason had been in the family thirty-five years, and he adopted
a proprietary interest in his master, even when the solicitude came
from the son.

"All right, Mason, thank you. Show Lieutenant Brandt in when
he comes."

"Very good, sir."

When the butler retired the young man continued to sort his
papers, but his manner was restless and preoccupied. Armistice!
The war over! Pauline! Thank God! Plans and anticipations jostled
each other in a joyous riot. He would be able to resign, to return to
civil life. He would be able to take his wife for a real honeymoon
at last. Italy, Algeria, Egypt! Then they would return and he would
go back to scientific research, and they would start that wonderful
home they had dreamed of and planned during the last years of
horror and suspense. Home, security, Pauline, children! It seemed
too wonderful to be true!...

Nearly half an hour passed amid these pleasant reveries when the butler re-entered and announced:

"Mr. Frazier Brandt."

A thick-set young American in officer's uniform swung into the room and gripped his hand:

"Why, Hignett, I'm mighty pleased to see you. How are you?"

"Fine, and how are you, Brandt?"

"Bully. I had some little difficulty finding this place."

"Yes, it's my father's house, you know. He's a widower. He lives here with odds and ends of relatives. Pauline and I are just camping here till we can find a place of our own."

"Well, that's fine. I'm real glad to see you, Hignett. You've heard the news, of course?"

"Yes, they're signing to-morrow, I'm told."

"Gosh! Isn't it wonderful? I just can't realize it. All the boys getting away back home. No more of these ghastly horrors, broken homes, broken limbs. Fancy being just a free man again, Hignett, and feeling you can do and act like a human being. I feel just crazy."

"I know. I shall go crazy to-morrow myself if it comes off. One has got so used to it one simply can't believe that there can ever be the old life again. Where and when do you think you'll be going, Brandt? I don't believe you ever told me anything about your people, when we met in Paris."

"I have a wife and three kiddies and an old mother and two sisters, waiting for me in the little burg of Trenton, and I am going to get right back on the first boat I can crowd on to going west. Oh, it's great; it's fine! Golly! there are good times coming to us yet, Hignett!"

Hignett stood up and laughed, and the two young men banged each other on the shoulder in sheer exuberance. They had met by pure chance at a cabaret in Paris, and had formed one of those quick war friendships, which in some cases lasted a lifetime.

"I'm just crazy to meet your missus," said Brandt.

"I'm crazy to show her to you," replied Hignett, and he pointed at a photograph in a silver frame. "She'll be home to dinner about eight."

"My! that's fine," said Brandt, examining the photo. "It makes me feel quite home-sick. Gosh! She's a peach—French, isn't she?"

Hignett nodded.

"I met her at Amiens. She's one of the best, Brandt. Poor child! It hasn't been much of a married life for her so far. But if the Germans sign to-morrow we'll be able to make all that up."

He was holding the photograph in his hand when there was another tap on the door, and Mason entered. He was carrying two visiting cards on a tray. He approached Hignett and said:

"These two gentlemen wish to see you, sir."

Hignett picked up the cards, examined them, and looked a little puzzled. Then he said quickly:

"Show them in, Mason."

When the butler had withdrawn he murmured:

"Anton de Thiepval! That's a queer thing, Brandt. This was the very chap who introduced me to Pauline. I didn't think he was friendly with me. I believe he was very keen on Pauline himself. I didn't get the whole story from her. I know he had been hanging about a lot. I know she liked him to a certain extent at one time. It's difficult to understand Frenchmen when it comes to their relations with women. You never can quite get the hang of how much they mean. They protest so much that their affairs are apt to lose all sense of proportion—"

The events of the next two minutes were so sudden and so astounding, that Brandt would be likely to remember them all his days. He saw the butler enter, announce two names, and retire. On his heels followed two very intense-looking men, one in the pale blue uniform of a French artillery officer. He heard Hignett exclaim:

"Hullo, de Thiepval!"

The next moment without a word of warning he saw the French officer give his friend a sharp rap across the face with an open glove. He exclaimed, "Gosh!" and sprang forward as though to come to his assistance. He felt Hignett's hand grip his forearm. He could tell by the latter's tense face and clenched fists that his instincts were the same as his own, but his startled expression seemed to be struggling to focus the amazing situation, and in some manner to keep it under control. He stood very erect, and merely muttered:

"This is my father's house."

The two Frenchmen were obviously waiting for him to make some further move.

After a momentary hesitation, he said quite calmly:

"May I ask, de Thiepval, what is the meaning of this—this unexpected attention?"

With a dramatic gesture de Thiepval declaimed:

"You are posturing, Captain Hignett. You know quite well you betrayed my trust in your honour. While my duties called me away to serve my country, you ran off with the woman who was affianced to me!"

"Pauline was never affianced to you to my knowledge."

"You lie! I loved her. She told me to wait till the war was over, *till the world was sane*. I trusted her. I trusted you. If the world was insane for me it was insane for you."

"Love, so far as I may judge, is not dependent upon any degree of sanity or insanity of an outside world... I am sorry you take it like this, de Thiepval. It was an open field."

"It was not an open field. You crawled in whilst my back was turned! You are, in your own language, a dirty traitor."

"I must ask you to withdraw that statement."

The other officer then stepped into the breach.

"I would draw your attention, Captain Hignett, to the fact that you have been insulted by my friend, Captain de Thiepval."

"I am vividly aware of that, Major Fougeret. And I deplore the fact that your friend should have thought it necessary to behave in this manner here, in my father's house. If he wants to make a row there are other places—"

"Good heavens!" exclaimed Brandt suddenly. "You see what he's after, Hignett? He wants to fight a duel."

This, surprisingly enough, had not so far occurred to Hignett. His expression was one almost of angry disgust. The situation seemed to him a little ludicrous, like a scene from an opéra-bouffe. People don't fight duels these days. Controlling himself as well as he could, he said:

"This is absurd. You have no right to come here and behave in this ridiculous fashion. If this were my house I'd kick you out. But my father upstairs is old and an invalid. If you wish to be rude to me, please do it outside, or anywhere you like to choose."

Fougeret bowed.

"I regard this, then, as an acceptance of my friend's challenge. May I assume that this gentleman here will act for you?"

"Oh, come now," said Brandt, in his heavy paternal voice, "let's cut all this out. To-morrow there's to be peace. Surely there's been enough blood-letting these last four years. Why can't you boys pull yourselves together? I'm sure my friend Hignett wouldn't play any underhand games. He's a gentleman. My view is that there was an open field for the hand of Mrs. Hignett and you didn't just happen to pull it off, Captain. Hignett won and that's all there is to it."

"He won while my back was turned."

Fougeret turned towards Hignett, and exclaimed:

"This is an affair in which my friend's honour is at stake. I shall be glad to know what you propose to do about it."

Hignett was still maintaining his puzzled, rather contemptuous attitude. He spoke testily.

"The whole thing is childish. I have no intention of fighting a duel."

The face of de Thiepval turned a shade paler. He said acidly:

"After these four years during which England and France have been allies, it pains me to have to call an English officer a coward!"

Hignett was patently uncertain how to act. His face was beginning to flush with anger, which he was at pains to control. At the same time his feelings appeared to be more bewildered by the unexpected outrage than profoundly stirred. Secure in his own sense of rectitude in the matter, conscious of the completeness of his triumph, absorbed in his own happiness, he could not but harbour a sneaking pity for de Thiepval.

As he hesitated, de Thiepval suddenly stepped forward and spat upon his uniform!

The face of Hignett underwent a strange transformation. Bewilderment, hesitation and forbearance vanished, nothing seemed to be left but the hard, cold anger of the fighting man. He turned to Brandt and said:

"Brandt, I think you understand the situation. I leave it to you to settle the details with Captain de Thiepval's friend. When you have done so, will you kindly ring the bell. The butler will show these gentlemen out."

With that he walked deliberately out of the room, closing the door very quietly after him.

Brandt was dumbfounded. When he had trundled out in a taxi to this dull-looking house at Teddington, he little expected to be suddenly whirled into the midst of a deplorable tragedy. He felt as though he had been chloroformed and awakened to find himself trajected across the centuries, or taking part in the sham posturing of a film. With Hignett absent he felt his powers of protestation to be useless. He listened attentively to the incisive suggestions of Fougeret.

One memory jumped vividly to the forefront of his mind. Whilst in Paris he and Hignett had visited a pigeon-shooting match. He had discovered that his friend was a deadly shot with a revolver. He promptly rejected Fougeret's suggestion of sabres or épées. For all he knew, Hignett had never handled "the darn things". He found himself making arrangements concerning duelling pistols for dawn near a small village in the *pas de Calais*, the affair to take place two days later. He made a note of the details. After the officers had gone, he sought for Hignett, but the butler told him he was upstairs "reading to the general". It was half an hour before he came down. Brandt met him on the staircase.

"Gosh, Hignett," he said, "why did you do it?"

"He spat on the King's uniform," replied Hignett quietly. "Listen, I hear my wife. Come on downstairs and I'll introduce you to her."

III

At eleven o'clock precisely the maroons went off. The King and Queen came out on the balcony of Buckingham Palace. A massed band of the Guards played "Land of Hope and Glory" in the courtyard below. The great concourse, which had already assembled, cheered. But their cheers had not the fervour and the frenzy which was to be their character later in the day. Drugged by the misery of four and a half years of war, the people appeared to regard this manifestation as one further episode in the story. They had not yet grasped the full significance of it. There was nothing about the familiar figures of their King and Queen, or the grey coats of the Guards, or the drab, characterless November sky, to suggest that this was one of the most momentous days in history. Nevertheless, the forecourt of Buckingham Palace remained throughout the day the pivot of the people's activities. From that hour they began to stream in the direction of the Palace, as though the news they had received by word of mouth, or in the newspapers, required some kind of material confirmation. When they had seen the King and Queen, or heard the solemn melodies played by the Guards, they turned to each other and exclaimed:

"My God, it's all over!"

And they went away with light hearts. By twelve o'clock the crowd was so dense that no traffic could get within half a mile of the Palace gates. And what a strange traffic it was! Every conceivable kind of motor and horse vehicle merged to this centre, weighted down by indiscriminate humanity. At the stupendous realization all social barriers snapped. Every vehicle was a public conveyance, restricted only by its cubic capacity. By midday the countless millions began to roar themselves hoarse in frenzied yells—of relief. For it may be said that throughout that day there was one simple emotion which stirred the multitude as though it were a unit, the emotion of intense relief. There existed no spirit of triumph, malice, recrimination—there was indeed little interest in the terms of the pact—there was only one thought expressed in the common formula of the day:

"Thank God, it's over!"

Having completed his business at the War Office, Hignett was one of the early arrivals outside the Palace gates. He too was not so far deeply affected by the significance of the affair. He was still shaken and exasperated by the events of the previous evening, still dominated by the claims of his personal preoccupations. His anger and disgust were being slowly penetrated by a greater disquiet. The previous evening's contretemps appeared so foolish, so unnecessary. The days that he had been living for, the days when he was to devote himself to Pauline, and to realize their united dream of happiness, were abruptly jeopardized at the very last moment. To have survived that awful war and then perhaps to fall to a bullet in a foolish quarrel! Or even to kill the other man!... And he could not tell his wife. She would not understand. And somehow it did not seem quite fair to her.

He wandered down the Mall, watching the crowd. In spite of himself its exuberant quality began to excite him. He saw officers and privates walking arm in arm, veteran "brass-hats" lying back in their cars surrounded by screaming little munition girls, waving flags. Flags seemed to spring up from everywhere. And the most surprising and un-English attitude was that everyone was talking to everyone else. All class distinctions had vanished; and not only were they talking, they were talking excitedly, and laughing, cheering, and singing, and even embracing each other.

He had appointed to meet Pauline, Frazier Brandt, and two women friends of Pauline for lunch at the Barborotti restaurant on the Embankment, and he arrived there well before his time. It was the natural instinct to share the magic of this hour with those one loved. The gay restaurant was already crowded with cheering people, the band was playing, and excited couples were dancing between the tables. New-comers greeted with shouts of "Hurrah! hurrah!" as though by their presence they were contributing to the entertainment of this wonderful experience. Frazier Brandt was the first to appear, with two other American officers, whose names Hignett did not catch—Brandt made some light-hearted apology for bringing them. One of them was an exceptionally tall man in uniform, but wearing a shiny black topper, which he had purloined from somewhere, and which he insisted on wearing all through lunch. Pauline arrived with an even larger party, some of whom were quite unknown to her. As the restaurant was so crowded, they all had to sit where they could. But their party was quickly absorbed into the larger party. There was in effect only one party, but Hignett, Pauline and Brandt managed to sit at the same table.

They drank champagne, not that they needed stimulant, but because champagne seemed the appropriate symbol of festivity, and their eyes shone as though with the lustre of revelation. They toasted each other, and life, and men, and strangers and even ideas. Suddenly two of them would rise and dance, or grip the hands of strangers.

At their table sat Dr. Caswell, the well-known osteopath, an elderly man with horn-rimmed spectacles and the manners of a judge.

"Watch them, Hignett," he said between the courses. "The readjustment of the rhythm of life has already begun. It is a notorious fact that after any such great upheaval the primary instinct of every people is to dance. For years now everyone will be dancing mad. When the street-bells have been jangled, out of tune and harsh, and all the ordered rhythms blown to pieces, the vital energy that survives instantly starts to reestablish the rhythms. War is a cacophony, but life is rhythm."

The tables were cleared, but the dancing went on. Some went and others came. They wanted to be everywhere at once, to meet old friends and to make new ones, to feel the warm vibration of human life around them, to know that everyone regarded his fellow-creature as a friend. Hignett was dancing with his wife, their bodies swaying in perfect unison. Suddenly he thought:

"Rhythm!... rhythm! and in twenty-four hours I may be dead."

"Darling," she whispered, "let's ask them all out to Teddington to-night. Everyone. Let us make what you call—a night of it."

To-night? Well, why not? There was no reason why one shouldn't dance *to-night*. "Make a night of it!" By all means. Ask everyone. Light up the old hall with youth and gaiety, and let his old father rejoice in the sight.

"Why, yes, Pauline, you are a genius! We will ask them all."

Hignett was seated talking to Pauline, who was breathlessly discussing the arrangements for the evening, when he was startled by the abrupt approach of two figures towards the table. It was de Thiepval and his friend! De Thiepval's eyes were glowing with a strange light. He appeared to be on the point of tears. Hignett jumped up, but the French officer gave him a ceremonious bow, then turning to Pauline, he took her hand and kissed it.

"Madame," he said, and his voice was hoarse with emotion, "you once said to me, 'When the world is sane'. Now... now I understand you."

Then he turned to Hignett and held out both his arms.

"Captain, forgive me. I have—I have seen a people *sane*. Everything false suddenly falls away from me. Madame was right, and I was wrong. I cannot—I cannot—you understand—forgive me for my rudeness—"

Hignett felt a lump come into his throat. For a moment he could not speak. Then he took the other's hand in a firm grasp, patted his shoulders, and said in that shy English manner:

"My dear chap!"

There was something childlike and a little pathetic about de Thiepval as he bravely tried to control his tears.

"I did not know—I did not think—there could ever be such a day, such a spirit. One sees everything clearly."

Frazier Brandt had been watching this reconciliation. He suddenly put his arm around the Frenchman and exclaimed:

"De Thiepval, old man, that's fine! Come and have a drink with us, and your friend too. I've forgotten his name. I'm a little drunk, as a matter of fact. Put it there. We're all friends now—eh? No more wars, no more troubles, all good friends—eh? Waiter, another bottle of Pol Roger."

The wine was brought, and the toasts started again.

"To France! To England! To America!"

"How will they be feeling in Berlin?"

"Relieved I should think. Poor devils!"

"Poor devils!"

Pauline suddenly stood up, her beautiful eyes aglow. She raised her glass to the two Frenchmen.

"My dear Anton, my dear Max, you must both come to-night to Teddington. We make a night of it."

"Teddington! But how—"

"There are no 'hows'. There is Dr. Caswell's car, and some taxis, or munition vans. One gets there. Then one either gets back or does not get back. There are beds and shake-downs, and sofas, and some food, and much dancing, and all goodwill, and love, and friendship. Anyone who says he is my friend comes back to Teddington, if only to prove that the world is sane. Will you come, Anton?"

De Thiepval bowed solemnly.

"Whatever the goddess decrees."

IV

The impromptu party arranged by Pauline on Armistice night at General Hignett's house at Teddington consisted of about thirty-five people, of whom no less than fifteen stayed the night. The telephone was kept busy, and the guests came and went in bewildering fashion. The old general himself dressed and came down, even donning his Boer War medals. He did not join the party at dinner, but he appeared soon after for a short period, and insisted upon being presented to the young officers, to each of whom he made a ceremonious little speech, formally thanking them for their services to the allied cause. The irresponsible gaiety of the evening seemed to puzzle him a little.

A gramophone was already emitting the strains of a foxtrot, and with it the glamour of Armistice Day seemed to take on renewed life. Young men and young women, strong of body and keen of mind, and the gloomy menace of four and a half years abruptly removed by the stroke of a pen! To be free to make one's life as one desired! How simple seemed the claims of personal love and personal success unhampered by the grinding machinery of State control!

The young people glanced over their shoulders to admire the wonderful diamonds of Madame Beneventuros. She was the wife of an Argentine senator and cattle king. Her diamonds were famous. Hignett had met her husband over Government business, and as Beneventuros had to go to Barcelona for a few days on family affairs, he and Pauline had asked Madame Beneventuros to stay with them.

These gleaming gems seemed symbolic of the unexplored riches of this newly awakened world.

De Thiepval had quickly succumbed to the spirit of the day. His jealousy had evaporated. His spirits were as gay as they had formerly been morose. He danced with Pauline, and in a quiet corner of the hall spoke freely of the quarrel and of his contrition.

By midnight Frazier Brandt was garrulous. He had drunk more champagne than he was accustomed to, and the result had heightened his natural bias towards kindliness, good-fellowship, and universal love. He was disposed to embrace everyone, men and women alike, and tell them what fine and noble specimens of humanity they were. There had been a halt in the evening's activities, and the whole company had reassembled in the dining-room, where more drinks and sandwiches were being served. It was at this moment that his garrulousness received an inspiration. He got on to his legs and made a speech.

"Ladies and gentlemen, I love you all. This is the greatest day in the history of the world. The greatest day, believe me. You will come to know it and look back on it. What we have to do, my good friends, is to keep it up. Keep up Armistice Day for ever, and ever, and ever. D'you get me? And it's not only in the big things, it's in the little things. Armistice Day! No more wars, no more envy, jealousy or malice. No more petty quarrels. Just all good friends, free… free men, free women, loving one another. Now I'm going to put across a proposition. All of us in this room, we've determined there's going to be no more war, no more bloodshed. There was very nearly—no, I can't tell you, it's a personal affair; anyway, I guess it's not up to me to talk about it. But, listen, I want to suggest that right here and now all we officers, and any others of you who've got guns, stilettos, or any other implements, put the whole lot into a sack, and that we then proceed down the garden to the boat-house and solemnly commit the whole lot to the bosom of your ancient River Thames. And we make a prayer and say:

"'Oh, Thames, here is our burnt-offering. See to it that there is no more war, no more strife, but that henceforth all men live in peace and goodwill towards each other.'"

Brandt's speech somehow fitted into the mood of the party. Everyone laughed, clapped, or cheered. Hignett was specially enthusiastic, although he was laughing too. A sheet was procured, and every man who had a weapon of any sort deposited it in the heap, which was then tied up. Then the whole party, including the women, some in overcoats and mackintoshes, and some even carrying umbrellas, formed into a procession, and, to the strains of "The Marseillaise," played on combs and whistled, they marched down to the boat-house. Hignett took the bundle, and, leaning over the edge of the platform, he said:

"Oh, Father Thames, at the inspiration of our bright young friend from America we commit this bundle to your keeping. We are fed up to the teeth with war and strife, and envy and jealousy. We pray you see to it that these things never happen again. Let the world remain free, and simple, and pure in heart as it has been on this Armistice Day. Amen!"

The bundle went plomp into the dark waters. The action produced on the whole company an almost involuntary effect of awe, then they turned and marched solemnly back to the house to the strains of "Land of Hope and Glory."… And still the dance went on.

Sometimes they would break up into little groups and talk, but for the most part dancing held sway.

Madame Beneventuros retired at half-past one.

It was not until nearly 3.30 that the rest of the party, with final embraces and benedictions, eventually retired to their various shake-downs and sleeping quarters, and it was not until they lay down that each member realized his or her extreme fatigue. For within a quarter of an hour or so all were in profound sleep.

In order to follow the amazing event which happened within the next hour and a half it is necessary to visualize roughly the plan of the ground floor of General Hignett's house.

The main entrance door, which was in the centre, led into a small vestibule, serving no other purpose than that of a buffer between the front door and the lobby which led into the large central hall. This lobby was about fifteen feet long and eight feet wide, and had one door leading into a cloak-room on the right. The other rooms on this floor, the dining-room and the L-shaped drawing-room on the west side and the library and billiard-room on the east side, all had doors leading into the central hall. In line with the entrance door and the lobby was a staircase which led up to a balcony on the north side, overlooking the hall. On the west side, but separated from the main balcony, and entered by a separate staircase, was another small section of balcony. This was the part occupied by the General and his personal servants. The only three guests sleeping on the ground floor were the two French officers in the library, and an American—the same who had paraded the streets of London in a topper—who had comfortably settled down on a lounge in the billiard-room. All the others were scattered in various rooms upstairs or above the garage.

By half-past four the whole household was in a profound sleep, with the possible exception of Hignett, whose mind was still semi-active with the events of the extraordinary day. He was half dream-ing—pleasant riotous dreams interlarded with airs of fox-trots and

jumbled phrases, and a sense of the promise of some newly awakened happiness. Suddenly he heard a loud scream. He jumped out
of bed and ran to the door. The balcony and hall were in complete
darkness, but he was vaguely conscious of movement. There was
the sound of a banging door, a rustle, and a dim vision of something white, and then, pitched on an hysterical note, the voice of
Madame Beneventuros:

"He's got my diamonds!"

He called out at random. "All right, Madame!" and groped for
the switch. For some moments he could not find it. During that
interval he heard the louder screams of Madame Beneventuros,
and the opening of other doors, and voices calling out:

"What is it?"

When he got to the switch it only lighted the balcony, the switch
for the hall being below. The hall, however, was dimly visible. He
saw two figures, one lurking by the lobby entrance, the other hurrying across the hall. They were both masked.

Hignett's mind came out of its torpid condition with a violent
jerk. A crowd of small facts impressed themselves upon him at the
same instant. One salient feature was that the men were armed,
for he saw the tall American standing by the billiard-room door,
holding up his hands. He was covered by the revolver of the
man from the lobby. He could also hear the muffled throb of an
automobile engine outside the front porch. The other man was
moving with professional deftness in the direction of a cabinet
that held some gold plate and gems. He hardly appeared to be
in a hurry.

"This is a carefully arranged plot by highly skilled expert thieves.
They came for the diamonds of Madame Beneventuros, but this
gentleman thinks he might have a few extras as well. We'll see—"

Hignett made an instinctive spring on to the staircase, and an equally instinctive spring back, for a bullet grazed his elbow. He scrambled towards his bedroom only to bump into Pauline.

"Get back, darling, get back! It's all right," he said, and then uttered a curse. He had gone back to the bedroom for his revolver. And suddenly the ironic truth struck him. Every single weapon of defence had been consigned to the gentle care of "Father Thames"! Of all those men in the house, not one had a weapon. These men must have been watching their every movement. It was a damnable situation. He heard other cries and screams, and crept back to the balcony. Quite a number of men were there in dressing-gowns and pyjamas, all helpless! For one of the thieves had his revolver covering the whole scene of operations, whilst the other calmly began to remove the contents of the cabinet into a large black bag. And then in a flash the whole bizarre business had reached a crisis of tragedy.

Without observing how she got there, Hignett suddenly observed Pauline at the foot of the stairs rushing in the direction of the thief and crying out, "No, no!"

He sensed in an instant the cause of her onset. In the cabinet were the jewels and little trinkets which had belonged to her mother and which had been temporarily placed there. His heart gave a throb of dread as he rushed after her. He sprang down the stairs in two bounds, but even that was not quick enough to avert the tragedy. The one thief continued to pack, but the other fired, and the bullet went clean through the heart of—de Thiepval!

The French officer had made a spring from the library door! Hignett caught Pauline in his arms and turned, and as he did so, he was aware of a new element in the conflict. For there was the ping of a rifle-shot followed by a scream of pain from the man who had fired. In spite of the danger of his position with his beloved burden,

Hignett could not help but turn, and the truth became evident to him at a glance. Up in his own section of the balcony, the General was busy with an old Lee-Metford rifle, such as was used during the Boer War. He was taking cover behind the projections in the balustrade, and calmly proceeding to snipe the enemy.

At this unexpected onslaught both the marauders dashed into the lobby and through the front door, each leaving a trail of blood. A car was heard to start. They had the diamonds, it was true, but little else, and each was wounded. Some of the men rushed after them, others hastened to the telephone. The police were informed and a doctor sent for, although all knew, alas! that the doctor's services were a mere matter of form. De Thiepval had died in the gallant way that he would have chosen. They placed his body in one of the bedrooms and, setting two candles, Pauline, weeping a little, knelt and prayed for his soul… With the raw light of dawn came the news that the thieves had been captured, and a bedraggled company met over tea and coffee and rolls and discussed the night's adventure.

The old gentleman had been badly shaken, but he insisted that he wished to see all the young officers and speak to them.

"It's an order from G.H.Q.," said Hignett, shrugging his shoulders, and he went upstairs, the others following him. The old man was sitting up in his bed; his eyes were very bright, and his lips moving jerkily. The men stood around the bed, and he looked at them, nodded and smiled. Then he said:

"Where is that other young Frenchman?"

Hignett coughed. "He—he fell in the conflict, sir."

The old General nodded slowly. Almost inaudibly, as if talking to himself, he suddenly said:

"You young men!…"

Then he raised himself and called out as though it were a military command:

"The strong man may lay down his arms, but he does not throw them away."

He lay back as though exhausted after that, and smiled once more.

"You young men... you young men..."

He closed his eyes, but his lips continued their jerky movement...

ARMISTICE

Francis Brett Young

collected in *The Cage Bird and Other Stories* (London: Heinemann, 1933)

Young (1884–1954) was a trained physician who served with the Royal Army Medical Corps in German East Africa during the war, and was no longer able to practise medicine after being invalided out of the army in 1918. He published a memoir about his wartime experiences, *Marching on Tanga: With General Smuts in East Africa*, in 1917. Set in November 1928, his story 'Armistice' relates the notable occasion when the narrator and his old wartime pal George, with whom he served in East Africa, meet and are reconciled with a former enemy in the course of their annual celebration of Armistice Day. Young's story reminds us of the impact of the First World War on the British class system; the narrator's thoroughly middle-class wife is appalled that he still associates with George, a working-class man she considers beneath her husband's attention. Shared experience of an increasingly marginalized war experience far from the Western Front serves as a bond for a group of veterans, across both class boundaries and (former) enemy lines. Unfortunately, the story gives us little insight into the war experience of native African soldiers.

I F THERE'S ONE DAY IN THE YEAR MORE THAN ANOTHER MY wife can't abide it's the Eleventh of November. She calls it a black-letter day: like our last of the seaside, the one when Jim's school-bills come in, and the one when I get my Income-tax Demand Note. On these days, she says, my barometer goes down bump from *Changeable* to *Stormy*. But November the Eleventh, the anniversary of the Armistice, is the worst of the lot. On that day, for the last ten years, I've made it a habit to go out to dinner with George Hollins and talk over old times. As for barometers—there's one thing that ours doesn't point to on these occasions, and that's *Very Dry*. Well, if we *do* celebrate a bit, that's our business, I say, and nobody else's. If anyone's earned the right to do themselves well old George and I have.

Of course, Maggie can't see it. She's been brought up that way—too refined. The first thing she asks herself about everything is what people will think. A man is known by the company he keeps, she says, and George Hollins is vulgar. Well, war, as I've told her a hundred times, makes strange bedfellows. As for that, we shouldn't have got married ourselves if it wasn't for the war. You couldn't make the World Safe for Democracy, like George and I did, without being democratic yourself. What really sticks in her throat is George being a sanitary plumber. She says he's no class— which means that when I have to go to church in a frock-coat and carry the plate round, old George reads the *News of the World* and smokes a pipe in his shirt-sleeves. As a matter of fact, in the war, it was just the other way round. Old George was a sergeant—*and* let you know it—while I was a lance-corporal; and as for us having nothing in common, as Maggie maintains, well, when George and I were prisoners in German East we had something in common with a vengeance, and that was one shirt. Whenever I start telling people the story of that shirt Maggie gets uneasy. She says the subject's in very bad taste and had better be buried. That, as I tell her, is what ought to have been done with our shirt. But when it comes to George Hollins she simply can't see a joke.

Well, joking in good taste or bad taste apart, there's one point on which I'm firm, and that is my evening out with old George on Armistice Day. If Maggie doesn't like it she can lump it, I tell her, and she knows that I mean what I say. This year was the tenth anniversary—you'd hardly believe it—and George and I had fixed up to meet at a pub downtown for a short one before we went out to dinner. Thanks mainly to Maggie I hadn't set eyes on the old devil for months, and it did my heart good, I can tell you, to see his honest face again. There he was, with all his medal ribbons stitched on to his waistcoat. Of course, I don't do that myself, Maggie says it isn't good form, but if anyone has a right to, old George has. Well, anyway, women know nothing about war, as I say...

We sat down, and we had a double whisky to start off with, and George asked me how Maggie was, which only shows what a good heart he has, when you come to think of the sniffy way she's treated him. We felt a bit strange just at first, not having seen each other for so long; but after we'd ordered another it began to feel just like old times—us talking Swahili, the lingo they speak down there, and all the old jokes popping up as fresh as paint. By the time we were ready for dinner and set off arm-in-arm down the street we were so far back in the thick of it that it wouldn't have surprised me if

I'd seen a giraffe poke its head round the corner lamp-post. Those giraffes were a bally nuisance in East Africa, you know; the brutes used to carry away the field-telephone wires round their necks.

This year George had found a new place for dinner he said. It was kept by a Swiss, and the proprietor was a friend of his, because George had done him a favour by fixing him up in a prompt and business-like way when his water-pipes froze and burst. He had a lager on draught, this chap, and, say what you like about the Boche, he can brew a good beer. George had asked him to make us a German meal, smoked sausage and sauerkraut, out of sentiment, like, just to remind us of the time we were in prison, though, God knows, he and I didn't get much to eat except mealies in those days. Still, it was a bright idea of George's. He may be a plumber and all that, but the chap has a vein of what you might call poetry in him.

We sat down at the table together, and I must say the food, though foreign, was first-rate. Then, when once we'd got going, we started in, like we do every year, trying to remember everything that happened on the day we were taken prisoners. Pretty rotten at the time it was, I can tell you; but when you come to look back on it, after nearly twelve years, you can't help seeing the humorous side.

You see, in those days, George and me were in the Mechanical Transport, driving lorries and box-Fords from the base, at a place on the Tanga Railway called Korogwe, down to the front where Smuts and the South Africans were. We used to average about two miles an hour. There weren't any roads—not what you or I would call roads. The troops that went down in front of us had cut a sort of track through the bush—great thorn-trees, with spikes on them up to six inches long. Then, what with the trampling of the soldiers' boots and the wheels of the bullock-carts and the guns and limbers, a strip would get flattened out in the sandy soil. Red sand... Don't I know it! Why, sometimes the wheels of our lorries would get stuck ten hours at a time, so that we had to wait—buried up to our axles and scared stiff of lions, if you want the truth—until some other blighter rolled up and dug or towed us out. And even when we got going again, as you did with luck, the radiators of those old lorries would boil the way you could have made tea at any moment, if you'd had any tea to make. I can tell you that driving a lorry through German East, with the sky grilling above you and the engine boiling underneath was next door to hell!

And so damn lonely, too! It's hard to imagine it now, when you go into business by the eight-fifteen every morning in a carriage so crowded with "seasons" that the odds are you can't find a seat. Lonely? Why, often, when you stopped for the night in the bush, you wouldn't be far out if you guessed that there wasn't another human soul within forty miles of you. There weren't many native villages in that part—too much malaria—and all the niggers that happened to be about had cleared off, because the Boche—the "Germani" as we called them—had cut down or burnt all their crops so that the enemy—that's us—shouldn't find any food.

Not a soul within forty miles! It got on your nerves—on mine more than George's. We used to rig up a tarpaulin at night as a sort of tent, and sit smoking native tobacco, to keep off the mosqui-toes, and talking about home. And then, when you stopped, that silence would bear in on you. Lord, you could feel the emptiness of it—hundreds of miles! And later, when you tried to sleep, you'd hear something worse than silence: the bodies of animals slinking through the bush, and the old lions snuffling round. You see, all that country was stiff with lions in those days, because hundreds of the South African's horses had died with fly and horse-sickness—your

nose didn't half tell you that!—and since our columns and the
Germans' between them had scared all the game away, the brutes
used to pick up a supper of gamey horse-flesh to keep them from
starving. They were welcome to all they could get as long as they
left *us* alone. But then, you could never tell the moment when they
wouldn't fancy something fresher in the human line. So we used to
build a sort of fence—a *boma* they called it—of thorn, and light a
fire of brushwood to scare the brutes off. Even if it hadn't been for
the lions, I can tell you, we should have needed a fire. For though
we got roasted by day we pretty nearly froze at night. I tell you,
it's not a health-resort, isn't German East Africa!

Then water... Well, that was the most important of all. The
lorry-engines got so hot, with the sun, you know, and ploughing
through sand, that they drank it up all the time. There was always
the chance that your blessed bearings would seize. We had to treat
water as if it cost more than champagne. You see, when old Smuts
went off chasing the Germans southward he had no time to spare
to think about details of that kind. The whole of that country's
about as dry as a bone—just muddy water-holes, here and there,
near the villages. The cavalry had gone down in front of us, drinking up everything; so when we chaps came along afterwards there
was nothing left but stuff like moist coffee-grounds. We had to
filter it through a cloth before we could put it in the radiators. You
people who can turn on a tap don't know your blessings! As for
drinking—we had to remember that the engines came first; we
couldn't touch a spot till we knew that the radiators were filled. I
give you my word, we used to dream about water, old George and
me. Honest Injun, we used to dream about it!

Let's see... Where was I? Ah, water. Of course. On the way
from our base to the front there was one place—M'bagwe, they

called it—with running water. Well running is hardly the word. I suppose it had once been running, before the cavalry got at it. At any rate, just near the track that the army had made, you could see the course of a stream—the only one, as far as I know, in all that damn country. By the time we got down there it was pretty nearly dried up—a series of deepish puddles among the rocks; anyway, enough to fill up the radiators and water-bottles and have a good drink as well. And that was how George and I came to have one shirt between us.

Wait a bit… I'll explain. When we got to that place one evening, I'm telling you the gospel truth when I say I hadn't had a wash for nearly a month. So I said to George: "Sergeant," I said, "I'm going to take a bath." "And who's going to drink it," he asked, "after you've done that?" "Well," I said, "it's good honest dirt, as clean as the horses anyway; and if you want a drink, Sergeant, you'd better look sharp about it."

He didn't like it at first. In those days we hadn't got intimate as we were later, and George was a bit puffed up with his sergeant's stripes. However, when he saw me splashing about like a hippo in the mud, old George got off his high horse. "Here, don't stir up the mud," he said, "I've a good mind to try it myself. Anyone would imagine, from the way you behave, that that river was your private property." "Come on, then," I said. "Judging from the colour of your face, a wash wouldn't hurt you." So old George, he sat down on the bank and began to strip off his shirt, like I'd done, and, just at that moment, the damn Germanis appeared!

There were four of them: one white officer and three black *askaris*. They used to send out little patrols like that to lay landmines all down the road. You never knew when you and your lorry wouldn't be blown sky-high!

"Hands up!" says the white man, pointing his rifle at George. He was taking no risks, that blighter, although, if he'd had one eye, he could see that neither of us was armed. Of course I knew we were dished—not an earthly chance! I can tell you, I felt pretty helpless, all stripped to the waist.

"Wait a mo', sir," I said. "I'll come quietly if you'll let me get my shirt."

"Shirt?" he says. "We've no time for shirts! Look sharp, get a move on!"

From the way he spoke English you'd never have thought him a German.

In two seconds old George and myself were tied up together. It was no use arguing, and this Zahn—that turned out to be his name—was in a hell of a hurry. No wonder! You see, any moment, another of our convoys might come along the road and mop him and his party up just as he'd mopped up us. He told the *askaris* in German what to do with us. While they marched us off into the thick bush, Zahn went back to the road. He didn't give another thought to my shirt; but, a moment later, we knew what he was thinking of when we heard two explosions, which meant that he'd blown up the lorries. I tell you straight, I could have burst into tears when I heard them. I'd driven that old bus for three months; she was like my own child, in a manner of speaking; and, apart from a bit of play in the big-ends, as good as when she left the works at Coventry. I thought about Herr Zahn, at that moment, as if he were a murderer…

The next twenty-four hours were just about as bad as anything I can remember. Those niggers of Zahn's went hareing like mad through the bush, and George and me had to keep pace with them. We must have travelled a good thirty miles through the day and the night; and I tell you that that's no joke in the African bush when you haven't a shirt to your back and your arms are roped up!

I can't say I blame Zahn for that, mind you. After all, we were a small party, in the middle of enemy country. We had to go fast and quietly, miles out of our way, to avoid the South Africans, and slip in, so to speak, behind the German lines. Old George never spoke a word the whole way; he just went sulky. But I knew what he was thinking, all the same, from his looks: he was thinking it was all my fault. Which it was, in a way. If I hadn't left my rifle in the lorry and gone off to bathe, it's quite possible that Zahn's patrol wouldn't have dared to attack us. Anyway, George had a shirt, and I hadn't. I used to remind him of that later on when he started blaming me.

Well, to cut a long story short, we got there eventually. To the German lines, I mean. We both had a pretty thin time, the Germans questioning us about the numbers of troops and the names of the units on lines of communication and that. They tried to starve us into telling them everything. I was thankful that George and I had had a good drink at that water-hole. The officers, on the whole, weren't so bad—they acted like sportsmen as far as a German *can* act like one, I will say that for them. It was later, when they sent us down the line to a place called Morogoro that we got to love the Germans as men and brothers. I tell you we did!

You see, just as luck would have it, Zahn got promoted. I suppose they considered him smart for having nabbed me and George, though really it was easier than shooting a sitting rabbit. Anyway, we hadn't been five days in the prison at Morogoro when Zahn was put in charge. And then we knew all about it!

To begin with, having captured us with his own hands, he regarded me and George as his private property. Then, George, who, being a plumber, is naturally independent, had a special knack of getting Zahn's goat, and then leaving me to take the consequences. And Mr. Zahn took it out of us to some purpose, I can tell you.

He was a typical German under-officer—well, typical?—By that I mean the kind you used to see caricatured in the newspapers. He wasn't very hefty; in fact I'd say he was on the small size; either George or me, given our hands free, could have knocked the stuffing out of him. But he had a head that went up straight and square, back and front, and hair like a nailbrush, and rather short-sighted eyes. It was because of his sight, I suppose, that they'd sent him back to look after prisoners; that also was why it had been such a score for him capturing us. I've met some good Germans, mind you; but Zahn would have been a nasty bit of work whatever country he'd belonged to. What he lacked in impressiveness he certainly made up for in truculence; and in that prison, I can tell you, he was just as much boss as Satan in hell.

He had lived in England, it seemed. That's why he spoke the language so well. What's more, he had had a bad time of it there, or imagined he had. He didn't say what he'd been, but George reckoned he'd been a "boots" in a hotel or something of that kind. Anyway, whatever he'd suffered in the way of kicks and humiliations he was glad to get back now he had us two in his power. He was clever as a monkey, too—oh yes, Mr. Zahn had brains—he must have kept awake at night thinking out ways in which he could put it across us. He seemed to know, as if by instinct, just where our corns were—particularly George's.

I can't tell you all he did to us. Some of it seems too petty now, and some's too disgusting. He'd got a revolting mind, had Mr. Zahn. It was even too much for George; and George, as I've told you, is a sanitary plumber by trade. All that sort of thing... We were the only Englishmen there, mind you; all the rest were Indian Sepoys that had been captured earlier; and there was nothing that wasn't particularly humiliating to an Englishman that Zahn didn't put on us.

Injustices! Lies, too! I never met anyone who could tell a lie better than that blighter. He half made us believe that the British Fleet had been sunk at Jutland; that London had been bombed from the air and reduced to ashes. He made poor old George begin to get anxious about his wife. Well, whatever was happening in London, the Germans were losing in Africa. We knew that when, a few weeks later, Morogoro was evacuated, and we had to clear out with them. We were glad of that, anyway; for the barracks where they kept us were only fit for natives, and we thought when they sent us back we should get clear of Zahn.

Not a bit of it, though! It seemed Mr. Zahn was a permanency. You'd almost have thought he'd taken a special fancy to us two and asked for the privilege of keeping us by him, for company. When they packed us off south, he went with us; and when, a bit later, four other white prisoners, South African Dutchmen, arrived, the brute took the opportunity of making it hotter than ever for us—partly, no doubt, because George, as I've said, got his goat, but mostly because we were English and he wanted to show off before the South Africans.

Things came to such a pass, in fact, that the day before the Germani were forced to abandon us—the place where they'd stuck us was surrounded and friend Zahn only got away by the skin of his teeth—on that very day George and I made a solemn compact: we took an oath, we two, that if ever, when the war was over, either of us ran up against Zahn we'd make it our business to kill him and damn the consequences. Quite serious, mind you. George felt even worse than I did. He said if he spent every penny he'd saved, he'd go to Germany, to a place named Oberhausen, where Zahn came from, and finish him off, the same as you would a snake. I can tell you that Zahn had got properly on both our nerves.

Well, this night at dinner, we were talking it all over, bringing it back again, as we do every year on Armistice Day. It's a queer thing how time alters everything. Ten years makes a lot of difference. All the dangers and hardships of those old days in Africa—the lions and the sun and the mosquitoes and the sand in your throat—we seemed to have forgotten them. Not forgotten, but almost remembered as if they'd been pleasant. Somehow it's only the good side of those times that comes back to us now—the cool air in the morning, the minty scent of the bush, the smell of a wood-fire at night—little things like that. There must be something queer about Africa that gets you. Here was George, on his own, doing well at his trade, and me in a first-rate billet, with prospects of a rise, both of us married, too, as happily as one can reasonably expect—and yet, do you know, our hearts just flew back to Africa!

"War or no war," said George, "I'd go out there to-morrow if I had the chance."

"And so would I, I'm damned if I wouldn't!" I told him.

"Those were champion days, Will," he says, "when you come to look back on them. I must say I enjoyed that war, son, though it sounds blasphemous to say so."

"Well, there's one thing you've forgotten," I told him.

"What's that?" he says.

"Why, Zahn," says I.

"Old Zahn? That blighter! *Have* I…?"

"D'you remember the compact we made? How you swore you'd spend your last farthing on tracking him down when the war was over?"

George laughed. "Well, he *was* a swine. There's no denying it. D'you remember how you and me used to scrap about who should have first go at him if ever we got the chance?"

"Don't I half!" I says. "Well, if there's a God in heaven he's probably dead by now. Still, if I *did* meet him, I'd rather not be Mr. Zahn!"

We went on talking like that for a long time. The food wasn't bad, as I've said, and the beer was first-rate. We got so engrossed that we never noticed the place emptying till there was nobody left in the room but ourselves and a waiter clearing up the tables. He made such a clatter with his plates and knives that it looked like a pretty good hint to us that it was time to go.

"Don't take any notice of him," says George. "I'm going to stick here till closing-time."

"It can't be far off that now," I said. And just as I spoke the clock struck. The waiter came up in a hurry and cleared his throat.

"If you don't mind, gentlemen," he said. Then he stopped: "God in heaven," he says, "if it isn't my old friend George!"

"That's my name," says George; "but who the devil are you?"

We didn't have to look at him twice. That waiter was Zahn!

If that wasn't a knock-out! I wondered what George would do. I shouldn't have been surprised if he'd picked up a table-knife and stuck him, there and then. But George was like me—too flabbergasted to move or speak. In fact it was Zahn who spoke first, as cool as a cucumber.

"I thought I'd seen you chaps before," he says. "But, you know, I'm short-sighted. I never thought to set eyes on you two again. It's a small world, isn't it?"

The nerve of the blighter was too much for both of us. George looked ugly first. Then, suddenly, he burst out laughing.

"You devil!" he says. "Have a drink?"

"I don't mind if I do," says Zahn. "The boss has gone home. Just you wait, while I shut up the shop."

And he went off to pull down the blinds and lock the door.

"What are you going to do about it, George?" I asked.

"*Do?* What *can* you do?" says George. "You can't knock a fellow out when you've asked him to have a drink with you."

A moment later Zahn came back with three big pots of beer. He was smiling all over his face, as innocent as a lamb.

"Look here, this round's mine," he says. "Here's to old times! *Prosit!*"

And he emptied his mug like a man. "Now it's my turn," I said.

So, to cut a long story short, we made a night of it, George, Zahn, and me. Well, we had a good bit in common, when you come to think of it. We went through it all over again, from the day when Zahn nabbed me without my shirt by that water-hole at M'bagwe; and I must say old Zahn enjoyed it as much as we did. He felt just like we felt, he said, about Africa. He'd go back there to-morrow, if the chance came his way, he said; but his old boss, the Swiss—the chap whose drains George had put right—had offered him this head-waiter's job, and he couldn't refuse it. You see, though his parents were Germans, he'd been born in Switzerland, at a place they call Berne, so there wasn't any difficulty about his getting a Swiss passport.

"And if I can't go to Africa," Zahn said, "I'd as soon be in England as anywhere. You see I've married a girl here," he said, "you must come round some Sunday and see her. There's no friends like old friends," he said; and we had another round on the strength of it.

I suppose it was pretty near one o'clock in the morning by the time we'd finished. George and Zahn, they insisted on seeing me all the way home; and Zahn, who in spite of his eyesight, could see better than either of us, very kindly found the keyhole and opened the door for me. Before he and George went off arm-in-arm we made an arrangement that we'd all meet again and talk over old times next Armistice night. And, mind you, I must confess I look forward to that. When you come to think of it, we're all of us human, thank God!